EVIL'S VOW

"Great sorcery requires much blood," said Jambres. "When I obtain the staff, I will finally possess the power necessary for the greatest feat of sorcery in the past three thousand years. In that hour, when the moon and stars are right, all your questions will be answered. The ancient gods of Kamt will again walk the earth and thirty centuries shall be ripped asunder."

Carl frowned. "What about your promise?"

The dead man smiled. "Your enemies will die by the thousands." His voice grew louder. There will be deaths by the tens of thousands." Then louder yet. "By the millions."

Praise for Robert Weinberg's *THE BLACK LODGE*

"Scary, witty, suspenseful, and fascinating. *The Black Lodge* is both a detective novel set on the seamy streets of Chicago, and a roller coaster ride of horror and mystery. . . . The kind of horror novel I love—taut prose combined with a journey through the dark, occult country of fear. . . . **One of the top dark fantasies of the year.**"

—Douglas Clegg,
author of *Neverland*

Books by Robert Weinberg

The Black Lodge
The Dead Man's Kiss

Published by POCKET BOOKS

THE DEAD MAN'S KISS

Robert Weinberg

POCKET BOOKS
New York London Toronto Sydney Tokyo Singapore

An *Original* Publication of POCKET BOOKS

POCKET BOOKS, a division of Simon & Schuster Inc
1230 Avenue of the Americas, New York, NY 10020

ISBN: 0-671-73269-2

First Pocket Books printing November 1992

10 9 8 7 6 5 4 3 2 1

Cover art by David Fishman

Printed in the U.S.A.

To the Horskys and the O'Boyles,
for relative reasons

As long as midnight cloaks the earth
With shadows grim and stark,
God save us from the Judas kiss
Of a dead man in the dark.

ROBERT E. HOWARD

1

▲ Carl's dream always started the same way.

He was walking down a long, narrow passageway cut through solid rock. No lights illuminated the tunnel, but the air itself glowed with an unnatural shine. He was not sure where he was going, or why, but he never stopped. His legs moved without any conscious thought on his part. He was only along for the ride.

The dream had been going on for more than a week. No trace of it remained with him during the day. He forgot every detail when he awoke. Yet as soon as he drifted off to sleep, the memory of his long trek returned. Like some bizarre videotape, his nightmarish journey continued from where he had left off the night before. Deeper and deeper, he plunged into the darkness.

Tonight he sensed a change approaching. Looking ahead, he could see the walls of the tunnel curving back and away. The passage was coming to an end. A shiver of fear ran through his body. Carl wasn't sure he wanted to know who or what waited at the mouth of the corridor.

Unmindful of his anxiety, his body continued forward. There was no hesitation in his step as he walked out into a huge underground cavern, so vast that it could never truly exist. Size meant nothing here, in a world where walls stretched a thousand miles up into the darkness and all traces of the horizon were lost in a majestic gray mist.

He was on a narrow tongue of sandy beach which reached out from the cavern wall to a vast underground river of immeasurable width. A solitary pier jutted into the flow, and it was there that he headed. Docked at the side of the jetty was a small boat. A solitary figure stood in the bow, waiting. Unbidden, the title "Ferryman of the Dead" entered Carl's thoughts.

Drawing closer, Carl noted with relief the long, dark cloak that covered the ferryman from head to toe. A deep cowl shadowed the boatkeeper's features. Carl felt certain he did not want to know what secrets lurked beneath that hood.

"Who are you?" asked the ferryman. His lifeless voice rang hollow in the emptiness.

"I am the one who is called," replied Carl, the words not his own.

"Where do you dwell?" asked the ferryman.

"On the island of the flame," said Carl.

The cowled figure nodded. "What is the secret of the bark?"

"The ferry came from the boatyard of the gods. You found it there in pieces, much like the dismembered body of Osiris. Only through use of the art of magic was it rebuilt."

"I bow to your knowledge," said the ferryman. "I will take you to the island of the magician."

Carl climbed into the bark and took a seat on the bench at the front of the boat. Using a long pole, the ferryman pushed the vessel away from the dock and into the sluggish flow of the river. A strong current took hold of the bark, and within seconds they were out of sight of the shore.

A thin mist rose from the dark surface of the water, making it difficult to see. In the distance, Carl could faintly make out huge shapes moving in the fog.

"The entrance to the Underworld and the Judgment of the Dead," said the ferryman, answering Carl's unspoken question.

"Is that where we're going?" said Carl, surprised to find he could speak on his own.

"No." The ferryman raised a cowled arm and pointed.

"Our destination lies ahead." A small island emerged from the mist. "The domain of the sorcerer," said the ferryman.

They docked at a stone pier much like the one they had left only a few minutes earlier. Trembling, Carl climbed out of the bark onto dry land. Without a word, the ferryman pushed his boat back into the current. Soundlessly, the vessel disappeared in the darkness.

The island was little more than a sandbar. At its center stood a jet-black obsidian throne. Sitting in the chair waited a small, ivory-skinned man, clad in a dull yellow robe and matched sandals. With shaven head and hawk-like nose, he resembled a human vulture waiting for its prey. Carl knew without asking that this was "the One Who Called."

"Welcome to my prison," said the man as Carl approached the throne. His voice sounded surprisingly mild, almost friendly. "Please excuse this intrusion in your dreams, but it was the only way I could contact you."

"Who are you?" asked Carl, once again in full possession of his faculties. "Where am I?"

"This is the Isle of the Dead-Alive," said the sorcerer, rising from his throne. His eyes, blacker than his throne and without pupils, stared deeply into Carl's. "I am Satni Jambres, master of magic. When I open my eyes, the light rises."

"When I close my eyes, night spreads over the Earth," said Carl, completing the couplet.

Jambres smiled. "I knew I chose well when I summoned your spirit to me."

Closing his eyes, the magician traced a mystical pattern in the air. "I am the Bull of the East."

"I am the Lion of the West," answered Carl, sketching the same design on his chest.

"You know the secrets of Osiris," said Jambres. "What is your rank?"

"I am an adept of the third level," said Carl.

Jambres shook his head. "The spell requires a member

of the Seventh Circle. You will need the help of another to perform the Ceremony of the Opening of the Mouth."

"What are you talking about?" said Carl, suddenly struck by the unreality of the situation. "I never heard of any ritual with that title. And why does it matter, anyway? This whole crazy scenario is taking place in my unconscious mind. You're only a figment of my imagination."

Jambres laughed, a nasty sound only vaguely human. Without warning, one clawlike hand shot out and grabbed Carl by the neck. Effortlessly, the sorcerer squeezed, sending a shock wave of pain through Carl's body.

"If you die in this dream, you will never awaken," said Jambres, cruelly twisting his fingers tighter. "Now, do you still doubt my existence?"

Unable to speak, Carl desperately shook his head.

Grinning, Jambres released his grip. "Listen, and you shall learn why I called your sleeping mind to me," said the sorcerer.

"For three thousand years, my *ba,* my inner spirit, has dwelt on this accursed island, stranded between the land of the living and the kingdom of the dead. I am unable to enter the Underworld because my *ka,* my physical soul, remains imprisoned on Earth in a golden statue of Anubis. That is the punishment I suffer for a crime I did not commit. Unless the two halves of my spirit are joined together once again, I will remain trapped here for all eternity."

"Why should I bother?" said Carl, his mind jumping two steps ahead of the conversation. "What's in it for me?"

"Power," replied Jambres. "The realization of all your dreams. Through me, you can strike back at all those who have tormented you over the years. I control forces beyond your wildest imagination. The gods of Kamt—the land you now know as Egypt—stand behind me. My magic can crush your enemies into dust."

"Wait a minute," said Carl, not sure what he was hearing. "You make it sound too easy. I'm no sorcerer. I can't perform miracles."

"Only an adept of my skill can manage the necessary rites," said Jambres slyly. "My spirit and soul are reflections of each other. What I know here, it knows as well. There are certain acts that must be done in the land of the living. My *ba* is trapped here in the realm of sleep. But my *ka,* my exact double within the statue, can escape from its prison. That is why I need your assistance."

"You want me to bring you back to life?" said Carl, shaking his head in disbelief. Then, suspiciously, he asked, "Why have you waited so many years before finding someone to try this ritual? Three thousand years seems a pretty long time to be patient."

"For untold centuries, I struggled to communicate with the world of the living," said Jambres. He sounded puzzled. "My attempts never met with success. Times beyond counting, I tried. My cries for help were too weak to be heard.

"Then, recently, I experienced a sudden surge of power. It was as if I had been exposed to a source of tremendous mystic energy. Evidently, the statue containing my *ka* was moved into the vicinity of some sort of mighty talisman. That additional power filtered through my soul and provided me with the necessary strength to contact the proper disciple."

"Talisman?" said Carl. "What talisman?"

"I do not know," said Jambres. "But I intend to find out."

The sorcerer leaned close, his black eyes fixing Carl with an unblinking stare. In the darkness around them, Carl sensed vast unseen figures intent on Jambres's words.

"Listen carefully now, so as to remember my instructions when you awake. These are the things you must do so that I may live again."

Carl listened. And remembered.

2

▲ Grinning broadly, Oscar Hinkley reached into the canvas sack and pulled out the gold statue. A little more than twelve inches high, it depicted the seated figure of an unusual creature with the body of a man but the head of a jackal. Narrow slits of eyes glistened in the candlelight as if watching all those present.

Proudly, Oscar displayed it to the three other people in the chamber. "It was easy," he said to no one in particular. "They never suspected a thing."

"You sure?" asked Carl Garrett, sounding unconvinced.

"Positive," said Oscar. "I signed in late. I had my hat and overcoat on, and the timekeeper never saw my face. The other guards were already making their rounds. I knew exactly what to do. The fuse box for the Egyptian display was exactly where I remembered. Once I shut off the alarms, it took me less than a minute to locate the statue, grab it, and replace it with the replica. Unless someone on the staff checks real close, no one will ever know that it's a fake."

"We plan to eliminate that possibility as soon as possible," said Carl. "You switched the sensors back on when you left?"

"Of course," said Oscar, somewhat annoyed at the question. "I'm no dummy. Don't forget, this isn't the first time I stole something from the museum."

"You got caught the last time," said George Slater, from the corner. His voice rumbled like an old steam engine. The size of a small house but with the brains of a mouse, the big man frightened Oscar. A bit of the dark world peered out from behind George's eyes. "Yer sure nobody followed you to the hideout?"

"I was just a kid then," said Oscar defiantly. "Besides, the cops pinched me when I returned the mummy, not when I first borrowed it. And nobody followed me tonight."

"No reason to argue with each other," said Carl smoothly. "Sam and Jasper monitored Oscar's trail once he left the museum. There was no sign of surveillance."

Carl smiled and patted Oscar on the shoulder. "You did a fine job, Hinkley. Blood and Iron needs men like you. Now, hand over the statue so I can put it where it belongs."

A circle of white wax candles burned on a small altar in the middle of the room. The candles provided the only illumination in the chamber; the gold carving was placed between the burning tapers.

"Are we ready to start the invocation?" Carl asked the fourth person in the room.

"Almost," she answered, her voice quivering with emotion. A slender, very attractive blonde with large breasts and dark eyes, she wore a sheer white robe that glistened in the candlelight. Oscar knew Sarah Walsh from her visits to his uncle's house. The old man thought she was hot stuff. Staring at her brown nipples pointing through the cloth, Oscar had to agree. "I have a few more knots to tie."

"Where's Uncle Joe?" Oscar was curious. "Wasn't he supposed to attend this ceremony too?"

"Those plans changed," said Carl. He glanced over at George and nodded slightly. "Your uncle proved to be more stubborn than we expected. He refused to come."

"He ain't hurt, is he?" asked Oscar, his eyes fixed on the big man. He didn't trust the giant. George was on his feet now. For all of his immense size, he moved with the silent grace of a wild beast.

"Nothing for you to worry about," said Carl. "Booze did the trick. It took two bottles of rum before he showed any signs of tiring. That old geezer could drink a still dry. He talked a blue streak until he finally folded. He was dead to the world when we left. Don't fret. You'll see him soon enough."

"Enough explanations," said Sarah. "I am ready to begin. Take your places before the altar."

Grumbling under his breath, Oscar knelt on the hardwood floor in front of the ring of candles. He knew what was coming next from a week's worth of practicing. All of the mumbo-jumbo garbage made him want to puke. He didn't believe in any of this crap—it was all a big crock.

Why they needed him to participate in this weird ceremony he had no idea. By rights, stealing the statue should have been enough for him to join Blood and Iron, but he knew better than to argue with Carl Garrett. In his quiet, polite way, the leader of the organization scared Oscar even more than the brutish George Slater.

"We come here tonight as the four children of Horus," said Sarah dramatically, bowing low before the statue.

Along with the others, Oscar chanted in response, "I have seen my father in all his forms."

Standing before the statue, Sarah gently touched its mouth with her right index finger. Reaching into her robe, she pulled out a glass bottle and a small brush. Carefully, she painted the mouth of the idol with a thick red liquid. Oscar swallowed uncomfortably. The stuff in the bottle looked a lot like blood. Once again, he wondered what had happened to Uncle Joe. He didn't like the way Carl brushed off his questions.

"I have come to embrace thee, for I am thy son, Horus. Thy mouth was sealed, but I have set it in order. I have opened for thee thy mouth. I have opened for thee thy two eyes."

Reaching again into her robe, Sarah pulled out a small metal rod resembling a dental pick. Gently, she touched the mouth and eyes of the statue.

"I have opened for thee thy mouth with the instrument of Anubis. I have used the iron implement with which the mouths of the gods were opened. Horus, open thy mouth!"

Oscar stifled a yawn. His knees ached. If the ritual followed the rehearsals exactly, it would be over in a few more minutes. Then, no matter what the others planned, he was going to have a beer.

"The deceased shall walk," said Sarah. Oscar looked up, surprised. He didn't recall that line from practice. "The deceased shall speak. The deceased shall move among the living."

Suddenly, a pair of huge hands grabbed Oscar by the shoulders and shoved him face first to the floor. His temple slammed hard against the wood. Powerful fists pounded his head and body like sledgehammers. Desperately, he tried to roll out of the way. There was no escape. Oscar knew plenty about street fighting, but he was no match for George Slater.

With a grunt of triumph, the giant wrenched Oscar to his feet. One massive arm held his victim motionless, waiting. Barely conscious, Oscar had no idea what was taking place. Dimly, through beaten and battered eyes, he glimpsed Sarah Walsh standing a few feet away, holding the gold statue. Ignoring the droplets of Oscar's blood staining her white robe, she extended the carving until its gory lips touched his. The gold felt cold, icy cold. He tasted blood, not his own.

"Bring me the knife," she said.

Oscar screamed, but the statue shoved up against his mouth muffled the sound. Desperately, he lashed out with both feet. That accomplished nothing. George merely tightened his grip, sending waves of pain rippling through his arms and chest. He was helpless in the giant's grip.

"I'm sorry about this, Oscar," said Carl Garrett, from somewhere out of view. He sounded like he almost meant it. "We need a warm corpse, and you fit the bill. You aren't Blood and Iron material anyway. Say hello to your uncle Joe for me."

"The touch of steel," whispered Sarah, placing the

knife point directly over Oscar's heart. The razor-sharp point pierced his skin.

"Then comes the Dead Man's Kiss," she said, slamming the blade home.

3

▲ Ellen Harper loved her job. Even on nights like tonight, when she worked well past ten, she never complained. She only wished that museums could afford to pay more.

As a young girl, growing up in New York City, she had first encountered Egyptian antiquities on a school field trip to the Museum of Natural History. Something clicked the instant she saw the intricately designed mummy cases of the pharaohs. Scarabs, pyramids, and animal-headed gods blended into one huge melange that overwhelmed her senses.

From that moment on, she knew exactly what she wanted from life. Ellen spent the next seventeen years on a single-minded quest to achieve her ambition. First came her bachelor's degree, then her master's, and then finally her doctorate, all in archaeology. A half-dozen trips overseas on digs during that period rounded out her education.

Ellen dreamed of heading her own department of Egyptology in a major museum or college. That day was still far off in the future. Still, as chief archivist at the Petrie Institute of Oriental Studies in downtown Chicago, she was making her mark in the field. At twenty-eight, she had time on her side.

With a sigh of relief, Ellen turned off the computer

monitor. After three weeks of working till the wee hours of the morning, she had finally finished cross-indexing the Rivington collection. Yawning, she glanced at her watch. Time for her to head home and hit the sheets.

Pushing back her chair, she stood up and stretched. Her body ached from too many hours spent hunched over a desk. The weekend beckoned. She had spent the last few Saturdays and Sundays entering data into her computer. With the Rivington project completed, she could finally devote some time to herself. *Maybe,* she thought, *I could even take in a movie or go out to dinner.*

Instinctively, Ellen glanced over at Andy Yates's desk. She spent much of her free time with Andy, the purchasing agent for the museum. They had shared this office for the past six months and were close friends. But their relationship had never progressed beyond the friendship stage.

Andy was five years older than Ellen and had gone through a painful divorce six months earlier. He probably wasn't ready for a new relationship. Nor did he appeal to Ellen other than as a pleasant companion. She wanted a lover who was exciting, romantic, and a tad mysterious. Andy was too wrapped up in his work to fit those requirements.

Andy had not come to work the past two days. She assumed he was off on a buying spree for the museum. Ellen couldn't help but wonder about the papers scattered all over his desk. Normally Andy hated a mess. Neatness obsessed him. He always straightened up his desk if he planned to be out of the office for any length of time.

Ellen shrugged her shoulders. Andy was probably suffering at home with the flu. Still, he usually called when he couldn't make it to the office. She wondered if anything else might be wrong, and decided she would give him a call tomorrow.

Putting on her winter coat and hat, Ellen shut off the office lights and exited into the hallway. The upper level of the Institute was pitch-black this time of night, but she knew her way by heart. After nearly a year on the job, she had the entire layout of the building memorized.

"That you, Miss Harper?" a man called out from the darkness ahead. The beam of a flashlight inched along the floor in her general direction.

"Just me and my mummy, Gus," said Ellen, recognizing the voice of one of the night watchmen.

Chuckling quietly, the guard shuffled forward. "Working late again? You never leave at quitting time."

Ellen laughed. "I'm just doing my job. The rest of the staff stays late if necessary."

"Sure," said Gus, gently mocking her. "I've worked here six years, and I see how often they stick around. Five o'clock comes, and they fly out the front door."

He swung his flashlight around. "I'll walk you to your car. No reason to take chances this time of night."

Ellen knew better than to argue. She expected no less. Whenever she ran into Gus, he insisted on escorting her to the parking lot. A retired cop, he imagined rapists and murderers lurking everywhere. A product of big-city life, Ellen half agreed with him. Anyway, she saw no reason to make a big deal about it. She accepted his courtesy with thanks.

Together they descended the wide marble steps to the first floor of the museum. The scuffing of their shoes on the slick surface broke the otherwise absolute silence of the huge entrance hall. The vastness of the building dwarfed them, making Ellen feel very small. Countless centuries of history surrounded them. The weight of the ages hung heavy in the air. Sometimes, walking through these dark halls, Ellen felt like she was violating the tomb of an ancient, forgotten god.

"Awesome, isn't it?" said Gus, as if reading her thoughts. "No matter how many times I walk through this place, it always gives me the shivers."

"Enveloped by the past," said Ellen. "I love it."

Then a stray thought struck her. "Aren't you normally off on Friday nights? Where's Joe Hinkley?"

Gus looked distinctly uncomfortable with her question. He coughed and cleared his throat several times before answering. "Joe hasn't shown up for his shift in nearly a week, Miss Harper. Me and the other guys have been covering for him. You know Joe. Sometimes he hits the bottle a little. It takes him a while to recover."

Ellen frowned. "Does Dr. Henderson know about this?"

Henderson served as curator of the museum. A strict, by-the-rules administrator, he tolerated no lapses in conduct by his employees.

"Of course not," said Gus. "Old man Henderson would fire Joe in an instant if he could. He never liked the poor guy. Luckily, the boss skipped work the past few days. You won't tell, will you?"

"No," said Ellen. "But Hinkley better get back on the job soon."

"Yeah," said Gus. "I don't know what ails the dumb slob. It ain't like him to disappear for so long. We tried calling his place a few times, but no answer. He must really be on a bender. Probably out boozing with that crazy nephew of his. Remember that slob, Oscar? Didn't he ask you for a date once?"

"I turned him down," said Ellen. "I'm single but not desperate. At least, not *that* desperate."

"Pretty girl like you should be going out on dates more and working less," said Gus. The guard frowned. "Kinda weird, ain't it? The way old man Henderson stays home the same week that Hinkley don't show up for work? I can't remember the last time the boss took a holiday. He's a workaholic, just like you. It almost makes me believe in fate, the timing and all that."

Ellen nodded her head slowly, vaguely troubled by Gus's remarks. A logical, orderly person, she disliked coincidence. Three unexplained absences in one week among the museum's small staff seemed odd. She made a silent promise to call Andy Yates early the next morning.

4

▲ Fear enveloped Satni Jambres like a shroud.

Looking down at his chest, he grimly counted five more green splotches marring the white flesh. In the last hour, the corpse he controlled had started to rot. Putrefaction attacked from within, spreading like wildfire. Jambres felt like dozens of rats gnawed at his insides. Constant burning pain threatened to overwhelm him. Unseen maggots tore at his brain.

Dissolution and decay challenged his unbreakable will. The preserving spell still held both forces at bay, but he sensed their growing power. In this newly resurrected state, he did not yet possess his full strength. Within a few hours, corruption would claim this worthless shell. An-mut, Eater of the Dead, awaited hungrily.

Jambres shuddered, contemplating an eternity of utter darkness, his mind trapped inside the brain of a rotting corpse. Immediately, he forced the thought from his mind. Such nightmares led only to madness.

Still, the threat of decay served a good purpose. It reminded him that his continued existence depended on finding a fresh, healthy body. Without it, all of his plans meant nothing.

Forcing himself up from his chair, Jambres walked across the small room. There was only one door, locked from the outside. His allies still worried about him trying to escape. He smirked at their useless precautions. If he wanted to leave, no wood door or bolt lock could stop him. At present, he needed their help as much as they desired his. When their usefulness ended, so would their worthless lives.

He rapped hard on the paneling until someone moved in the corridor outside.

"What do you want?" his jailer called anxiously.

Jambres rejoiced when he heard that voice. He recognized the soft tones of the seeress, Sarah Walsh. Good fortune smiled on him tonight. The only woman of the group, she possessed incredible psychic powers. Those unique mental gifts they shared forged an invisible link between them. Of all his captors, she was the most susceptible to his will.

"Open the door," he said slowly. Sucking enough air into his lungs for speech took time. His body no longer functioned properly. Muscles shrieked in protest as he forced his lungs to work. "I must talk to you."

"I am not allowed to talk," said Sarah. "Carl and George went out for a while to get supplies. They left me in charge. They'll return in an hour or two. You can talk to them then."

"I can't wait that long," said Jambres. "By then it will be too late. Do you hear me, Sarah? *Too late.* I need your assistance now."

A few seconds passed. Then a key turned in the lock. With a squeak of rusted hinges, the wood door swung open. Peering about fearfully, as if suspecting someone lurked in the shadows, Sarah entered the room.

Jambres stepped back, trying not to frighten her. The seeress was a good-looking woman around twenty-five years old, tall and slender with light blond hair that contrasted nicely with her dark brown eyes. Her narrow cheekbones formed a delicate symmetry Jambres found pleasing.

Cautiously, Sarah closed the door behind her. She leaned against it, as if blockading his passage with her body. "Carl will be very angry if he finds out I disobeyed him."

She paused for an instant, gathering her thoughts.

"What did you mean, too late?" she asked. Her curious eyes looked directly at Jambres for a second, then darted away. No one could stare at his features, frozen in death, very long. "Too late for what?"

"You resurrected my spirit," he said, grasping for the right words, "but this body died a week ago. Even my magic cannot animate it much longer."

Dramatically, he pointed to his shirtless chest. Feeling neither heat nor cold, he needed a minimal amount of clothing. "This corpse decays as we speak. The forces of corruption cannot be denied their due."

As he spoke, Jambres reached out with his mind and tried to touch her *ba,* her inner soul. The task proved to be much harder than he expected. Her mind was a swirling mass of emotions. He could sense her surface thoughts but little else.

Bitterly, he realized again how little energy he actually possessed. His success the previous evening using the dark forces had given him a false sense of confidence. It would take days, perhaps weeks, for him to regain his true strength.

Sarah shook her head. "Carl forbid me to do anything until he returned."

Nervously, she bit her lower lip. She seemed agitated by his presence. His unblinking eyes, sunken cheeks, and bloodless features frightened everyone. Yet beneath that fear, he sensed another, stronger emotion.

The seeress bore most of the responsibility for returning him to life. An adept of the Seventh Order, she correctly performed the intricate ritual necessary to release his *ka* from its millennia-long imprisonment. Carl and George supplied the necessary strength. An unsuspecting Oscar Hinkley provided the body for him to inhabit.

Unfortunately, as happened with many powerful witches, Sarah's psychic gifts had played havoc with her mind as a child. Poorly trained in the rigorous disciplines of sorcery, she barely controlled her talents. Extremely unstable, she hovered on the borders of sanity.

Jambres understood Carl Garrett's motives perfectly. A fanatic, he schemed to alter the world according to his own design, and black magic was the ultimate tool for that ambition.

The dreams of fools remained unchanged over the centuries—they hungered for the temporal pleasures of wealth, fame, and kingship. Only magicians and priests knew that true power came from the gods. At present, Jambres cooperated with Garrett willingly. Killing cost him nothing. He only wished that Sarah's desires were as clear as Garrett's.

The seeress paced around the room, flitting from one corner to another. Her body shook, as if gripped by a powerful emotion. Finally, she stopped at the foot of his useless bed. Undead, Jambres never slept.

"The statue," she said, pointing to a heavy tarpaulin, rolled tightly together and stored beneath the cot. "We could . . ."

"Never," said Jambres emphatically. "I refuse to endure that torture again. Besides, the ceremony would take too long. This body continues to decompose."

Beginning to feel the first touches of panic, he reached out and grabbed Sarah by the arm. "If we don't act soon, the maggots will claim me."

Desperately, he searched Hinkley's brain for the right words. "Enough stalling. Help me!"

Sarah trembled helplessly in his powerful grip. Yet she made no effort to pull away. A strange expression crossed her face. It was a look older than civilization and one that Jambres recognized immediately. He still remembered lust. The touch of his hand had sexually aroused the seeress.

A surge of triumph swept through him. Dark, unnatural passions obsessed Sarah Walsh. No wonder she instinctively feared him. He represented her innermost suppressed desires. Working with those secret, unspeakable lusts, he would bind her to his will.

"I require a strong *male* body," he said, still holding her tightly. "One to serve *all* of my needs."

Sarah blinked her eyes furiously, as if sensing the hidden meaning of his words. She pursed her lips, as if deep in thought. "You'll treat him the same way as Hinkley?"

When he nodded his agreement, a sly smile crossed her lips. "I'm thinking of one man in particular . . ."

"An enemy," said Jambres, silently relishing his success. "Perhaps a lover who left you for another."

He measured the accuracy of his guess by the expression on her face. Sarah scowled bitterly as she spoke. "He calls himself Tom Darrow. I'm not even sure if that's his real name.

"I met the handsome son of a bitch at a bar last year. No one ever treated me like Tom. He had a smooth, smooth line. I was a fool. The night we met, I brought him home, and we spent hours screwing. He was incredible in bed.

"I fell for him hard. After a few days, he moved in with me. I supported him for the next six weeks. He spent my money, ate my food, drove my car. Then one day, out of nowhere, he dumped me for some bleach-bottle blonde with a bigger bankroll. And when he left, he stole everything in my apartment that was not nailed down."

Her voice grew high-pitched and shrill. "That scum. He leeched off me until he met a high-class tramp wanting to get laid. He never loved me—just my money."

Her face twisted with hate. "Parasites like him deserve to die."

Not a hint of mercy echoed in her voice as she repeated the death sentence. "He deserves to die."

"So he shall," said Jambres. "Or at least his spirit will face the judgment of Anubis. His body will continue to serve me." His eyes looked deep into hers. "His strong, handsome, *desirable* body."

Sarah shivered, aroused by his words. Calming herself, she pulled away from him. "We'd better leave right away. Carl and George will return in a little while."

Sarah opened the door to the hall. "The other men are

playing cards upstairs. The less they know, the better. I'll go find my car keys. They won't question anything I tell them. You meet me outside."

"One more thing," said Jambres as Sarah turned to leave. "I need a knife to perform the sacrifice. Bring me one from the kitchen. The sharper, the better."

He smiled at the hatred that flashed across her face. Like lust, revenge remained the same after thousands of years. Jambres knew Sarah would obey him no matter what the cost.

"The jackal-headed god demands payment in human blood," he declared. "Without it, the ceremony will not work. Hinkley paid, and so shall Darrow. It is the only way."

5

▲ The room stank of death and decay.

The clock on the mantel chimed midnight. Moe Kaufman snorted loudly, as if showing his lack of surprise at the time. Normally, his shift ended at twelve-thirty at night. But once a murder investigation started, the detective in charge was expected to stay on the case until all the loose ends were tied up. He probably wouldn't get home till after four in the morning.

Moe shook his head in disbelief. In his ten years working as a detective for the Violent Crimes Unit of the Chicago police force, he had seen some pretty grisly sights, but nothing matched the condition of this cadaver. The body, tinged green from putrefying flesh, sprawled face first on the living-room floor.

Gas swelled the corpse to nearly twice its size. Arms

and legs took on the appearance of obscene sausages trapped in cloth casings. The dead man smelled like raw meat left out in the sun on a hot day. The stench of decay filled the room.

Just staring at the remains made Moe feel lightheaded. Behind him, the floor vent belched out wave after wave of hot, dry air. Droplets of sweat formed on his forehead. Desperately, he fought to keep down his dinner. "Can't somebody turn down the thermostat in here?" he asked.

"I tried that already," answered one of the several uniformed cops in the room. A half-dozen policemen searched the apartment for clues. "The whole building works from one master panel. We can't shut it off until we find the superintendent."

"Then open a window at least," said Moe. Wrenching loose his tie, he ripped open the top button of his shirt. Feeling queasy, he drew in several deep breaths. It didn't do much good. He needed some fresh, clean air.

"Can't do that either," said the same cop, the expression on his face reflecting his misery. None of the officers in the apartment appeared happy with his work. "They're painted shut. It would take a crowbar to open one."

"Shit!" said Moe vehemently, prompting a few grins among the patrolmen. "When you find the damned super, throw the book at him. Cite the jerk for violating city building codes. Anybody running a rat trap like this must be guilty of something."

Trying to ignore the overpowering stench, Moe squinted at the coroner, who was carefully studying the corpse. "What's the story, Art?" he asked, anxious for answers.

The medical examiner looked up at the mention of his name. "You picked a winner this time, Kaufman," he said softly. His words caught Moe by surprise. Usually, the M.E. never offered any sort of judgment. He did his job and left. His reports were always short and to the point. Moe couldn't recall the last time Art Marlowe had commented on a murder case.

A chubby, short man in his late forties, the examiner had the whitest skin Moe had ever seen. If sunlight touched Marlowe's flesh, it left no impression. He belonged in a vampire movie. Unconfirmed rumors circulating at the station claimed that he only went out at night.

Art Marlowe won no popularity contests in the homicide department. He enjoyed his work a little too much for most detectives' tastes. Tonight he sounded anything but pleased.

"The facts don't add up," said Marlowe, frowning.

"See over there," he continued, pointing to the corpse's right side. The dead man's hand tightly clutched a butcher's knife. Flecks of dried blood dotted the ten-inch blade. "The fingers locked stiff around the handle. Normally that indicates rigor mortis. Yet the body is quite cold. It shows every sign of algor mortis. The two conditions can't exist at the same time. At least, I never heard of it happening before."

"You're not talking sense, Art," said Moe, upset by what he was hearing. Like most detectives specializing in homicide, he knew quite a lot about dead bodies. "How long ago did this guy die?"

"In my professional opinion," said Marlowe, his expression glum, "judging primarily by the degree of putrefaction present and the temperature of the cadaver, I would say this man has been dead at least a week, perhaps longer."

The medical examiner shook his head in bewilderment. "Several other things bother me about the body. The position of the legs, for one. It appears that the victim stood in this spot just a few hours ago. However, that contradicts the advanced state of muscle decomposition present in the corpse. Even propping up a body in this state of decomposition would be extremely difficult.

"Besides that, all of the blood has pooled in the lower

regions. This condition, known as livor mortis, takes place several days after death. Once that happens, any movement bruises the skin and leaves a mark. I can't find any such blemishes. So I have to guess that this body has not been moved in days. It makes no sense at all."

"Don't look so worried," said Moe, trying to sound confident. "These oddball murders all seem mysterious at first. Once we uncover all the facts, things fall into place fast enough."

"I hope so." The M.E. sounded anything but convinced. "I'll be interested in how you explain the caked blood on the knife. How could another person use the blade the corpse holds so tightly? Or, more to the point, why?"

Marlowe nodded, as if answering Moe's unspoken question. "Yes, the blood type matches the stains in the carpet. They're all quite recent. None of it comes from the corpse. One thing I can say for sure: The stabbing victim lost a lot of blood. You might have another corpse on your hands before long."

"Great news," said Moe testily. "Fortunately, we heard about the second man some time ago. Our witness told the first officer on the scene about him. There's an APB on the radio now. He should turn up soon."

Moe rose to his feet. "Let me and Calvin worry about the methods and the madness, Marlowe. All we want is for you to provide us with facts. All the facts."

Without a word, the medical examiner returned his attention to the corpse. Seizing the opportunity to escape the vile smell, Moe pushed open the swinging door leading to the kitchenette. He gasped in relief as he entered. Over the stove, a noisy exhaust fan hummed furiously, drawing out some of the foul air.

Two people sat at the kitchen table. One was a skinny, short woman, perhaps sixty years old, with a shock of bright red hair. Clad in a faded maroon robe, she had coarse, thick features and a shrill grating voice that started Moe's ears aching. Listening to her and patiently scribbling notes was a big black man. His name was Calvin Lane. He was Moe's partner and best friend.

Lane looked like a boxer gone to seed. His large pot belly and sleepy, half-closed eyes fooled a lot of people into thinking he was slow and fat. Actually, a powerful layer of hard, trim muscle hid beneath the surface flab. Calvin Lane could tear phone books in half without working up a sweat.

His blank stare also deceived the unwary. Born and raised in one of Chicago's worst neighborhoods, Lane worked his way from beat patrolman to homicide investigator in the course of only a few years. His brains matched his brawn. A smart, savvy cop, he knew the value of looking stupid at the right times.

He and Moe had worked together as partners for nearly a decade in Chicago's toughest district. The two of them owned a near-eighty-percent arrest record, best in the department.

"This is my partner, Detective Kaufman," said Lane slowly, directing all of his attention to the redhead. Calvin used his most neutral tone, which immediately signaled to Moe that his friend needed a break. They usually interviewed people as a team anyway. Together they could ferret out information that alone they might miss. "Moe, meet Mrs. Claire Wronski. Mrs. W. is a widow. She lives in the next apartment."

Moe inclined his head in a short, polite bow. He always tried to establish good rapport with possible witnesses. "You called the police," he said, remembering the woman's name from his preliminary reports. Swinging himself into an empty kitchen chair, he sat down next to Lane. "We really appreciate your cooperation in this matter, Mrs. Wronski. Perhaps you wouldn't mind repeating to me, in your own words, what happened here tonight."

"I already told Detective Lane everything I know," said Mrs. Wronski, sounding annoyed. Breathing heavily, she emphasized every other word. Moe found her unusual sing-song accent unnerving. "And I talked to the policeman who arrived after my telephone call. How many times do I have to repeat myself?"

"We like to check over a statement several times," said Moe smoothly. "It's police department policy, based on years and years of experience. Often, when the witness recounts information for a second or third time, she remembers some small fact she overlooked in her original statement."

"I guess that makes sense," said Mrs. Wronski, not sounding like she meant it. "Where should I start?"

"Why not begin when you first heard the buzzer," said Calvin Lane quickly. Moe stifled a yawn. From his partner's pained expression, he suspected Mrs. Wronski rambled on and on if given the chance.

"Well, don't forget to put those wild parties in your report, Mr. Lane," she said sharply. "It wouldn't surprise me one bit if this whole mess resulted from something that took place at one of them. You know what I mean—some jealous boyfriend trying to get even."

"Yes, ma'am," said Lane, nodding respectfully. He held up a notebook thick with scribbled pages of information. "I wrote it all down here. Detective Kaufman and I will review your whole transcript. For now, though, could you just go over the events of the past few hours?"

"All right," said Mrs. Wronski, wrinkling her nose in annoyance. "Though I still think it's a waste of time."

She began her story again. "It was a few minutes after ten o'clock. I know that for a fact because they were still on the local news. It had to be before ten-fifteen because they still hadn't gotten to the weather. I hate the way they do that, holding the important stuff until halfway through the show. If I ran the network, the weather would be on first."

She paused, drew in a deep breath, and then continued to ramble. "I only watch the news for the weather report. That way, I know what to wear for work the next day, if the weather forecasters are right, which half the time isn't the case.

"Usually, I skip the first part of the show and turn on the TV around ten after. That way, I don't listen to the news stories. It's all too depressing. You know what I mean? All those rapes and killings and stuff like that—who wants to hear about that?"

Moe sighed. The look on Calvin Lane's face said *I told you so.* "Let's keep to the story, okay, Mrs. Wronski? You've convinced me it was around ten-fifteen. What happened?"

"The buzzer rang in Mr. Darrow's apartment." The way she said the man's name left no doubt of her low opinion of him. "The walls in this building are so thin, you can't help hearing everything that goes on. Not," she hastened to add, "that I would eavesdrop on my neighbors."

"Of course not," said Moe. Sarcasm was wasted on the woman. "Did Mr. Darrow often entertain visitors in the evening?"

"Entertain?" She laughed nastily as she repeated the word. "If you call screwing cheap young sluts all night entertainment, then he was a regular entertainment industry."

Mrs. Wronski's face twisted in disgust. "I mean, the man acted like a regular gigolo. One woman after another. Not nice girls, either. Janine, Gina, Sarah, and a bunch more. He never stopped. Week after week, rutting like a dog in heat. It made me sick. What a terrible life."

Moe shrugged. To him, at forty, happily married for fifteen years, it didn't sound *that* terrible. At least, not from a distance. Not that he would say anything like that to his wife, Miriam. Some fantasies were best not shared.

"After the buzzer rang, what happened next?" asked Moe, trying to keep the conversation on track.

"He buzzed the person right in," said Mrs. Wronski. "The super warned us never to let anyone into the building without checking their identity on the intercom first. That's why we live in a limited-access building, isn't it? But Mr. Darrow never bothered with such formalities. Why should he? It was always some floozy or another wanting to say hello. Well, this time," she said, her voice filled with self-righteous satisfaction, "he paid the price."

"Then . . . ?" asked Moe, letting the word hang, hoping to nudge the woman along.

"A few minutes passed. Enough time for somebody to make it up here from the foyer. I heard Darrow's door open. He never bothered keeping it locked. Right after that, he started screaming."

"There was no exchange of words first?" asked Moe carefully. He didn't want to be accused later of leading a witness. Still, most belligerent relatives or boyfriends shouted a few choice words before committing violent acts.

"You heard me," said Mrs. Wronski belligerently. "The door opened, and *boom,* like that, Darrow screamed."

"Screamed what?" said Moe.

"Crazy stuff," said Mrs. Wronski, suddenly looking very uncomfortable. "You know, curses, swears, words like that. None of it made any sense. Right away, I called 911."

"Smart move," said Moe. "Then what did you do?"

"The officer on the line told me to stay in my apartment until the police arrived. But . . ."

"But what?" asked Moe, as the woman hesitated for a moment.

"I hung on the phone for a minute. Then, all of a sudden, Darrow stopped screaming—right in the middle of a word. You know how I mean. It was as if a faucet had been turned off. One second there was sound, the next instant nothing. I had to find out what happened."

Moe shook his head. After all these years on the police force, he still did not understand why people acted the way they did.

Mrs. Wronski smiled at the expression on his face. "You're wondering, after all the things I said about Darrow, why I cared. Because, Mr. Kaufman—and you, too, Mr. Lane—when I grew up, my parents taught me that you helped a neighbor in distress. No matter how stupid or obnoxious they acted, when they were in trouble, you lent a hand. That was the way it used to be many years ago. It ain't that way anymore, but I'm a product of my times. So I rushed over there, like a foolish old lady."

"If more people felt the way you did," said Moe seriously, "there would be a lot less crime. What happened next?"

"You ain't going to believe me," said Mrs. Wronski, her voice barely above a whisper. "He," she said, gesturing at Calvin Lane, "thought I was crazy. I could tell."

Lane shrugged his massive shoulders. "I've heard weirder stories, ma'am. You tell Detective Kaufman exactly what you saw. Don't change the facts because of me."

"They were kissing," said Mrs. Wronski, leaning across the table and speaking so low that Moe could hardly hear her. "The door to the apartment was wide open, and I could see inside. A man I never saw before and Mr. Darrow stood in the middle of the parlor, kissing."

Moe glanced over at his partner, but Lane studiously avoided his gaze. "Kissing?"

"I know, I know," said Mrs. Wronski, her voice growing louder. "It sounds nuts, but I swear that's what they were doing. The stranger held a bloody kitchen knife in one hand. His other arm was looped around Darrow's neck, holding his face close. Their lips pushed against each other's so hard it must have been painful. It wasn't like there was any passion involved. These men weren't gay lovers. It was something else, something weird. If anything, it reminded me of mouth-to-mouth resuscitation. They stayed that way for almost a minute."

"Then what?" asked Moe, sighing deeply. His head ached from this insane story.

"I asked Mr. Darrow if everything was all right. To be frank, I couldn't think of anything else to say." Desperation edged Mrs. Wronski's voice. She obviously sensed Moe's disbelief.

"Did he respond?" asked Moe.

"Not at first. His eyes were closed, and his body sagged in the other man's arms. I almost thought he was dead. Then, all of a sudden, his eyes popped open. He stared right at me and then started to laugh."

"What did the other man do?" asked Moe. "The one holding the knife."

"He also acted strange," said Mrs. Wronski. "When Darrow's eyes opened, the stranger collapsed to the floor and didn't move. It reminded me of a puppet whose strings are cut. All the life went out of him."

"So the corpse on the floor isn't Tom Darrow," said Moe. "It's the stranger."

"That's right," said Mrs. Wronski. "It's the man who stabbed Mr. Darrow."

"What?" said Moe, not sure he'd heard what she said correctly.

"I forgot to tell you that," said Mrs. Wronski. "When Darrow first pulled back, I saw blood all over his shirt. The other guy must have stabbed him fifteen or twenty times in the chest. What a god-awful mess."

"Well, that clears up one minor mystery," said Moe. "There's an APB out already on Mr. Darrow. Once we find him, things will clear up quick enough."

"I wouldn't bet on that," said Mrs. Wronski. "He dashed past me like a madman. He moved pretty fast for a guy bleeding so bad. By the time the cops arrived, he was long gone."

"We'll find him," said Moe, expressing a confidence he didn't truly believe.

He rose to his feet. "I think we've troubled you enough for one night, Mrs. Wronski. How about if I send a patrolman to accompany you back to your apartment? Just for peace of mind, of course. Thanks again for your cooperation. You've been a big help."

Alone a few minutes later with his partner, Moe groaned. "What do you think?"

"I meant what I told her," said Lane. "I've heard crazier stories." Then he grinned broadly. "But not for a long, long time. And not from anybody near as sober."

"She sounded so sincere reciting that fairy tale," said Moe. "I almost believed her."

"Wait till we find Darrow," said Lane with a snort. "I can't wait to hear his version. It wouldn't surprise me if Mrs. Wronski did the chopping. She struck me as the kitchen knife type. You keeping an eye on her?"

"Of course," said Moe. "I put Harris and Doyle on stakeout. They'll watch for Darrow, too, in case he returns unexpectedly."

"I'm not holding my breath," said Lane.

"That corpse in the other room has been dead for a week or more," said Moe, shifting topics. "Or so Marlowe claims. How do you explain that?"

"I don't," said Lane. "Black plague? Biological warfare?"

"You've been reading too many spy novels," said Moe. He shook his head, a worried expression on his face. "We're in for big trouble with this case, Calvin. Big trouble. This investigation is going to be a major pain in the ass."

Lane nodded. "Tell me about it. You're only considering it from a cop's viewpoint. Think of the publicity the old lady's story is going to generate. If you feel bad now, wait till the newspapers interview Mrs. Wronski. Her account will make the front pages. I can see the headlines already."

6

▲ "I'll take two of the jelly doughnuts right there in the front of the case," said Carl Garrett, pointing out his choices to the convenience-store clerk. "No need to wrap them up or anything. I'm going to eat them in the van. Just stick a few napkins in the bag. Damn things are always so messy."

"Yes sir," said the boy behind the counter. A tall, gangly teenager with slicked-down black hair, he couldn't have been much more than seventeen years old. "You want me to ring up your total now?"

"Yes, thanks," said Carl pleasantly. The doughnuts joined a stack of nearly five pounds of deli meats, two loaves of bread, and four six-packs of beer on the counter. "What's the damage?"

Methodically, the teenager rang up the purchases, packing the food into a large shopping bag as he did so. From time to time, he cast a nervous glance at Carl and his companion. It was nearly midnight, and there were no other customers.

"That comes to forty-two fifty," said the boy, pushing the bag across the counter.

"Pay the man, George," said Carl over his shoulder. Smiling at the clerk, he picked up the paper sack.

Behind him, George Slater reached beneath his coat, searching for something. Suddenly wary, the clerk stepped back from the counter. Carl knew for sure the boy had his foot on the alarm button. He didn't blame the kid much. George intimidated most people. Even Carl sometimes felt a little uneasy around his huge companion.

Standing six-foot-seven and weighing a little more than four hundred pounds, George was a walking mountain of muscle and bone. With his thick black hair, bushy eyebrows, and full beard, he resembled an old-fashioned lumberjack. No matter what the season, George always wore long-sleeve flannel shirts, rolled up to the elbow. His only concession to the cold weather was a heavy down vest and a Chicago Cubs baseball cap.

"Here it is," said George, his voice rumbling like thunder. He pulled his hand out from his coat. In his huge fingers, he held a crumpled fifty-dollar bill. "I knew I had this son of a bitch in my pocket."

Smoothing out the greenback, he laid it on the counter. "Keep the change," he said cheerfully, and grabbed all four six-packs. "You stay cool now."

"Yeah, sure," said the clerk faintly as the two men left the store. "Take it easy. And thanks."

Ten minutes later and five miles away, Carl steered the van into a deserted parking lot and killed the engine. Patiently, he watched and waited. He always checked his back trail before heading home. Others not so careful had paid the price in blood and disaster.

They were twenty miles south of their hideout in Chicago's far north suburbs. Carl never bought supplies from the same store twice. He favored convenience stores over supermarkets. There were never long lines at the checkout counter, and the big front door was always only a few steps away.

"That kid was scared to death of me," said George casually as they sat in near-total darkness. "I thought his eyes would pop out when I put that big bill on the counter."

Carl nodded as he bit into one of the jelly doughnuts. The pastries were his only vice. Otherwise, food meant nothing to him. Eating provided fuel for his body. Normally he rushed through his meals, considering it wasted time. He felt the same way about sleep, bodily functions, and sex. The only thing he really cared about was his "mission." His entire life revolved around his cause.

"We should've killed him just to be on the safe side," said George, talking softly to himself. "The fifty surprised him. I could have reached over and grabbed him by the neck. One good squeeze would have done the job. It only takes a few seconds to break the bones. No chance for him to reach the alarm."

"The boy caused us no harm, George," said Carl, carefully wiping the sugar off his mouth. By now, he felt sure no one was on their trail. Time to head for home. The other men got restless lately when he was gone too long. He knew the reason. They feared the living corpse who walked among them.

He didn't blame them much. Raising the dead was gruesome business. But he was prepared to deal with the devil himself if it would rescue his enslaved nation.

America will be free someday, Carl swore silently to himself as he started up the van. *No matter how many people have to die, white Christians will again control their sacred destinies.*

"Why didn't you let me do it?" asked George, sounding slightly annoyed. "The punk saw our faces. He could be on the phone right now, calling the FBI."

"I doubt that very much," said Carl, trying to keep his voice calm. Getting angry with George only made things worse. The giant had the personality of a spoiled child. When he didn't get his own way, he sulked for days. "He probably went back to his comic book as soon as we left."

Carefully looking both ways, Carl steered the van back onto the road. The last thing he needed was an accident.

"I told you before we left the house tonight, no violence," he said, once they were on the highway. "Nobody knows us in this part of the country. As long as we maintain a low profile, we're safe. All the law enforcement agencies think we're still out west. The FBI goons spend all their time hunting Blood and Iron in the north woods. One killing, and all our plans go flying out the window. Don't forget, according to the government, we're dangerous criminals.

"The Jewish bankers cartel worries about our group, George. They realize we know the truth about them secretly ruling the country. Their masters in the Kremlin want us silenced before we can spread the word. That's why they have all those FBI stooges hunting us. They outnumber us a hundred thousand to one. The only thing we can do is stay low until the time comes to strike back. And that means no violence of any kind unless absolutely necessary. Now, do you understand?"

"I guess so," said George sullenly. He made no effort

to hide the disappointment in his voice. "I still think the punk recognized me."

Carl gritted his teeth in annoyance. He relied on the big man for too many things to have him unhappy. Somehow, he had to soothe the giant's damaged feelings.

Carl Garrett was a man with a mission. A brilliant, charismatic figure with delusions of grandeur, he was willing to make any sacrifice to achieve his goals. In his own eyes, any crime committed in the fight against the Zionists who secretly ruled America was an act of patriotism. In common with fanatics throughout history, he felt sure that the end justified the means.

The child of Wilson and Nancy Garrett, Carl had been born and raised in the small farming town of Redemption, Kansas, thirty years earlier. A few weeks shy of Carl's second birthday, his father died in a freak accident when a threshing machine slipped into gear and crushed him to death. A large out-of-court settlement with the manufacturer provided Nancy with a comfortable income for the rest of her life. She quit her job at the local restaurant and retired to a home life spent watching soap operas and eating TV dinners.

A lazy, uneducated woman, she raised Carl with a minimal amount of love and attention. Always dressed in secondhand clothes and without any social graces, he was constantly taunted and bullied by his classmates. He endured the punishment in stoic silence, mentally cataloging every insult, every torture. Gifted with a near-genius IQ, Carl possessed a photographic memory for detail. He never forgot or forgave those who made his early life miserable.

Books served as his only companions. While other boys his age joined scouts or baseball leagues, Carl spent all of his free time reading his late father's huge collection of occult and religious texts.

Wilson Garrett had been fascinated for years with obscure cults and supernatural phenomena. At the time of his death, he had assembled a library of nearly a thousand volumes on the two subjects. As a teenager, Carl read through the entire assemblage. Those books he found particularly interesting he read three or four times, committing certain passage to memory. His favorite among all the works was an esoteric religious tract written in 1871 by Edward Hine titled *Identification of the British Nation with Lost Israel.*

Central to the book's theme was the thesis that the British Isles were settled by the Lost Ten Tribes of Israel. According to Hine, that made the English the true chosen people of the Old Testament. Furthermore, those people calling themselves Jews were actually descended from Satan. Zionism actually masked a worldwide plot to wipe out the white Christian race.

Ignored and forgotten by the early twentieth century, Hine's beliefs gained new life after World War II with the founding of the state of Israel. Aid from the United States to the fledgling country enraged anti-Semitic extremist groups throughout America. Using *Lost Israel* as justification, they claimed an international Jewish bankers conspiracy controlled both the United Nations and the United States.

By the time Carl Garrett read the book in 1975, it served as the binding force between such diverse hate groups as the Ku Klux Klan and the American Nazi Party. Each organization found specific ideas in Hine's work to support their own version of world events. Searching through his father's library, Carl discovered a number of other books and pamphlets written by biblical revisionists furthering the Anglo-Israel doctrine. Their twisted message binding racial hatred and fervent patriotism found a willing convert in the lonely teenager.

By the time he graduated from high school, Carl knew his purpose in life. A well-built, handsome young man with clean-cut features, he preached endlessly to anyone who would listen about the Zionist cabal that controlled the government and the press. Strangely enough, for all of his anti-Semitic fervor, Carl had never once met a Jew. None lived in Redemption.

An outsider in his own community, thought to be half crazy by most of the townspeople, Carl dreamed of escape from small-town life. He knew he needed money—the one rule of survival he learned over the years was that cold cash, not good looks or a pleasant personality, paid the bills. Penniless and without a job, Carl decided to murder his mother.

Nancy spent most afternoons soaking in the bathtub, watching her favorite shows on a portable TV she kept perched on the bathroom sink. One summer's day, while he was supposedly out of town looking for work, Carl took advantage of her dangerous habit. He crept back into the house shortly after his mother had settled down in the tub to watch "All My Children."

Nancy kept the bathroom door locked, but Carl had made a duplicate key. His mother looked quite startled when Carl slipped into the chamber. Shocked and embarrassed, she tried to cover her naked body with her hands.

"What are you doing here?" she asked indignantly.

"I just came to say good-bye," answered Carl truthfully.

"Good-bye?" said Nancy. "Where are you going?"

"I'm not the one who's leaving, Mother," said Carl. "You are."

Something in his tone of voice must have alerted her to the danger. Or perhaps it was the plastic gloves he was wearing so as not to leave any fingerprints. With a whimper, Nancy struggled to get to her feet.

Carl waited until she was nearly standing before he tossed the portable television at her. With a shriek, Nancy instinctively grabbed for the set. Unable to keep her balance, she plunged back into the soapy water, clutching the TV set in her arms.

Nancy was electrocuted instantly, though violent convulsions jolted her dead body for several seconds more. The smell of burnt flesh filled the bathroom as Carl carefully checked for any signs of his presence. There was nothing to indicate he had ever been there. To all appearances, Nancy had slipped getting out of the tub, fallen, and accidentally knocked the appliance into the tub. Carl was sure the local authorities would rule her death an accident.

And so they did. A month later, Carl headed off for California with $140,000 in his pocket and a list of extremist organizations he wanted to contact.

For the next ten years, he drifted from one group to another, attending meetings of a dozen different racial purity organizations throughout the far west. Still an avid reader, he devoured every book or pamphlet available on the Jewish bankers conspiracy or the "black menace."

According to the modern version of Hine's theory, blacks and other nonwhite races were subhuman creatures created by God to serve true men, the white Anglo-Saxons. Inferior beings, they resented their betters and sought to bring them down to their level. The males, in particular, lusted after white women.

In their efforts to destroy those of pure blood, the Jews had rewritten the laws of the United States to encourage race mixing and preferential treatment of blacks. The amendments to the Constitution as well as the rulings of the Supreme Court were all part of the same conspiracy.

To Carl, there seemed only one answer to the undeclared war between the races. Violence had to be met with violence. The only problem was that most white Christians were unaware of the secret forces working against them. They had to be informed of their peril.

However, few people he met seemed willing to fight for their beliefs. Membership in the paramilitary groups consisted primarily of dissatisfied middle-aged men intent on playing soldier once a month. None of these "Anglo-Israelites" appeared in any hurry to actually engage the enemy.

Their leaders were no different. Drawn primarily from the ranks of the KKK and the American Nazi Party of the late 1960s, they had grown fat and lazy over the years. Comfortable with their position in life, the men spent much of their time promoting the church teachings that encouraged polygamy. They preached a great deal about rescuing their country from the Zionists but refused to take any action against the enemy. Suspicious to the point of paranoia, Carl concluded that most of the groups had been infiltrated and subverted by government agents.

Disillusioned, Carl decided to form his own organization. Over a period of six months in 1985, he recruited a half-dozen fanatics to his cause. They christened their group *Blut und Eisen,* the German phrase for "Blood and Iron."

Iron described Carl's personality. George "Sledgehammer" Slater provided the blood. A folk hero among extremists, he joined the cabal late that summer.

George had been on the run from the authorities for more than a year. He traveled from one extremist conclave to another, staying one step ahead of the law. Carl met him in August 1985 at a gathering of the Brothers of Gideon, an Idaho paramilitary group. By the end of the meeting, the two men were already planning their first strike against the U.S. government.

Originally a farmer in Nebraska, George had grown rich on paper during the boom days of the late '60s and early '70s. But when inflation went wild and agricultural prices plummeted, he found himself deep in debt to the local bank. The day two sheriff's deputies came to his farm with a warrant, George greeted them at the door with a sledgehammer. The encounter left both lawmen dead and earned George a place on the FBI's most-wanted list.

Extremist groups throughout the Northwest portrayed George Slater as the innocent victim of the international Jewish bankers conspiracy. In actuality, he was a borderline psychotic with a long history of violent run-ins with the police. None of that mattered to Carl. He knew now he controlled the necessary muscle to strike a blow against the hated Zionists.

Over the next two years, Blood and Iron conducted the

most daring series of bank robberies and armored car hijackings since the days of the Great Depression. Armed with high-powered automatic weapons and using the latest high-tech computer wizardry, the urban terrorists became the most feared gang of killers in the annals of American crime.

George Slater received most of the publicity. Notorious even before his exploits with Blood and Iron, the bearded giant made great copy for the newspapers. George enjoyed killing, and he ruthlessly murdered more than a dozen people, usually using his bare hands, during the course of their crime spree. However, Carl was the one responsible for the group's incredible success.

A genius at planning, Carl benefited from mistakes of past gangs. With his photographic memory, he remembered and avoided the mistakes that had brought about the downfall of his predecessors. Too many gangs perished because of spies or traitors in their midst. Carl ensured the fidelity of his troops by personally recruiting each new member.

Carl also refused to let money interfere with his sacred mission. Greed and envy brought ruin if left unchecked. The gang kept only enough cash to live in comfort and buy necessary equipment. The rest of the booty was mailed in plain brown boxes to other extremist groups all through the United States. During Blood and Iron's reign of terror, nearly six million dollars found its way into the hands of lunatic fringe paramilitary organizations.

For all of their successes, Carl remained dissatisfied. He realized how little the robberies and killings affected the evil cabal that ruled the country. The Zionist-controlled press twisted their exploits and made Blood and Iron into common criminals. He was still searching for new tactics when his strange dreams began.

A student of the occult, Carl recognized the opportunity Jambres offered. It was in the land of Egypt that black magic began. According to the ancient texts, a powerful sorcerer commanded forces unimagined by modern man. He was on equal footing with the gods. Working together, they could make the world tremble.

But, to do so, Carl needed the absolute cooperation of all his men. He couldn't afford to have George Slater angry. There had to be a way to soothe the giant's ruffled feelings.

"Forget that clerk," said Carl, trying to sound worried. "I'm more concerned about a possible traitor in our own organization."

"Who do you mean?" said George, suddenly not so sullen.

"Sarah," said Carl. The silence beside him indicated he had guessed right. George didn't trust the seeress. He disliked anyone who might be a rival for Carl's attention.

"She owes her loyalty to Jambres, not us," continued Carl. "Someday that could prove dangerous."

"Why not just kill her now?" asked George.

"We can't risk upsetting Jambres. At least, not until he makes good on his promises. Then, I think, we will reevaluate our relationship with this sorcerer. And his apprentice."

"What do you want me to do?" asked George, looking like an eager puppy, anxious to please. Gone was all mention of the convenience-store clerk. George could only concentrate on one thing at a time.

"Keep a close watch on Sarah. Report anything unusual to me. The same holds for Jambres. I don't trust him. He's not telling us the whole story about this statue. I'm patient, though. All good things come to those who wait."

"I'll do my best," said George fervently. "But one thing bothers me, Carl."

"What's that?"

"How do you kill a dead man?"

Carl grimaced. "That's one question I can't answer. At least, not yet. But I'll find a way. Nobody crosses Carl Garrett and survives. *Nobody.*"

7

▲ As they drove back to the hideout, Jambres surveyed the passing scene with curious eyes. On the ride into the city, he had been too concerned with the state of his decaying body to do any sightseeing. Now, safely housed in a fresh corpse, he could relax and concentrate on his surroundings.

The landscape was totally alien to him, yet at the same time very familiar. It was as if two sets of thoughts fought for space within his mind. He marveled at the wonders of the modern world.

During his life in Kamt, only a few magicians had ever performed the ritual known as the Dead Man's Kiss. They used the spell merely to remain alive a few hours or a few days longer to finish one last important task. In ancient Egypt, death was neither feared nor avoided. Death was recognized as an inevitable part of life, a moving-on to a higher plane of existence.

Jambres recalled a conversation he had with Sa-Asar, a fellow sorcerer, thirty centuries ago. Sa-Asar, a man many years older than himself, suffered from the wasting disease that gnawed at his insides. Death approached him with heavy steps.

For months, Sa-Asar's slaves labored feverishly to prepare his tomb for his journey to the Underworld. When it became clear that the edifice would not be completed in time, Sa-Asar had transferred his *ka* into the body of his chief supervisor through use of the Dead Man's Kiss.

His own body, without a soul, remained in a state hovering between life and death. Meanwhile, animating the corpse of his servant, the magician had been able to oversee the final stages of construction of his burial site.

"The effects of the spell are maddening," Sa-Asar confided to Jambres on the afternoon before the completion of the tomb. "The spirit has departed from this flesh, but some traces of the supervisor's *ka* remain. His thoughts, his feelings, and his experiences are open for my inspection. It is as if I lived his life as well as my own. My thoughts are those of two men, not one."

Jambres nodded, not exactly sure what Sa-Asar meant. Now, thousands of years later, experiencing the same sensations, he understood his friend's confusion.

"All of my chamberlain's pleasures, as well as all of his sufferings, mingle with mine," continued Sa-Asar. "His darkest desires stain my soul. Only now do I know the secrets hidden behind my supposedly loyal servant's bland smile. How he mocked me in private and cheated on the household accounts. How he spied on my family and laughed at our misfortune."

On the far side of the courtyard, Sa-Asar's wife loudly directed the servants making final preparations for the evening feast. She was an extremely attractive woman with flashing black eyes and a voluptuous figure. Many years younger than the magician, she possessed a sharp tongue and knew how to use it.

"My faithful wife," said Sa-Asar with a bitter laugh. "My deceitful servant noted her comings and goings carefully. Especially when I was out of the country. No wonder she let him run the household as he wished. She dared not let him inform me of her trysts."

He laughed again. "My *faithful* wife. I have made plans for her."

Sa-Asar shook his head. "We search for knowledge all our lives, my friend. But beware—the truth tastes of ashes."

They never spoke again. Later that day, Jambres was

summoned before Pharaoh. By evening time, he was on a bark many miles down the Nile, attending to secret work for the god-king.

When Jambres returned many months later, Sa-Asar had long since departed on his final trip to the Underworld. Gone, too, was his beautiful wife. She had vanished without a trace the night of the magician's entombment and was thought to be dead. Rumors had it that in her sorrow she had thrown herself into the Nile and drowned.

Other, darker stories, told only at night, described her being dragged kicking and screaming into her husband's tomb by the magician's vengeful spirit. Jambres, who had more than once enjoyed the ample charms of his friend's unfaithful spouse, considered this the more likely explanation.

"You're awfully quiet," said Sarah, dragging Jambres back to the present.

"I'm fascinated by this great city," lied Jambres. "Nothing in my wildest dreams prepared me for your world."

"Not much like Egypt, is it?" said Sarah.

"A difference of day and night," he replied.

Sarah smiled and settled back to her driving. Jambres saw no reason to elaborate on his feelings. Let the woman live with her delusions. The modern metropolis didn't overawe him, it disgusted him. Kamt had been a land of heat and sun, not this dark and dismal collection of untold millions stacked high in buildings like boxes.

But all this will change, he swore silently to himself. For now, he was content to wait and plan. Three thousand years of waiting made him very patient.

"Carl isn't going to be happy with what went on tonight," said Sarah a few minutes later. "Especially when he sees your new body."

"He's a reasonable man," said Jambres, suspecting that what he said was not true. "It had to be done."

"He won't see it that way," said Sarah, the first sounds

of panic evident in her voice. "I know the way he thinks. Carl likes to make all the decisions. *All* of them."

"Let me handle Carl," said Jambres. "And George as well."

Immediately, Jambres knew he had made a mistake. The mere mention of the giant's name started Sarah shivering. All color drained from her face. Hands tightly clutching the steering wheel, she huddled down in her seat. She was deathly afraid of the big killer.

Jambres desperately searched Tom Darrow's memories for a means to counterbalance her terror of George Slater. He relied on the seeress. His plans depended on her cooperation. Bound by fear, she would be useless to him.

A thousand images flickered through his mind in the space of an instant. Mentally, Jambres sneered at the picture they presented. Like most men obsessed with their own importance, Darrow never recognized the essential shallowness of his life. The dead man had spent most of his life in an endless search for pleasure—a worthless parasite on society. Jambres felt no remorse at having killed him. Not that it would have mattered in any case. His mission was more important than any one life—or any thousand lives. Soon the whole world would tremble before his rage.

Tom Darrow's interests in life circled around one person—himself. An arrogant, egotistical man, he considered himself God's gift to women everywhere. A bartender by trade, Darrow worked only a few nights a week. Instead of struggling, he let his various conquests support him. He moved from woman to woman as his mood shifted. He rarely remained faithful to anyone more than a few weeks. There were always plenty of other good-looking girls to pay the bills.

His seduction of Sarah Walsh had been done in his usual smooth style. Darrow was taken by the woman's long blond hair and dark brown eyes. It wasn't until he moved in with her that Darrow learned of Sarah's weird obsession.

In seconds, Jambres reviewed the entire story of their stormy relationship. The memory of those days was sharply etched in Darrow's psyche.

Death and dying fascinated Sarah Walsh. Both acted as powerful sexual stimulants. Darrow had no idea how strongly Sarah was affected until he allowed himself to be drawn into her fantasies. Afterward, he found himself both repelled and aroused by her bizarre tastes.

The first incident had taken place in a cemetery not far from their apartment. Sarah enjoyed taking long strolls in the early evening among the tombstones. Soon after Darrow moved in, she pleaded that he go there with her. A bit squeamish, Darrow at first refused. But after days of her constant badgering, he gave in.

They set out right after the sun went down the next night. It was a hot, humid evening, in the middle of the summer. Only the stars and a half-moon served as light.

The air weighed heavy on Darrow's chest. There had been a burial earlier in the day, and the smell of newly turned earth filled his nostrils. Sarah inhaled it deeply, as if smelling perfume.

Chatting merrily, she led him down one narrow path after another, threading their way deeper and deeper into the graveyard. From time to time, she stopped, pointing out a favorite spot or a curious tombstone. Face flushed red with excitement, she guided Darrow down paths only she knew existed.

Finally, they came upon a solitary tomb at the center of the cemetery. The white marble building glowed eerily from reflected moonlight. Only the sounds of crickets broke the stillness of the night. There was no one else about. Less than a hundred feet from the streets of the city, they could have been in another world.

"This is my favorite spot," said Sarah, leaning back against the solid metal door of the tomb. "I love it here. So close to the outside world, and yet so far away."

She licked her lips, almost as if in hunger. In the darkness, her eyes sparkled like a cat's eyes. Reaching up, she gripped the upper edge of her tube top. With one fluid motion, she pulled it forward and down, releasing her breasts. Darrow gasped in surprise. Her naked skin glowed white in the moonlight. Sensuously, Sarah rubbed her dark nipples until they grew hard and erect.

"The feel of cold marble drives me wild," she said, continuing to caress her breasts. Sarah leaned back so that her nude back rested against the mausoleum wall. "Right around now, I'd be willing to do anything. Anything at all."

Darrow didn't need any coaxing. He grabbed Sarah and pulled her close. Their lips met in a passionate kiss. Her tongue snaked inside his mouth, writhing with desire. Her breasts mashed hard into his chest. He had never been so aroused before. His body felt like it was on fire.

Savagely, Sarah spun him around so that now it was his back pressed against the cool stone. The fury of her kisses burned away his remaining inhibitions. There was no stopping her, no turning back.

Her hands fumbled with his belt, and then with the snap of his pants. In seconds, he was naked from the waist down. He shivered with desire as Sarah boldly grasped his erection.

Breaking off their kiss, Sarah dropped to her knees in front of him. There was no question what she intended. For an instant, Darrow fretted about someone stumbling across them in the darkness. He knew that most cemeteries employ a night watchman.

Then all of his protests died unspoken. Sarah wasn't concerned about being discovered. Sex was the only thing on her mind. Oral sex. Darrow moaned softly as her mouth engulfed his rigid shaft.

He only lasted a few minutes. What little control he still possessed disappeared when Sarah's hands grabbed him by the buttocks and forced him deeper into her throat. The combination of sensations from her hands and mouth proved too much. With a groan of release, he exploded in the most intense climax of his entire life.

After their first session of sex and death, Darrow

worried about being discovered by the authorities. But he had to admit it was his most memorable sexual experience ever, and Sarah had no difficulty persuading him to experiment with the combination again. And again. And then as often as possible.

When sex in local cemeteries grew boring, they sought new thrills. Visiting funeral parlors, they discreetly sought information about burial plots for fictional relatives conveniently near death. Invariably left alone for a few minutes' contemplation, they performed forbidden acts among the coffins. Sarah reveled in her power to bring him to a shuddering climax through a hurried act of oral sex.

Wakes served as the location for a number of memorable experiences. They went to all the ones listed in the newspapers, in the guise of old friends or coworkers. Late at night, as solitary relatives fought with grief or dozed quietly, they engaged in acts of mutual masturbation surrounded by huge bouquets of flowers.

Each excess led to even greater risks. They delighted in attending funeral masses in the many old churches that dotted Chicago's northwest neighborhoods. Ensconced in the farthest corner of the building, Sarah remained standing throughout the entire service. No one suspected that her lover crouched at her feet, hidden by the wooden pews, his tongue and fingers bringing her to climax after climax. Kindly priests, noting how her body shook during the mass, usually offered quiet words of sympathy when she departed, never guessing the truth.

In the end, it was not another woman, as Sarah claimed, that came between them, but her own twisted desires. Darrow was afraid of Sarah's fascination with exhibitionism. It wasn't enough for her to perform sexual acts in public places. Sarah wanted people to know exactly what she was doing.

Darrow suspected that one obsession fueled the other. By mixing sex and death, Sarah was proclaiming her triumph over mortality. She was showing her contempt.

At first, the act itself had been enough for her. But, driven by her success, she now wanted to demonstrate her bravery to the entire world.

Darrow refused to cooperate. A vain man, Darrow had an overwhelming fear of appearing foolish in public. The notion of being caught in a compromising position by the police drove him mad with worry. As Sarah's schemes grew increasingly bold, Darrow's passion cooled.

Her insistence that they make love at the city morgue brought an end to their relationship. Darrow agreed to meet her at the building at midnight. However, while she headed downtown for their late-night rendezvous, he drove instead to the apartment they shared. At twelve, he busily emptied all of his possessions into his car. In compensation for the time he had devoted to her, he took her valuables as well.

Sex and death, Jambres reflected silently, two of the most powerful forces in the universe. So it had been in his time, as it still was, thousands of years later. The combination would bind Sarah to him with unbreakable chains.

He decided on a bold course of action. There was not enough time to be subtle. Garrett was too dangerous to be trusted. Jambres needed an ally who was totally loyal to his wishes.

Impulsively, he reached out and rested a hand on Sarah's thigh. Surprised, she jerked her leg away. In reflex action, her hands spun the steering wheel in the same direction.

Out of control for an instant, the car careened to the left. Tires caught on the shoulder of the road, sending Jambres tumbling against Sarah. Almost by accident, his hand slipped between her legs.

"S-sorry," stuttered Sarah, guiding the auto back on course. Her gaze never wavered from the road ahead. Her voice quivered slightly as she continued, "You startled me."

Sarah made no mention of his fingers boldly stroking

her body. Instead, she slouched down further on the seat, opening her legs further to his touch. Her face flushed blood-red with excitement.

"Together," said Jambres softly, as he pulled up her dress to reveal her nakedness, "we will triumph."

"Together," repeated Sarah, thrusting her hips forward anxiously. She moaned as his fingers made contact with the wetness between her thighs.

"United," said Jambres, knowing exactly what mental image that word would summon. "The living and the dead."

8

▲ Sleep eluded Ellen. Normally she was out before her head touched the pillow. Tonight all of her usual cures for insomnia had failed.

After an hour of tossing and turning, she got out of bed, put on her robe, and went to the kitchen. The clock over the sink read ten minutes to one. Nervously, Ellen stared at the phone on the wall. One call could put an end to the jitters—or make them a hundred times worse.

For the twentieth time since arriving at her apartment, she mentally debated phoning Andy Yates. If Andy answered, what could she say to justify calling at one in the morning? She was worried because he hadn't come to work and a night watchman and the museum chairman were also absent. Even to Ellen, that explanation sounded awfully lame.

Her problem, she decided, was that she was too straitlaced and proper. She hated appearing foolish. It went contrary to her carefully cultivated professional image. A successful career woman didn't panic every time her overactive imagination kicked into gear.

Even among her closest friends, Ellen had the reputation for being cold and distant. In reality, she was just the opposite. Her emotions ran deep and true. The difficulty arose in expressing those feelings.

More than likely, a simple explanation existed for Andy's unusual behavior. Still, Ellen couldn't force the worry out of her thoughts. Too many detective and suspense novels warned her to mistrust the obvious.

Single, without many friends outside the museum staff, Ellen rarely went out in the evening. She disliked bars and refused to consider blind dates. Resigned to a static social life, she instead devoured mystery books.

She rushed through them the same way some people eat chocolates. A day rarely passed when she didn't finish a book or two. Spy novels and thrillers were her favorites. However, a steady diet of these books resulted in an abiding concern with secret conspiracies and dangerous plots.

Biting her lip, Ellen picked up the receiver. She had to call him—either that or stay awake all night. Slowly, she dialed Andy's number.

The heroines of suspense novels she read never worried about what to say in situations like this. They just relied on their wits to extract them from sticky entanglements. Reaching the last number, Ellen hesitated for an instant before punching it through.

She settled on a simple course of action. When Andy answered, she would hang up. No reason for him to know who was on the other end of the line. The sound of his voice was all she needed to calm her nerves. Any explanation of his actions could wait until he returned to work. Just knowing he was all right would be enough for now.

The phone rang. The breath froze in her lungs as she waited for a reply. And waited. And waited.

After twenty rings, she gave up. Putting down the receiver, she rose to her feet. "No reason to get upset," she said aloud, her voice trembling. "He probably was called out of town for a family emergency and forgot to turn on his answering machine."

Ellen fought to hold back the tears. Her explanation sounded terribly hollow. Andy always turned on his answering machine when he went away. He couldn't bear the thought of missing a message.

Standing there, in the center of her kitchen at one A.M., Ellen confronted her dilemma.

She marched back to her bedroom. She might not be the heroine in a novel, but she did know what was right and wrong. There was only one way to settle this mystery. Off came her nightgown, to be replaced by jeans and a sweatshirt. Andy's apartment was twenty minutes away.

Grabbing her purse, Ellen swept out the front door, filled with purpose. Her mind was made up; she acted without hesitation. She didn't care what time it was. She was going to visit Andy Yates tonight.

9

▲ Carl Garrett prided himself on never losing his temper. He felt it was a measure of his self-control. An angry man acted irrationally. A dangerous man stayed emotionally detached from events no matter how badly provoked.

He remained perfectly calm as he interrogated Sarah Walsh and Satni Jambres. There was nothing in his tone of voice to indicate he was discussing anything more important than the weather.

"You're confident that no one trailed you back to our

retreat?" he asked Sarah, rubbing his chin thoughtfully. He had been careful to question both Sarah and Jambres separately. Their stories had matched perfectly. Though he trusted neither of them, it seemed unlikely they were lying about the night's events.

"Definitely not," she replied confidently. "I'm not stupid. I doubled back and around several times. And I waited at the turnoff for five minutes before proceeding."

"Very commendable," said Carl dryly. "I'm sure such a long wait would try the patience of anyone following you."

Sarah smiled faintly, the sarcasm lost on her. Carl shook his head in disgust. She was a fool, an outsider, recruited on Jambres's suggestion. Her stupidity threatened the security of the entire organization.

Carl weighed the consequences of killing her before she could do any real damage. After several seconds, he regretfully rejected the notion. Jambres claimed that he needed the seeress to further his plans. If Carl murdered her tonight, it would be an admission of defeat. And he wasn't ready yet to abandon his dreams.

"I was only trying to help," whispered Sarah, obviously troubled by his silence. Her voice sounded desperate. "Jambres would have perished without a new body."

Carl knew she believed that. He suspected otherwise. Jambres was as cunning as a rattler and twice as poisonous. With or without Sarah's help, the sorcerer would have found a way to survive.

"I agree," he said, sounding as if he actually did. Nothing in his manner betrayed the contempt he actually felt for her. "But," and his voice grew cold and distant, "you disobeyed my direct command. George wanted you punished. He demanded that you be punished—severely. I think he wanted to do it himself."

Sarah's face turned ash-white. She huddled in her chair, terrified. Carl continued to speak, as if unaware of her reaction. "George can be very stubborn when he gets upset. He's not entirely sane, you know. When these rages take hold, it's difficult for me to control him. He wants to strike out and hurt people. Not merely kill them, but make them suffer first.

"It's quite fascinating. He's like a vampire, living off the pain of his captives. I've seen him at work. He spends hours at it, wringing scream after scream from his luckless prey. Most of the time, George concentrates on the face. Teeth are smashed, eyes gouged, features maimed. It gets pretty grisly after a while. Eventually his victims expire, but never while they're still sane."

Sarah was trembling violently now. She looked ready to puke. Carl felt satisfied.

"I told George to leave you alone," he said. "You have nothing to worry about. Not as long as you follow orders. Understand? I allow one mistake. Don't make another."

"Oh, I won't, Carl, I won't," Sarah promised, her voice quivering with relief. "You can count on me."

"I know," he said, rising to his feet, dismissing her. "Tell Jambres I want to speak to him again."

Sarah exited as quickly as possible. Alone for a moment, Carl breathed a sigh of relief. He had George watching Sarah. After his little lecture, Sarah would be keeping close tabs on George. His two wild cards would neutralize each other.

Carl had discovered the seeress on Chicago's north side, running a variation of the gypsy fortune-teller scam. Jambres, in his dreams, assured Carl that Sarah was no fake. She was a gifted psychic who possessed the necessary skill and knowledge to free his imprisoned spirit.

Moreover, Sarah passionately hated the government. An orphan of unknown parentage, she was a ward of the state, who had been shuffled from foster home to foster home for most of her childhood. She never stayed put at one house very long.

Her erratic mental powers involved her in constant mischief. A wild, unhappy child, she craved attention she rarely received. She was mistreated, abused, and often ignored by couples more interested in the monthly government stipend she brought than in her welfare.

At sixteen, she escaped the brutal sexual advances of her latest foster father by strangling him to death while he slept. Convinced she would face prison if caught, Sarah disappeared into the vast underground of runaway teenagers. Luckier than most, she had her psychic powers to protect her.

She spent the next ten years drifting among tarot readers, faith healers, and psychics of all types. Most were blatant fakes, but a few possessed legitimate mental powers. Little by little, she learned to control her own gifts.

One mystic, a certain Professor Drago, taught her the rudiments of black magic. He also put her in touch with others, who for a price were willing to teach her more. She paid—usually in cash, sometimes in blood. A bit squeamish at times, Sarah was otherwise completely amoral.

She blamed the government for all of her suffering and unhappiness. Nameless bureaucrats, more intent on finishing their paperwork on time than on doing a good job, had destroyed her childhood. Sarah knew from TV that growing up meant dolls and good friends and high school proms. She remembered only incessant hunger and constant beatings. Sarah meant to get even. Blood and Iron offered her the chance.

Carl had no illusions about any of his companions. Hard, dangerous killers, they were outcasts of society. George and Sarah were the worst of the bunch, but all of the members of his elite band were slightly off balance.

Hate drove them, motivated them, ruled their lives. Hatred of the Jews and the blacks, the Catholics and the race mixers who sought to destroy white America. Hatred of the bloated federal government whose agents dogged their footsteps, trying to destroy them. Hatred of all those who opposed their holy crusade.

They fought impossible odds. Their enemy numbered in the millions and controlled the wealth of the mightiest nation in the world. Carl's vision guided them, gave them purpose, kept them strong. Without his leadership, they were nothing. His unshakable beliefs sustained them. He was the rock of their faith.

Time worked on their side. Already, thousands supported them in secret. The longer they remained at large, the more desperate the Zionists became. The secret rulers of America knew they could not suppress the truth forever. One day, white Christians everywhere would rise up and exterminate their oppressors. And leading them would be Blood and Iron.

Or so Carl promised. Unknown to his compatriots, he wasn't quite so positive. The enemy controlled the newspapers, the radio, and the television stations. He had no way to broadcast the truth. Most people lived in total ignorance of the powers controlling their lives. Besides, years of subtle brainwashing had turned the population into a nation of stupid sheep. There was no sleeping army out in the heartland waiting to be awakened.

But the resurrection of the sorcerer changed all the rules. Jambres controlled powers beyond belief. With his help, Carl could change the world. But only with the Egyptian's help.

"You wanted to speak with me," said Jambres from the doorway.

Carl looked up, startled. The dead man moved without making a sound. Not even a breath betrayed him. Carl wondered how long Jambres had been standing there. Spying on him. Perhaps reading his mind. Carl wasn't sure what the sorcerer could do.

Jambres frightened him. There was no mistaking the Egyptian for a living person. He was a dead man, walking. Though he moved with the subtle grace of a cat, his pale skin and glazed eyes cried out, "I am death. I am corruption."

Carl motioned to the seat recently vacated by Sarah. Unable to meet Jambres's lifeless stare, Carl concentrated on a spot on the far wall as he spoke.

"You convinced Sarah that Hinkley's body was failing. I'll go along with that. But tell me. What if she refused to believe you? Or if I had left Luther or Sam guarding you? They might not have been so agreeable. What would you have done then?"

Jambres held up his right hand. He muttered a few words under his breath, so soft that Carl heard nothing he said. With an audible hiss, inch-long jets of blue flame crowned his five fingers. The magician murmured another phrase, and the flames extended six inches into the air.

Carl swallowed hard. He could feel the heat of the fires across his desk.

"I am not without methods of persuasion," said Jambres with a laugh. "I would have made them an offer they could not refuse."

Carl scowled. It spooked him when Jambres used modern slang. He had expected the sorcerer to be overwhelmed by the modern world. Instead, Jambres seemed perfectly adjusted to the wonders that surrounded him. For the hundredth time in the past week, Carl wondered if he had done the right thing in freeing the sorcerer's spirit.

"Don't fret over my trick," said Jambres, as if sensing Carl's discomfort. "I meant no disrespect. We are allies. There is no reason for us to quarrel. Your enemies are my enemies. We both strive for the same goals."

"Sure," said Carl, wondering if he actually believed Jambres. He suspected the sorcerer had plans of his own. Plans he felt sure had nothing to do with Blood and Iron or their mission.

"You caught me by surprise, that's all. I mean, changing bodies and all that."

"The fault was mine," said Jambres, as if in apology. "I should have realized that decomposition could only be postponed, not stopped."

The sorcerer hesitated for a moment, then continued. "You realize, of course, that I will need to change bodies frequently."

"How frequently?" asked Carl, not very pleased with this new revelation.

"My will alone holds the forces of decay at bay," said

Jambres. "Performing acts of sorcery forces me to direct my full attention elsewhere. In the meantime, corruption attacks my body. The more magic I attempt, the quicker my body rots."

"I told you before not to waste your time on these killings," said Carl. "These weird murders are bound to attract attention."

"I disagree," said Jambres. "I dare not take any chances."

The sorcerer chuckled. A harsh, barking sound, it made Carl shudder. Dead men weren't meant to laugh.

"Besides," he said, his face twisted in an obscene grin, "do you really think any policeman will believe what is taking place? They are trained to think rationally. And black magic is not part of the rational world."

Jambres stood up. "Hinkley kindly provided us with a list of those individuals at the museum who might cause problems. Night after night, I send out a demon to devour their spirits. Two are already dead. Soon the rest will follow. Swallow your pride and accept the inevitable."

The magician walked to the door. "Do you need me for anything else? If not, I leave to continue the hunt. The spell only works during the dark hours."

Carl dismissed the sorcerer with a wave of a hand. His eyes narrowed as he watched Jambres depart. More than ever, he felt sure the Egyptian planned a double-cross. Not that he expected any less. In this deadly game, only the ruthless survived.

Alone at last, Carl raised his hands onto the desk. Carefully, he laid down the Skorpion machine pistol he had kept hidden on his lap during the last half hour. For all of Jambres's bravado, Carl doubted that the sorcerer could survive the more than eight hundred rounds per minute the deadly gun fired.

A faint smile crossed Carl's lips. The dead man thought magic was the supreme force in the universe. The cold feel of the Czech machine gun told Carl otherwise.

10

▲ Biting her lip, Ellen pushed the intercom button above Andy Yates's mailbox. Holding her breath, she waited for someone to answer. Silently, she prayed for a reply. Nothing happened.

After a minute, she pressed the button for a second time. Again, no one responded. A tear formed in one eye. Angrily, she brushed it aside. She had expected no less. If Andy wasn't answering the phone, he surely wouldn't be opening the door.

Ellen hesitated for an instant. The possibility still existed that Andy had left town in a rush. In an emergency, he might have forgotten his answering machine. A power failure or a blown fuse could have put the device out of service. All of her earlier doubts rushed back to haunt her. Standing alone in a deserted hallway at two A.M., she suddenly felt very stupid.

Shrugging her shoulders, Ellen turned and walked out the front door. Wearily, she started down the steps to her car. Without thinking, she surveyed the other autos parked on the street. Her gaze fixed on a bright yellow Volkswagen—it was Andy's car.

Throat dry, Ellen rushed over to the vehicle. A piece of white paper peeked out from under the front windshield wiper. Ellen pulled the ticket out and scanned it quickly. There was no parking on this street from nine A.M. till five P.M. on Thursdays so the street cleaners could work efficiently. Andy had obviously parked his car here on Wednesday night, intending to drive to work on Thursday morning. The parking ticket offered mute evidence he had never done so.

Back in the apartment building foyer a few minutes later, Ellen ignored Andy's call switch. Instead, she pressed hard on the button to the superintendent's apartment.

"Whatcha want?" came the sleepy question, harsh and metallic over the intercom.

"It's Ellen Harper, Mr. O'Malley," she replied, trying not to sound hysterical. "You've got to let me into Andy's apartment. I think he's hurt. Or worse."

"Lady, it's two o'clock in the morning," said O'Malley. "Go home and leave me alone."

"If you don't help me, I'll call the police," said Ellen, playing her trump card. "How would you like that?"

Dead silence greeted her threat. Ellen had never met the superintendent but had heard many stories about him from Andy. A no-nonsense individual, he tolerated no wild parties or celebrations in his building. O'Malley liked things quiet. Ellen was gambling that the last people he wanted tramping through the apartments in the middle of the night were the police.

She guessed right. "I'll be right there," he finally answered. "But this better not be some sorta lovers' quarrel. Or your Mr. Yates will be looking for new lodgings."

Ellen waited nervously for O'Malley to arrive. Now that she was finally going to discover the truth, she wasn't sure she wanted to know. Droplets of sweat trickled down her back. By the time the superintendent opened the security door, she was starting to feel queasy.

"Now, what's this all about?" asked O'Malley, walking with her down the hallway to Andy's apartment. A short, burly individual of indeterminate age, he wore a bright green pajama top tucked into a pair of faded jeans. In one hand, he clutched a thick ring of keys.

Taking a deep breath, Ellen rattled off her suspicions. O'Malley frowned when she mentioned the parking ticket.

"I don't know much about Yates's workin' habits," he said quietly. "I'll take yer word on that. But I know he hates gettin' stuck with a fine."

O'Malley looked at her sideways and shrugged. "Begging your pardon, Miss, but your boyfriend's a bit on the cheap side."

They stopped in front of 2D, Andy's apartment. O'Malley glanced around suspiciously. "Ain't none of them photographers lurking about, are there?" he asked. "I'm not looking to be involved in one of those divorce scandals."

"No, no, no," said Ellen, trying to stay calm. "Please, I'm telling you the truth."

"I hope so," said O'Malley, and he rapped his knuckles on the wood paneling. No answer.

O'Malley knocked harder. Still no answer.

"Mr. Yates," the superintendent said softly. "Are ya in there? It's me, O'Malley."

No reply. O'Malley lifted his key ring and hit the door sharply several times. The distinctive sound of metal hitting wood rang sharp and clear in the hallway. No answer.

"I'm likin' this less and less," said the superintendent. He carefully sorted through his keys until he found the one he wanted. It slipped into the lock smoothly. With an audible click, the bolt slid free.

"Now we'll see what's the matter," said O'Malley, and he pushed at the door. Then cursed as it opened only a few inches, then halted with a thump.

Ellen peered into the crack between the door and the frame. She spotted the problem immediately. "There's a metal security chain holding the door closed."

O'Malley rubbed one hand across his eyes. He shook his head, annoyed. "I'll be back in a minute. You stay here."

Ellen waited impatiently for the superintendent to return. It was more like five minutes than one. When he finally reappeared, he held a heavy-duty wire cutter in both hands. Behind him trailed another man carrying a small black medical case.

"I asked Doc Mayfair from 1C if he wouldn't mind lending a hand. This is Ellen Harvard, Doc, Mr. Yates's girlfriend."

"Harper," corrected Ellen, shaking the doctor's hand.

Mayfair was a short, slender man, around forty, balding, wearing thick horn-rimmed glasses. He wore a blue bathrobe and a pair of oversized slippers. Despite his attire, he was crisp and alert.

"I gather from Mr. O'Malley's description Mr. Yates may have suffered a heart attack or stroke. Do you know if he has a history of heart problems?"

"He never mentioned anything like that to me," said Ellen. "But we weren't very close. Good friends, nothing more."

"Best we find out for ourselves," said O'Malley, raising the wire cutters. A few snips, and the chain was gone. Gently, O'Malley pushed the door open.

The three of them entered the pitch-dark parlor. "Anybody home?" asked O'Malley, sounding foolish.

Ellen, knowing her way about from previous visits, turned on a lamp. The light revealed nothing unusual.

"The bedroom," said Dr. Mayfair, pointing to the closed door. "He's probably in there."

Tentatively, Ellen tapped on the bedroom door. "Andy, it's Ellen. Open up."

No answer.

"Enough delayin'," said O'Malley. "Whatever's troublin' the man, we'd best find out."

He pushed open the door and walked into the room. Somewhat reluctantly, Ellen followed. All of the anger and annoyance had burned away, leaving only a feeling of dread. Dr. Mayfair walked behind her, his medical bag already open.

O'Malley flipped on the wall switch. Light flooded the room. Again, nothing seemed amiss. Except for the unmoving man-sized lump covered by a heavy down comforter at the center of a king-sized bed.

"Smells pretty pungent in here," said O'Malley, his nose wrinkling in disgust.

"Urine," said Dr. Mayfair, stepping forward. "A bad sign. Miss Harper, you might want to look the other way. Such sights are often not pleasant."

Mayfair grabbed hold of one end of the comforter. With a jerk of the wrist, he tossed the blanket back, revealing the figure beneath.

Ellen, no longer brave, stood at the foot of the bed. Face turned to the side, at first she caught only the reactions of the two men.

The doctor, closest to the body, gasped in shock. Eyes bulging in disbelief, he staggered back, arms waving about like a drunken sailor. His medical bag tumbled to the floor. Horrid, retching noises came from deep inside his throat.

"Mother of God," said O'Malley, both hands clenched tightly into fists. His nails dug so deep into the skin of his palms that droplets of blood fell to the carpet. "Don't turn, Miss Harper," he shouted. "Don't turn around!"

His warning came too late. Ellen pivoted and stared at the body on the bed. Expecting death, she encountered worse.

Andy Yates had died in his sleep. But it had not been a pleasant death. His body lay face up and spread-eagled on the bed. His arms stretched out on either side of him to their limits, fingers clutching the mattress with such force as to rip through the sheets into the pads below. His legs were thrust out straight, rigid as boards, toes curled and frozen in a last spasm of incredible agony.

The pajama bottoms covering his stomach and groin were stained black with blood. In his death throes, Andy had both urinated and emptied his bowels. The smell was nauseating.

Staring at Andy's face, Ellen felt faint. His mouth gaped open wider than possible. His lower jaw had cracked and hung loosely down across his neck. A blackened piece of his tongue, cut to pieces by gnashing teeth, rested on one cheek. Crusted blood caked his eyes and nostrils.

She heard Dr. Mayfair muttering to O'Malley.

"I've never seen convulsions like these before. It's beyond belief." Mayfair paused, as if trying to make sense out of the unexplainable. "I mean, look at the blood stains on his groin. It's like something inside him ripped his intestines to shreds."

Ellen couldn't fight the madness that swept over her. She screamed and screamed. And screamed until oblivion swept over her.

Five minutes later, she returned to consciousness in the front room, lying on the sofa. Dr. Mayfair was bending over her, a wet washcloth in one hand. O'Malley was nowhere to be seen.

"Take it easy," he cautioned, lifting her head so she could sip from a cup of water. "You've had quite a shock. Rest for a few minutes."

He helped her up into a sitting position. Reaching inside his medical bag, he pulled out a small bottle of brandy. Hands none too steady, he poured a small amount into her cup.

"Drink it," he said, taking a swig right from the bottle. "You can use it. We both can."

Ellen didn't argue. The warmth of the liquor helped combat the coldness that clutched at her insides.

"The super went to call the police and an ambulance," said Mayfair. "We thought it best not to touch anything in the apartment, in case there's an investigation."

He sighed. "Not that it'll mean much. This is a job for the medical office, not the law. Yates died in bed, inside a bolted and locked apartment. I'm not sure what killed him. But I'm positive no human being had anything to do with it."

Ellen shivered. *No human being.* The words echoed in her thoughts. Vague memories stirred, touching the surface of her mind. She recalled reading the description of similar deaths in a tale of demonic attack—inscribed in a manuscript three thousand years old.

11

▲ Sarah waited nervously for Jambres to return to his room. She sat there quietly, reviewing Carl's threats. In some ways, Garrett's relaxed manner was more frightening than George Slater's madness. After the lecture she received tonight, Sarah felt positive that both men wanted her dead. She knew too much about their schemes. Only her short-term importance to Jambres stayed their hand.

She was realistic enough to know that escape was out of the question. The only path open to her was to kill them first. And to do that, she needed Jambres's help.

She harbored no illusions about the sorcerer. He considered her a useful tool, nothing more. Their sexual escapade in the car had been entirely for her benefit. She knew Jambres would sacrifice her if necessary, without a second thought. Mercy meant nothing to him. Yet he was neither unnecessarily cruel nor sadistic. He killed out of necessity, not pleasure.

As if summoned by her thoughts, Jambres entered the room. He smiled when he saw her. For a moment, Sarah forgot her problems. A feeling of unreality gripped her senses. Jambres was more than a foreign spirit inhabiting Tom Darrow's body. He walked, talked, and acted like Darrow. It was as if the gigolo had returned to life.

"You brought the necessary items?" asked Jambres.

"As you commanded," answered Sarah. She pointed to a corner of the room. "I left everything in the box over there."

"Good. Let us begin the ceremony. Only a few hours of

darkness remain. The spell does not work during the daytime."

"Carl threatened me tonight," said Sarah as she helped the sorcerer empty the contents of the box onto the floor. "He wants me dead. I sensed his emotions. He no longer trusts me."

"There is nothing to worry about," said Jambres, examining each item carefully. "Carl trusts no one. That is what makes him a good leader."

Jambres turned and looked at her with unblinking eyes. "He knows that I depend on your skills. He dares not cross me. You are perfectly safe."

"George . . ." began Sarah.

". . . is a minor annoyance, nothing more."

He quieted her unspoken protests with an upraised palm. "I have my plans for George Slater. Be patient. You have my word that no harm will come to you from either Carl or George."

Sarah nodded. Jambres's promise satisfied her for now. Later she could raise the possibility of eliminating the two men.

She squatted down next to the magician. He was carefully stacking up a small pile of charcoal in a small Weber kettle. Jambres needed a hot fire for his spells. The barbecue pot worked perfectly as an alternative fireplace.

A splash of lighter fluid and a match started the blaze. Within minutes, the gray coals were at the proper temperature. Silently, Sarah placed a thick lump of white wax onto the grill. It wasn't long before droplets of hot wax were dripping onto the fire.

Impervious to pain, Jambres retrieved the soft paraffin from the metal rack. The heat was so intense that the skin on several of his fingers blackened and crackled like paper. Sarah gagged as the smell of burning flesh filled the room.

Working swiftly, before the wax could harden, Jambres molded the substance into the semblance of a human figure. Five inches long, it had a barrel-shaped body with sticklike arms and legs. Crude breasts made it female

Sarah knew from previous conversations that this wax doll was the substitute body for Jambres's next victim. Through it, Jambres could perform incredible acts of black magic.

"I am ready for the marker," said Jambres, holding out a hand.

Sarah placed a sharpened pencil in his palm. Carefully, the sorcerer etched a simple face on the figure's head. First came the eyes, then the nose, mouth, and ears. By now, the wax had set. Jambres used the pencil tip like a knife, carving thin white slices off the surface of the doll.

On the back of the figure, he inscribed a series of minute hieroglyphics. Ancient words of power, five thousand years old. Egyptian sorcery was the oldest codified system of black magic on Earth. Unlike similar spells performed by lesser magicians in other cultures, the use of a substitute body required nothing from the intended victim. Jambres had no need of hair clippings or fingernails to work his magic. Instead, his powerful will bridged the gap between wax and flesh.

"Sheila Parsons," said Sarah, responding to his unspoken question. "That is the name of the woman who supervises the displays in the Egyptian room of the museum."

"She dies tonight," said Jambres, checking his scribbling on the doll for any mistakes. One wrong mark, and the spell would not work. "How many others?"

"Two more," answered Sarah, checking the short list given to her by Oscar Hinkley. "A man and a woman. One is the member of the museum board who arranged the actual donation. And the other is chief archivist for the exhibit."

"A few more nights, and they join their companions in the Underworld," said Jambres. "Then I can turn my attention to more important matters."

Passing the wax figure to Sarah, Jambres lifted an inch-wide piece of linen from the floor. Unrolling it, he held it before his eyes and recited a powerful spell against nightmares.

"Horus stands before me. Set waits at my right hand. The great gods protect me. Let none disturb my rest. Those who attack me do so at their peril. I will cut off their hands, bind their eyes, and close their mouths."

Sitting down with his legs crossed, Jambres allowed Sarah to wrap the bandage around his neck. The ritual of protection completed, he took the wax doll away from her.

Raising the white figurine to his lips, Jambres whispered the name of his victim into the doll's ear. Now the two were linked as one on the spirit plane.

All of the preparations completed, the sorcerer motioned Sarah to back off. It was time for him to summon the forces of darkness.

Eyes closed in concentration, Jambres silently mouthed insults so bold they could not be said aloud. In the most vile of terms, he challenged the demon, Shakek, to a duel of magic. A creature of sky and earth, Shakek was the most obscene of all monsters of Egyptian lore. Tongue in his anus, he was known as the eater of excrement.

Having participated in this ritual twice before, Sarah knew what to expect. Still, nothing could prepare her for the advent of Shakek. Covering her nose and mouth with a wet cloth did little to filter out the incredible stench that signaled the arrival of the demon.

A creature of nightmare, Shakek had no material form. Instead, dark black smoke swirled about Jambres, coiling around his face and chest. The demon sought entrance to the magician's body. One breath was all it needed. Once inside, it could rip his intestines apart with invisible claws.

Sarah could sense the monster's growing frustration. The strip of linen about his neck protected Jambres from all spiritual harm. Already dead, the magician never breathed, denying Shakek access to his body. He was completely insulated from the demon's attack.

Not so the wax doll he held clutched tightly to his chest. As if sensing new prey, the black cloud encircled the small figure. Within seconds, the mist started to congeal. A thick, oily substance, resembling tar, coated the statue. As the sludge increased, the cloud around the doll lessened in direct proportion. The white wax figure became like a giant sponge, sucking the contents of the demon into its center.

Sarah knew exactly the opposite was taking place. Shakek was forcing itself into the substitute body, and from there into the unsuspecting body of Sheila Parsons. Sarah shuddered with the thought. According to Jambres's description, the demon's attack amounted to a soul-consuming, psychic rape. No one ever survived Shakek's attentions. It was a monstrous way to die.

Five minutes later, there was no sign of the demon other than a thin layer of black film coating the wax doll. Cautiously, Sarah walked over to Jambres and tapped him on the shoulder.

"It's finished," she said.

Wearily, the magician opened his eyes. With a nod of his head, he indicated she should help him to his feet. Performing magic drained him of all his strength. He could not stand without her aid.

Together they shuffled over to the narrow cot. Despite her fears, Sarah couldn't stifle a tingle of excitement. A host of erotic fantasies whipped through her mind.

"Soon," whispered Jambres, as if reading her thoughts, "our flesh will join in passion. The time is near."

Strong fingers tightened on her shoulder, digging into her soft skin. Waves of sexual pleasure raced through her body. The muscles in her thighs tightened almost in orgasm.

"Be patient," said the sorcerer, dropping onto the cot. "I need time to recover. Guard my body while I commune with the gods."

Jambres's eyes glazed over as he focused his mind inward. Only the stillness of his chest betrayed the fact he was not a normal man sleeping. Resting in this manner, he did not look dead.

Physically exhausted, Sarah sat down on the floor at the foot of the bed. She needed sleep. No reason to return to her room. She was much safer here.

None of the members of Blood and Iron dared enter this place. They all feared Jambres too much to intrude. And she was an extremely light sleeper. Not even George could enter without waking her.

Drifting off into sleep, she made a promise to herself. Tomorrow she would ask Jambres to kill Carl and his stooge.

12

▲ David Ross lived alone in a restored nineteenth-century Victorian home a few blocks off Sheridan Road. He had paid cash for the place six years ago, which was located only minutes away from Lake Shore Drive. Every morning from March till December, David rose at six A.M. sharp, put on his jogging suit, and walked over to the park that hugged the drive from the north to south sides of Chicago. He spent the next two hours running.

Neither rain nor snow, cold nor heat, kept him from his exercise. On rare instances, a blizzard forced him to stay indoors. A summer thunderstorm shook the rafters of his house once, and rain came down in sheets, stopping him. Otherwise, he never missed his morning workout.

His routine never varied. He ran for ten minutes, then slowed down and walked for five. After that, he ran again, repeating the cycle. It was an ancient Indian trick used for tracking. It was more demanding than jogging, but much less boring.

This Saturday began the usual way. Darkness still hugged the lake as David did his warmup exercises.

David moved with the fluid grace of a jungle cat. Speed mattered little to him. He ran for stamina and mental discipline.

Unfortunately, many criminals viewed early-morning joggers as easy prey. Police rarely patrolled the long stretches of trail along the beach. There were too many miles and not enough officers. The past few years had seen a dramatic increase in crime on the lakefront. Most runners bunched up in groups for protection, but David maintained his solitary ways despite the growing threat of muggers and gangs.

At five-foot-nine, one hundred sixty pounds, he made a tempting target. Nothing about his curly black hair or his delicate features spoke of trouble. A certain hardness in his eyes served notice of hidden depths of violence lurking within. Word on the street warned he should be left strictly alone.

David relied on his speed and quick wits to extract him from dangerous situations. He stayed in the open, avoiding wooded areas and gullies. As much as possible, he avoided contact with strangers. But sometimes events conspired against him.

A thunderstorm caught David several miles from home. In a matter of minutes, the skies darkened from gray to black. A cold wind swept down from the northwest, bringing the rain. Instantly soaked, David searched for a place to wait out the storm. Rain didn't bother him, but he had no desire to be struck by lightning.

He found shelter in a narrow drainage ditch beneath a cement walkway. He also found trouble.

Three young punks were busily ripping the clothes off a middle-aged black woman. Her terrified screams rose above the roar of thunder. The gang members made no attempt to muffle her cries. Their coarse laughter proclaimed their indifference to the outside world.

"All right, that's enough!" shouted David.

His appearance caught the trio off guard. Shocked

silent, they turned to face him. Grins broke out on their faces when they saw David standing alone at the edge of the ditch.

"Get movin', piss-face," said the biggest of the three. A tall, skinny teenager with an orange mohawk and yellowed teeth, he glared crazily at David. "We don't take kindly to chicken-shit heroes interrupting our fun."

Behind him, his two companions started giggling. Both short and fat with greased-down black hair, they couldn't have been much more than fifteen years old.

All three wore soiled white T-shirts, jeans, and expensive athletic shoes. Etched on their shirts in pink neon were the words "Born to Be Wild." Middle-class members of the new generation out for a thrill. Wilding.

Trapped between them, naked and afraid, their victim whimpered in pain. Bruises covered most of her body. A thin trickle of blood dripped from her nose.

"Leave her alone," said David, clenching his hands into fists.

"Fuck you," answered the boy with the orange mohawk. Grinning, he pulled a switchblade from one pocket. Waving the six-inch blade back and forth, he stepped forward.

"I'm gonna cut off your balls, Lone Ranger," he declared. His friends howled with anticipation.

David drew in a couple of deep breaths, filling his system with oxygen. He disliked violence, but sometimes it was necessary. A wise man knew when to stop talking and start fighting.

As if suddenly realizing his mistake, the big teenager halted six feet from David. The grin faded from his lips, and he took a tentative step backward. But it was too late for retreat.

With a hop and a skip, David leapt high into the air. Balancing on empty space, he whirled with the fluid motion of a ballet dancer. His right leg lashed out with incredible force. The heel of his foot caught the bewildered teenager flush in the mouth. Bone and teeth cracked on impact.

Face spurting blood, the boy went flying headlong into his friends. All three crashed to the earth in a flurry of arms and legs. The switchblade went flying high into the air and disappeared in the brush.

David didn't give his foes a chance to recover. His hands flashed out with incredible speed. Gifted with unnaturally fast reflexes, David used them with deadly effect.

Callused, hard fingers caught one of the black-haired hoods in the throat as he tried to rise. David pulled his punch slightly. Otherwise, it was a killing blow. Gagging, the boy collapsed to the ground. He wouldn't be able to breathe without pain for a week.

The second black-haired thug fared no better. A flurry of closed-fisted blows hammered his nose into bloody shards of bone and cartilage. Shrieking in pain, he fled into the storm, leaving his companions to fend for themselves.

Cursing savagely, the orange-haired leader of the band struggled to his feet. David waited until the teenager was standing, then kicked him hard in the groin. Howling in agony, the boy dropped to a sitting position, hugging his smashed testicles.

Reaching out, David pulled the thug with the battered windpipe to his feet. The teenager cringed as fingers like steel clamps dug into his shoulder muscles. "Start running," said David. "Before I get really angry."

Gasping for breath, the young thug disappeared into the rain. Now only the orange-haired leader remained. The big teenager cringed as David approached.

"You smashed my nuts," he said through smashed lips, tears trickling down his cheeks. "That's assault, man. My dad's a big-time lawyer. You'll pay for this."

David laughed. He reached out, grabbed the boy by the hair, and shoved him flat. Dropping to one knee, David twisted the teenager's head so that his eyes were parallel to the ground.

"A jerk of the wrist," said David, applying a small amount of pressure, "and your spine snaps. Wouldn't that be fun? Spending the rest of your life in a wheelchair, paralyzed from the neck down?"

The boy froze, his eyes huge with fear.

"I don't care who your father is," said David, all of the laughter gone from his voice. "If I catch you in this park again, you're dead meat."

David rose to his feet. Turning his back on the teenager, he walked over to the woman he had rescued. She was busily struggling to reassemble her ripped outfit.

"I owe you my life," she said, her voice trembling with emotion. "Those hoodlums surprised me in the woods this morning. I like to watch the sun rise over the lake whenever I have a chance. The three of them dragged me here, then you came along. How can I ever thank you?"

"Don't take shortcuts through the woods anymore," said David, smiling.

Behind him, pebbles rattled. Glancing over his shoulder, David glimpsed the gang leader scrambling up the side of the ditch. The boy hesitated at the top of the ridge, as if about to shout something, then he thought better of it. In seconds, he was gone.

"Shouldn't we have held them for the police?" asked the woman, buttoning together remnants of her blouse.

"That might have proven difficult," said David, "considering the odds."

He saw no reason to mention his intense dislike of publicity. His profession required anonymity. Having his face plastered all over the newspaper as a hero could ruin his career.

"You handled the three of them so easily," commented the woman as she critically eyed her smashed shoes. Shrugging, she tossed them away.

"I taught self-defense for a few years," said David. "Roughing up some punks barely qualifies as exercise."

"They were too much for me," said the woman.

He looked up at the sky. "The rain seems to be stopping. Come on. I'll find you a cab."

Together they climbed out of the shallow gully.

"I'm not a spiteful person," said the woman. "But I'm glad you hurt them. They deserved it. I mean, they treated rape like a big game." Her voice shook. "Those scum."

"Calm down," said David, his voice steady and relaxed. "It's all over."

"I'm glad you hurt them," the woman repeated.

"I taught them a lesson they won't forget," said David, not believing his own words. "The only thing punks like them understand is violence. You won't see that gang in the park again."

He knew better. Teenagers never learned from their mistakes. He already regretted letting the trio escape.

"I hope you're right," said the woman, her doubt reflecting his own uncertainties.

"I'm sure of it," said David, feeling anything but confident. Somehow he knew he had not seen the last of the orange-haired punk.

13

▲ Calvin Lane looked up as Moe shuffled over to his desk around eleven A.M. the next morning. Chuckling, the big black man put down the report he had been thumbing through.

"About time you showed up. How we gonna solve this case if you waste all morning snoozing?"

"Oh shut up," said Moe. "There any coffee left?"

"I knew you'd need a fix," said Calvin, handing Moe a cup filled to the top with the steaming liquid. "There's a few doughnuts left. You want one?"

"Bring me two," said Moe, sipping his drink. "My body needs the sugar."

Moe gasped as the hot coffee scalded his insides.

"Still no sign of Darrow," said Calvin. "Did I mention that the blood on the knife matched his? Ditto for the stuff on the floor. My gut feeling says that dude won't show up alive.

"No headlines in the paper, either. Though a couple of reporters called this morning. Tomorrow," he concluded gloomily, "we should make the front page."

Munching on a jelly doughnut, Moe thumbed through the report his partner had been reading. It was a summary of the medical examiner's findings, along with pertinent data from the police computer files.

"I warned the lieutenant about the newspapers. He agreed to cut us off from any other assignment. We're to concentrate on wrapping this mess up as quick as possible."

"Wonderful," said Moe, licking the sugar off his fingers.

Frowning, he continued reading. "The guy died a week ago. Tell me something I don't know. Like how his body made it into Darrow's apartment."

Moe turned the pages, skimming paragraphs for important details. Most of it was material he'd learned at the scene of the crime. Halfway through the document, he came across something that caused him to raise his eyebrows.

"Our friend died of a stab wound to the heart? Isn't that terrific." He waved the report at Lane. "You read this crap. According to Marlowe, the angle of penetration indicates an overhand blow, perhaps done with the victim on his knees. How the hell can he say something like that?"

"Dunno," said Calvin, shrugging. "That's what he gets paid for. I can't stand the geek, but he knows his business. The part about the victim being on his knees ring any bells with you?"

"You damn well know it does," said Moe, grimacing. "That satanism stuff we investigated last year. Human sacrifice and all that shit." He groaned. "Why in the name of God do we get all the weird ones?"

"Lucky, I guess," said his partner.

Shaking his head in disgust, Moe dropped the report back on his desk. "You coming to dinner Monday night?" he asked Calvin, changing the subject. "Miriam told me to remind you. And don't forget Wednesday night, too. All the relatives are expecting you." Moe grinned. "I think they like the way you sing. It adds a little extra to the blessings."

"I circled the days in red ink on my calendar," said Calvin. "Your wife making potato latchkeys on Monday?"

"Latkes," said Moe, grinning. His partner loved the deep-fried potato pancakes his wife made using an old family recipe. Whenever Calvin visited, Miriam cooked them special for him.

"Of course. Plus, she bought a nice brisket yesterday. Along with a kishke, a jar of sour tomatoes, and a nice challah. And I heard her promise the kids she'd bake a mandelbrot. But it has to be all eaten in two days. No bread allowed in the house after Wednesday. Think you can manage?"

"I'm only human," said Lane, holding up his big hands in protest. "But I'll do my best. You can count on me."

A confirmed bachelor, Calvin ate most of his meals at restaurants. His diet consisted mostly of pizza, ribs, and fried chicken. Miriam Kaufman considered it her civic duty to feed the big detective real home cooking at least once a month. His visits had become a family tradition at the Kaufman house.

Over the years, Calvin had developed a taste for what he called Jewish soul food. Blintzes, corned beef on rye, and kasha knishes had become staples in his diet. From time to time, he admitted to Moe sheepishly, he had even tried frying up some matzo and eggs. But nothing compared to the culinary expertise of Miriam Kaufman. To Calvin, she was living proof that the Jews were God's chosen people.

"Hey, would you guys stop jawing about food?" asked Joe Fisher, another one of the detectives in the room. "You're making the rest of us hungry. Besides"—he held up a sheaf of papers—"the make on your victim just arrived. Boy, the two of you always land the good ones." Fisher grinned. "I wish I had your luck."

"Oh, drop dead," said Moe, grabbing the report. He quickly scanned the file. Lane followed along, reading over his shoulder. The dead man had been identified by his dental work. Along with his Chicago rap sheet, listing his previous brushes with the law in the city, an ambitious clerk had provided a copy of the state rap sheet as well. Both ledgers ran to the bottom of the page. Their victim's earlier encounters with the men in blue made depressing reading.

"Oscar Hinkley," said Moe aloud. "For a young man, he compiled quite a record. It's incredible that this jerk managed to stay out of the slammer."

"You can thank the I-bond program for that," said Calvin. He spat out the words like a curse. "According to the stats, our buddy Oscar was released from custody three times without having to post a cash bail. Doesn't make much sense to me. A habitual criminal is let loose on his own recognizance because the docket is so crowded it might be years before he ever gets tried. In the meantime, the bum keeps right on committing crimes. What a crock."

"Listen to this case in point," said Moe, scanning one of the write-ups. "Last year, several neighbors registered complaints about loud noises coming from Hinkley's uncle's place. A search turned up a primitive bomb construction plant in the basement. Seems that Oscar belonged to all the local hate groups—the KKK, American Nazi Party, the skinheads, and so forth. Using stolen gunpowder and gasoline, he was stockpiling Molotov cocktails and crude hand grenades in the cellar, waiting for the upcoming revolution."

"A jury let him walk on that one?" asked Calvin, flabbergasted. "I'm sure the people on his block were thrilled when they heard that verdict."

"Case never made it to trial," answered Moe. "Hinkley's lawyers kept on getting it continued."

Calvin laughed. "Hope they collected their fee in advance. 'Cause their boy ain't in any shape to pay them now."

Moe shuffled through the pages. He read off the crimes each one contained. "Assault, assault and battery, destruction of private property, sending threatening letters through the mail. Hinkley worked hard at being rotten."

Fascinated by one case in particular, Moe studied it carefully before speaking. "Talk about bizarre stuff. Hinkley was busted when he was sixteen trying to smuggle a mummy *into* the Petrie museum."

"Say what?" said Calvin. "You're joshing me."

"No joke. Hinkley's parents threw him out of their house years ago. He lived with his uncle, Joe, a night watchman at the Institute. The old man evidently had a weakness for the bottle. One night, when he was out like a light, Oscar put on his uniform and snuck into the museum. For kicks, he stole a mummy from the Egyptian exhibit. Took it home and put it under his bed."

"Very, very weird," said Calvin, shaking his head.

"I guess Oscar expected the Institute to offer a big reward for the return of the relic, no questions asked. Problem was, they never realized it was gone. He took it from a closed mummy case, and there was no reason for anyone to check inside to see if the contents were still there.

"After a week, he started worrying his uncle would find the body in his room. So he tried smuggling it back into the museum. That's when he was caught. Under questioning, the whole story came out. Uncle Joe received a severe reprimand but kept his job. Oscar got a six-month sentence, suspended, because of his age, and a lecture from the judge."

"You thinkin' what I'm thinkin'?" asked Calvin.

"Time for us to pay a visit on Uncle Joe," said Moe. He scribbled down an address on his memo pad. "Maybe the old man can shed a little light on his nephew's murder."

14

▲ "You want . . . history books?" said Carl, not believing the request.

"Yes," replied Jambres patiently. "I want to learn what happened in Kamt . . ." He paused, as if searching for the right words. "The land you know as Egypt . . . after my passing."

"Since when did you learn to read English?" asked Carl.

Thunder roared and lightning flashed outside as an early-morning storm battered the old house that served as their hideout. Carl had awakened a short time before to find Jambres waiting by the side of his bed. Night and day meant nothing to the sorcerer. He never slept.

"It is an unexpected side effect of my spell," said Jambres, obviously reluctant to reveal his secret but knowing he must. "The bodies I inhabit possess a certain psychic residue left over from the original spirit. A dim memory of their entire life and knowledge. That is how I managed to adjust so easily to this modern world; it is only foreign to part of me.

"I inherit the skills impressed upon the brain cells of my host. Hinkley was a moron, barely able to read or write your language. Fortunately, Darrow received a much better education. I learned a great deal from his memory. But I want to know more. A great deal more."

Carl licked his lips, calculating the possibilities. "What's in it for me?"

Jambres stared at him with cold, unblinking eyes. "A sorcerer of Kamt does not bargain like a servant in the marketplace. Do not push me too far, Carl Garrett. Weak as I am, I can still crush you and your band like lice beneath my feet."

"Take it easy," said Carl hastily. He knew when to retreat. "I'll send Luther out to the bookstore when it stops raining. He'll buy you all the damned history books they handle. I'm warning you, though. They're all filled with lies."

Jambres settled back in his chair. "After a few thousand years, fact and fiction merge into one. My concern is not with people or places, but with ideas. Certain beliefs are like stones striking a pond. They send waves rippling through time, growing wider with the passing centuries."

The sorcerer sat silently for a moment, as if debating whether or not to continue. Finally he spoke. "You worship one god, do you not? Hinkley's mind was muddled with thoughts of three divine beings."

"The Father, Son, and Holy Ghost," said Carl, wondering why the Egyptian cared. "All aspects of the Lord, Jesus Christ, Christian. The true God of all white Aryan people."

Jambres paused, as if reflecting on the name. After a few seconds, he nodded. "I understand. Darrow's mind contains all the details I need on your religion. Finding it is the problem. I am like a child in a great library. Anything I wish to learn is available—if I knew which volume to read. And I am hampered by the fact that one author wrote all the books, and his prejudices and opinions color all of the facts."

Eyes fixed on Carl, Jambres continued. "Minor events take on great meaning when observed through the eye of time. In Kamt, we worshiped many gods. There was Osiris, Set, Horus, Anubis, and a host of others, too numerous to mention. Pharaoh, too, was considered a god, living among mortals. Deities filled our land, our thoughts, our lives. Worship governed every aspect of our existence. So had it been, with only a few brief aberrations, for two thousand years before my time.

"Yet there were those who wished it otherwise. Chief among them were the members of the cult of Aton, the Forbidden God."

Carl shook his head. "Never heard of him."

"Perhaps," said Jambres mysteriously. "Perhaps not. About a hundred years before my birth, the pharaoh Akhunaten proclaimed that Aton, God of the Sun, was the only true god and all other gods were false. He ordered the people of Kamt to abandon the immortals and worship only Aton."

"I'll bet he didn't last very long," said Carl.

Jambres nodded. "The opposition he encountered was so overwhelming he abandoned Thebes and found a new capital to the north. A weak leader, Akhunaten cared little about affairs of state. Only his god mattered to him. He spent all his time preaching his new religion while ignoring important affairs of state. The country suffered greatly under his rule, which fortunately lasted less than a decade.

"When he died, the priesthood immediately declared Aton a false god and ordered all traces of his name destroyed. Worship of Aton was forbidden upon penalty of death. Kamt returned to normal.

"However, there were those who still worshiped the one god in secret. Fanatic in their beliefs, they plotted to someday overthrow Pharaoh and replace him with their high priest. Generations passed, but the cult never abandoned its goal of once again ruling the Two Kingdoms."

Carl suppressed a yawn. Jambres was leading up to something important, but he had no idea what.

"The cult flourished among the poor and dissatisfied

who longed for the wealth of their betters. Slaves longing for their freedom embraced it. The priests of Aton welcomed them all. The disciples of the Forbidden God numbered in the thousands. Posed for revolt, the cult lacked one man."

"A strong leader," said Carl, without hesitation. "A man of vision," and, he almost added, *a man like Carl Garrett.*

"Correct," said Jambres. "The cult needed a commander willing to dare anything in his quest for absolute power. The revolution could not succeed unless the god-king, Pharaoh, was killed. But only a master sorcerer could challenge the might of Pharaoh and his inner circle of magicians."

Jambres paused. "After waiting nearly a century, the cult found one such man. He was a great sorcerer, living in exile from the court of Pharaoh, a dynamic, ruthless leader. They persuaded him to lead the revolt that almost toppled the empire.

"Alone, he stood against the combined strength of Pharaoh's magicians and defeated them all. Only the timely intervention of the army saved the god-king from death. The usurper and his allies fled for their lives."

"*You* were that man," said Carl, remembering his first dream meeting with Jambres.

Carl knew instantly that he was wrong. Jambres's dead face twisted with emotion. His clawlike hands reached out as if to rip Carl to pieces. Then he stopped, and his arms dropped to his sides. He shook his head.

"I served all of my adult life as master magician to Pharaoh. In all the land, I was second only to him in power and importance. Whatever I desired was mine. There was no reason for me to betray my king. No, it was not me who rebelled against his lord." Jambres's voice sank so low Carl almost didn't hear what he said next. "It was my son."

"Your son?" Somehow it was impossible for Carl to think of Jambres as a father. It made the dead man almost seem a living person.

"He was my only child, the result of a youthful passion with a lady of noble birth. His mother died giving him life. I raised the boy myself. Like his father, he possessed a gift for sorcery. At my knee, the Son of Jambres learned the dark secrets of magic. A brilliant pupil, he never forgot anything I taught. He was my pride, my joy, and my undoing."

"The Son of Jambres?" asked Carl, bewildered by the expression.

"As was the custom in Kamt, many fathers gave their favorite child their own name. Much as in this world, male children are named Junior. So it was practiced in times gone by. In my excessive pride, I named the boy Son of Jambres."

"What happened?" said Carl, prodding the magician to continue. He sensed Jambres, in his despair, was revealing secrets he meant to keep hidden.

"He grew to manhood in my shadow. He was a powerful sorcerer, and it was common knowledge that upon my death he would become chief magician unto Pharaoh. Like many his age, my son was a proud, arrogant young man. Those traits proved to be his nemesis.

"When a noble of the court mocked him in public, my son foolishly cursed him aloud. Needless to say, the man, a relative of the king, died soon after. Even my influence could not save my child. He was forced to flee for his life.

"Eventually, he settled in the lands north of Kamt, far from the wrath of Pharaoh. It was during those bitter years of exile that the priests of Aton found him. With cunning words, they seduced him with their stories of the Forbidden God. In his vanity, my son saw himself as Akhunaten reborn. He agreed to lead their revolt.

"He returned to Kamt, the master of dread sorcery. In the course of his wanderings, my son had stumbled upon an ancient artifact of incalculable power. A relic of an earlier age when legendary beings walked the Earth, it enabled him to perform incredible acts of magic. The

Two Kingdoms trembled beneath his wrath. Pharaoh's magicians, myself included, were like children before him."

"How did he lose?" asked Carl, intrigued by the tale.

"Treachery from those he trusted the most. The high priests of Aton grew fearful of his powers. They worried that if my son defeated Pharaoh, he would declare himself a living god and not bow down in worship to Aton. So the betrayers of their gods betrayed their own leader.

"In a carefully planned ambush, the rebellion was crushed by the loyal armies of Pharaoh. My son and the remnants of his followers escaped into the desert. Those who pursued him perished. He never returned.

"As a reward for their treachery, the priests of Aton were granted a swift, painless death. My fate was much worse."

"Huh? Why were you punished? I don't get it."

"The usurper was my child. As his father, I was held responsible for his actions. If not for me, he would never have been born—and the royal house of Kamt never threatened."

"That's insane. It doesn't make sense."

"You are thinking like a commoner, not a king," replied Jambres. "What better threat to hold over a potential lawbreaker than the knowledge that his parents and family will be held responsible for his crimes? Death not only to himself but to all those he holds dear?"

"It wouldn't stop me," said Carl.

"I know," said Jambres. "Nor did it deter my son."

The sorcerer rose from his chair. "You know my fate. My spirit and soul were drawn from my body. My *ba* was banished to the Isle of Dead-Alive. My *ka* was imprisoned in the gold statue of Anubis. Then my empty shell was burned and the ashes scattered in the desert. In that manner, I was denied entry to the Underworld and eternal life after death. For more than thirty centuries, I have suffered for the crimes committed by my son."

"So now what?" asked Carl, not expecting an answer. Jambres always grew vague when pressed on his plans.

"What was done . . . can be undone," said the sorcerer mysteriously. "The sins of my child must be erased. The gods of Kamt demand it."

"What do you mean?" asked Carl, caught off guard by this new revelation.

But Jambres refused to speak further.

15

▲ The shrill ring of the telephone greeted David as he pushed open the front door of his house. With a hop, a skip, and a jump, he made it to the instrument just before his answering machine switched on.

"Ross here," he gasped, slightly out of breath.

"David?" The voice was high-pitched, heavily accented, and instantly recognizable. "It's me, your uncle Eli. How are you?"

"Eli," said David, recovering quickly. "It's good to hear from you. It's been months."

"Over a year," corrected the voice on the phone. "I'm in your neighborhood. How about if we meet at Kaplan's Deli for a late breakfast and catch up on old times?"

"Sounds fine to me," said David. "I just came in from my morning run. I'll see you there as soon as I shower and shave."

"Good. I'll order for the two of us."

Eli hung up before David could object. Not that it would have mattered. The old man operated by his own set of rules. Eating with him was a unique experience.

Smiling, David headed for the shower. It had been a long time since he last dealt with the Israeli secret service. Working for Mossad always paid well. He wondered what new operation they had planned.

Eli Richter was not related to David other than by profession. It was merely a convenient cover story they used when they needed to meet. David also had "relatives" and "army buddies" who spoke with Swiss, German, and Japanese accents. His extended family was not only multilingual but multinational. David believed in equality among nations. He worked for whatever friendly country paid his price.

The demands of a swiftly changing world scene created problems for even the most sophisticated intelligence-gathering networks. More than any army, these global spy systems were responsible for the security of their country. They fought a war waged behind closed doors, often without a shot being fired. Their secret budgets were routinely approved without dissent in capitals around the world.

The political complexities of the last quarter of the twentieth century strained even the best-funded operations. Often, when all of their agents were busy in the field, branch offices turned to independent operators for help. These "stringers" primarily handled internal security problems or cases of industrial espionage. It was a small but lucrative field for the right men.

David was one of the best stringers in the business. He charged a flat fee of twenty-five thousand dollars per assignment, and none of his employers complained about the price. Four or five jobs a year enabled him to live in the moderate luxury his tastes required.

Eli Richter was a wealthy North Shore businessman, famous for his lavish life-style and extravagant parties. Few people knew he also headed the Midwest branch of Mossad, the Israeli secret service. A brilliant strategist, Eli had the reputation of spotting trouble before it happened. In the past five years, David's activities for the old man had ranged from stopping neo-Nazis attempting to firebomb the Israeli consulate to bugging the Russian consulate. Working for Eli was never boring.

David arrived at Kaplan's Deli exactly twenty minutes after nine. Looking around, he spotted Richter sitting at a booth in the rear of the restaurant. A short, chubby man with rosy red cheeks and bright white hair, Eli was busy talking to Leo Kaplan, the deli's owner.

"So, the gypsy woman says," concluded Eli, pausing for dramatic effect, "'Mr. Arafat, any day you die will be a Jewish holiday.'"

Shaking his head, Leo Kaplan rose from the table. "Mr. Richter," he declared, "your jokes are so old they sound new." He nodded and smiled at David. "Here's your nephew. Entertain him with your stories. I gotta get back to business."

"David," said Eli, making the one word into an entire sentence. "Sit. Take a load off your feet. Have some lox and bagels."

There was enough food on the table to feed a small army. Bagels, smoked salmon, herring in cream sauce, miniature danish, and a half-dozen other delights crowded on a space meant for half the amount. David settled for a plateful of small cinnamon rollups he particularly liked.

There would be no mention of his assignment until after they ate. Eli refused to discuss business over food.

"Nu?" he said as David munched away at the pastries. "How is that girlfriend of yours? Leah, Lana, her name escapes me."

"Leigh," said David. "She's history. We split up six months ago."

David suspected Eli was well aware of his social situation. Like any good spy master, he kept close tabs on his employees. Even the part-time ones.

"I'm sorry to hear that," said Eli smugly. "Though I do recall telling you that it wouldn't last."

David nodded. In many ways, Eli treated him like a

true nephew. He always called to wish him a happy birthday, sent a card at the holidays, and commented at length on his social life. The worst thing about his remarks was that the old man was usually right on target. Especially in regard to the women David dated.

"You need to find a nice, intelligent girl," said Eli, as if reading his mind. "Enough with these empty-headed blondes you meet at the health club. Physical stimulation is fine for a little while, but you can't build a relationship on sex alone."

"Leigh was pretty thick," said David, chuckling. "She thought Stravinsky's *Firebird* was the name of a new foreign car."

Eli snorted in disgust. "Exercise your mind for a change," he said. "Make an old man happy."

"I'll try, Eli," said David. "I promise."

"Enough socializing," said Eli, brushing the crumbs off his shirt. "Finish up. I'm due back at my office shortly. Time to discuss your assignment."

"I'm ready," replied David, gulping down the last danish.

Eli scratched his head, as if hesitant to speak. David noticed that Eli lost much of his accent when talk turned serious. "I want you to discover why certain people are dying in their sleep," he finally stated. "And to do it as quickly as possible."

"What are you talking about?" asked David, baffled by Eli's odd request.

"The problem is," said Eli, agitated now, "that I really don't know what I am talking about."

"Huh? You want to repeat that? And make sense this time?"

"David, let me tell it my way. Then you'll understand."

Eli leaned forward, resting his elbows on the table. "You know the Petrie museum downtown? Of course, everyone does. It's world-famous. Well, strange things are happening to members of the Egyptian department.

"The curator of the place died three days ago under very unusual circumstances. The police were keeping the incident quiet while they investigated. However, last night the body of a second employee, another man, was discovered, in much the same situation. And early this morning I learned of the death of a middle-aged woman who also worked in the Egyptian section."

"You suspect foul play?" asked David.

"I'm not sure what to think," said Eli. "That's why I called you. My government wants to know what is going on at the museum—and why these specific people are dying in their sleep."

Pausing, Eli shifted subjects. "At the present time, Israel and Egypt are engaged in extremely delicate talks regarding a joint industrial project in the Sinai desert. Talks are entering a critical stage. If the agreement is signed, it will be a historic breakthrough, one sure to have major repercussions throughout the entire Mideast. Needless to say, certain parties are working day and night to sabotage the discussions."

"I don't see the connection between the talks and the three deaths," said David.

"It appears unlikely that one exists," admitted Eli, "but we dare not take the risk. My orders are to investigate any disturbances involving Egypt or Egyptians. What if terrorists plan to blow up the museum, destroying its fabulous Egyptian collection? The resulting publicity would ruin any chances for a secret treaty."

"Sounds like a wild goose chase to me," said David, "but you're footing the bill."

"I assure you," said Eli, not smiling, "that this month we are chasing many wild geese."

"You mentioned unusual circumstances?"

"As I said, all three victims died in bed. Evidently, they were frightened to death by their dreams. I checked with several sleep specialists. None admitted ever encountering such phenomena before. Nightmares keep people awake, but they don't kill them. The only explanations they offered were heart attacks or strokes. Both were checked out and rejected by the authorities.

"I wish I could tell you more, but there isn't anything else. The police are baffled. In none of the cases was there any sign of a struggle or lethal drugs. One man died in an apartment locked and bolted from the inside."

David whistled. "A locked-room murder? I thought they only occurred in mystery novels."

"Perhaps you can write one after you determine the cause of these deaths," said Eli. "And put an end to them."

"Where do I start?" asked David.

"See what you can learn from a young woman named Ellen Harper. She discovered the second victim, a fellow employee. According to Ms. Harper, she grew worried when the man missed work for several days and didn't answer the phone."

"A fellow employee?" repeated David. "You suspect she might be involved with the murders?"

"Perhaps. Your job is to find out. For all we know, she could be slated as the next fatality," said Eli.

"Protecting people from their dreams is beyond my skills," said David. "You need a mystic, not a mercenary."

"I have great faith in you, David," said Eli, smiling. "You will find the answer."

"I'd strongly advise you to assign stringers to keep an eye on other members of the department," said David. "If what you say is true, they could all be in deadly peril."

Eli eased himself out of the booth and stood up. "I've already taken care of that. I've grown extremely cautious in my old age. All of my bets are covered."

The old man took a slip of paper from his coat and handed it to David. "Here is Ms. Harper's phone number and address. The police questioned her most of the night, so she's probably indisposed at the moment. Don't wait too long before contacting her, though. We can't run the risk of her being killed before we discover the truth."

"She does what at the museum?" asked David, pondering his options.

"Chief archivist," answered Eli, pulling money from his wallet. A huge tipper, he was a popular customer at many local restaurants.

"That sounds important. I'll call New York and arrange a magazine spot on her," said David, also rising. "Time for me to cash in a favor."

"Stay in touch," said Eli.

"You know I will," said David.

They shook hands, the perfect picture of a young man saying good-bye to his favorite uncle. An attractive fiction. Two very dangerous men, about to encounter an unimaginable evil.

16

▲ Ellen slept right through the thunderstorm.

She didn't return to her apartment until nearly dawn. The police had no reason to hold her, but they were reluctant to let her go. No one said anything at the station, but Ellen was no fool. Andy's death had caused quite a stir. Especially when the police learned he worked for the Petrie Institute.

Throughout the questioning, she refrained from mentioning the two other missing men. She had no desire to draw any more attention to herself than necessary. Ellen recognized all of the signs from her detective novels. The police were treating this case like a homicide, not a natural death. That could mean only one thing. One or both of the other men had died in the same way.

The first thing she did when she reached home was remove the receiver from the phone. Anyone trying to call would get a busy signal. Better that, she decided, than a recording. The police assured her they would not release her name to the newspapers. Ellen knew better than to trust them. A private person, she was ill prepared to deal with reporters pestering her about Andy's death.

Door locked, shades drawn, phone unhooked, she stretched out on the bed. Still dressed, she feel asleep on top of the covers.

More than six hours passed before she awoke. Yawning, she padded out to the kitchen in her bare feet to grab something to eat. After wolfing down two bowls of cereal, a glass of orange juice, and a Twinkie, she spent the next twenty minutes steaming away her pains in the shower.

A baggy pair of old jeans and a sweatshirt fit her mood. Prepared for the worst, Ellen put the phone back on the hook. After five minutes passed without a call, she was ready to admit that the police had kept their word. At least she didn't have to deal with questions that she couldn't answer. At least, not yet.

Feeling slightly apprehensive, Ellen walked over to the huge bookcases that covered one entire wall of her living room. It only took a minute for her to find the volume she wanted. A remnant of her college days, the book was covered by a thick layer of dust. Ellen couldn't remember the last time she'd consulted the book. No one, not even archaeology majors, read *The Coffin Texts Decoded* for pleasure.

Dropping onto the sofa, she opened the textbook to the index. She found the listing for Shakek between Shabtis and Shed the Savior. With trembling fingers, she turned to the section of the book dealing with the supernatural entity.

It took her only a few minutes to skim the two pages describing "the demon of the sky and the Earth." When she slammed the book closed, Ellen felt extremely uneasy. Her memory had not played any tricks. Andy Yates had died in exactly the same manner as described in the section on Shakek, one of the most gruesome creatures in all of Egyptian mythology. Shakek haunted the dreams of the unwary, killing those unprotected by magic. It was one of the demons that gnawed in the shadows. *The Coffin Text* referred to it as "devourer of intestines."

In graphic detail, the book described a typical victim of the monster. Though killed four thousand years ago, the dead man could have been Andy. The conditions of the two bodies matched point by point, down to the expressions on their faces and the ripping of their guts from the inside. They perished in exactly the same manner.

According to the writings, only a powerful sorcerer could raise Shakek from the nether regions. Once summoned, the demon required a human sacrifice before departing. It existed only to kill.

Ellen rarely thought about religion. She believed in a supreme being but beyond that had no sympathy for the major faiths. She inherited her cynical outlook from her liberal parents, both lifelong agnostics. In college, Ellen always played the devil's advocate in dormitory arguments about God, the Devil, and the hereafter. She knew better than to laugh at the beliefs of her friends, but she smugly considered herself above their childish fantasies.

Not anymore. There was no escaping the facts. It appeared quite possible that Andy Yates had been murdered in his sleep by a demon four thousand years old. Though she still found it hard to believe, what she had seen last night half convinced her that the supernatural existed. And that a bit of darkness was intruding on the real world in a very deadly manner.

Fortunately, Ellen considered herself a pragmatic person. Confronted by the impossible, she readily embraced the unthinkable. It was either that or go mad. Ellen preferred staying sane. Very tentatively, she accepted the hypothesis that Shakek was responsible for Andy's death. And probably several others as well.

At the same time, she harbored no doubts that the police would think her crazy if she told them about Shakek. Or they would blame her for the murders. She deemed both options totally unacceptable. Either one put her career and probably her life in jeopardy.

Reclining on the sofa, she reviewed the facts. Someone had discovered the secret words of power used by ancient Egyptian sorcerers to summon demons. Using that power, this mysterious person had raised Shakek to murder his enemies. Andy Yates's mutilated body offered ample proof of the success of his plan.

After replacing *The Coffin Texts Decoded* on the shelf, Ellen drew forth *The Secrets of Egyptian Magic Revealed* by Claus von Gelb. Notorious for his decadent volume on early Grecian fertility cults, the German author had also written the definitive book on Egyptian sorcery.

Ellen turned to the section on defense from magical attacks. She breathed a sigh of relief as she carefully perused the transcript. Von Gelb included extremely explicit instructions to prevent dream assaults. He listed the specific items necessary to defeat the lurkers in nightmares. Blended together, the materials formed a paste to be spread over the forehead and cheeks before slumber. The taste and smell of the concoction frightened demons, forbidding them entrance to the sleeper's mind.

Ellen copied the list onto a piece of paper. They were mostly common household goods. She could buy everything at the local supermarket.

A simple spell accompanied the instructions. Ellen read it over several times, memorizing it. Von Gelb claimed that the words not only would repel any night gaunts, but would also send them howling back to their master seeking revenge.

Ellen laughed. She felt ridiculous. For a second, she considered ripping up the list and forgetting the whole thing. Then a vision of Andy's mutilated body flashed through her mind.

In the kitchen, the phone jangled. She picked up the receiver on the third ring.

"Hello," she answered cautiously, not giving her name.

"Hi, this is Marybeth Smith from New York. May I speak to Ellen Harper, please?"

Ellen frowned. She didn't know any Marybeth Smith. But the name struck a familiar chord.

"I'm Ellen Harper."

"Terrif," said Marybeth. "Maybe you've heard of me? I'm the editor of *Nineties Women* magazine."

Voice and name came together. Ellen remembered seeing the woman on a talk show a few weeks ago. Her magazine was the latest rage. Ellen, not current on recent trends, had never read an issue.

"I saw you on . . . Oprah," she replied, guessing.

"Great," said Marybeth. She sounded so upbeat, so lively, that Ellen, worn out from last night, wanted to strangle her.

"Listen, Ellen, we've run into a small problem on our next issue, and I'm hoping you can help us out."

"Me? How?"

"We were all set to run our feature story on Lydia Paulson, that zoo director from Hartford. You know who I mean, the girl who's always on David Letterman's show."

"Uh, oh sure," said Ellen, who usually shut off the TV after the ten o'clock news.

"Well, unfortunately, Lydia had the misfortune of getting herself fired last week. Bad timing there. If we published the piece now, the issue would bomb. That would make our advertisers quite unhappy. And we can't risk that.

"Needless to say, we killed the piece. All that work went right down the toilet. Which left us without a lead story. Anyway, to shorten a long story, we had you slated for a future issue. How about if we give you Lydia's spot?"

"But I'm not famous," said Ellen, bewildered by the offer. "I never appeared on television."

"Aren't you the chief archivist with the third largest private museum in the United States?" said Marybeth, not expecting an answer. "According to my files, Ellen Harper is twenty-eight years old, single, and moving up fast in her profession. Those facts make you exactly the type of woman our readers want to know about. Take my word for it, honey. I'm the expert. You belong on our cover."

"I'm awfully busy," said Ellen. "And a friend of mine died last night. It hit me pretty hard."

"Oh, you poor child," said Marybeth, most of the brashness gone from her voice. "We could postpone the article. But chances are it would be lost in the shuffle."

The editor sighed. "I hate to push you at a difficult time, dear. However, consider this tidbit before you make up your mind. There's three ways a woman reaches the upper management levels in today's world. Through hard work, sleeping with the boss, or lots of publicity. The first choice means you slave twice as hard as anyone else in your office to earn half the money. The second option only works if you're young and pretty and totally without morals. I'm handing you the third alternative on a silver platter. Can you afford to turn it down?"

"No," said Ellen, overwhelmed by events. "Of course not. What do you want me to do?"

"I'll make all the arrangements," said Marybeth. "We use a Chicago free-lance writer for Midwest features. He'll want to spend the next few days interviewing you, getting a feel for your work. After that, once we have his piece in-house, we'll assign a photographer to take specific shots to accompany the text."

"This author can't wait till Monday?" asked Ellen.

"No way," said Marybeth. "Our deadline is less than a week away. Every minute counts. Plus, we want an in-depth article, not some puff piece like they run in the tabloids. David will call you later today."

"David?"

"Ross. He's one of the best in the business. Oops, gotta run. Nice talking to you, Ellen. Sorry about your friend. Stay cool."

Ellen placed the receiver back on the hook, then rubbed her ear. It hurt, just like when she spoke with her mother. Why did most New Yorkers shout into the phone? It was one of the unexplained mysteries of the universe.

Hastily, she checked over the list copied from the von Gelb book. She wondered if there was enough time to dash out to the supermarket before this David character called.

The phone rang.

"Guess not," said Ellen, and picked up the still-warm receiver.

"Ellen Harper?"

"Speaking."

"It's David Ross, Ellen. I gather that Marybeth explained the situation to you. We have to squeeze a week's worth of interviews into three days. Are you free tonight?"

"Tonight?" said Ellen. "Uh, I guess so."

"How about dinner then? We can combine business with pleasure. Mexican okay with you? I know a great restaurant not far from where you live."

"Mexican's fine," said Ellen. "How do you know where I live?"

"Marybeth passed it on to me earlier today," said David, chuckling. "Actually, she talked to me before she called you."

"But she didn't know then that I'd agree to the interview," said Ellen.

"Nobody disagrees with Marybeth Smith," said David. "What she wants, she gets. See you at seven?"

"Seven is fine," said Ellen. "'Bye."

It was time to head off on her shopping trip. Then she had better pick out something nice to wear. This David Ross sounded pleasant enough over the telephone. Getting away from the house would take her mind off Andy's death for a while. Plus, talking about herself would be a novelty. She only hoped she lived long enough to see the article in print.

17

▲ Moe stared at the Hinkley residence with ill-concealed distaste. "Classy place, huh?" he said to his partner.

Calvin shrugged his massive shoulders. "I'm surprised the neighbors haven't burned the place down. This area is solid Polish with a few Hispanics thrown in for variety. They're all real concerned about property values. A wreck like that pulls down the market prices for the whole block."

A narrow ranch-style house, the dwelling needed more than a coat of paint to restore its dignity. Loose shingles dangled from the roof, small chunks of concrete were missing from the foundation, and the rusted gutters were choked with moldy leaves. The sidewalk leading up to the front door was pitted and cracked. An old metal fence, smashed and bent in a half-dozen spots, surrounded a small yard that resembled an abandoned auto parts graveyard. Bits and pieces from a dozen old cars littered the ground.

"Well, time for us to tell Joe that his nephew won't be coming home anymore," said Moe. This part of his job was never easy. Nobody coped well with violent death.

The two men got out of the unmarked squad car. As they approached the front walk, a small boy no more than nine or ten years old came darting out from the house next door. Dressed in jeans and wearing a Teenage Mutant Ninja Turtles T-shirt, he had eyes brimming over with curiosity. "You looking for old man Hink?" he asked in a high-pitched voice.

"That's right, dude," answered Moe. His two kids were heavily into the Ninja Turtle craze, and he knew all the popular phrases. Not bad, he felt, for a forty-year-old detective who only watched baseball games on TV.

"You guys cops?" asked the kid.

"That's right," said Calvin Lane, his voice rumbling from deep down in his chest. "We're cops."

"Old man Hink says all cops stink," continued the boy, completely innocent of guile. "You smell okay to me. My name is Tommy Gleason. Cops are pretty cool. Do you carry guns? Why don't you wear holsters? I think Mr. Hinkley's a little bit crazy."

"Sounds about right," said Moe, grinning. His own son chattered continually, in much the same manner. "Do you know if he's home?"

"Nobody's seen him all week," replied Tommy. "Ever since that giant guy came to visit. I heard my dad tell Mom that old man Hink was probably drunk again. My parents don't like Mr. Hinkley very much."

"Can't say that I blame them much," said Moe. "Time for us to pay our respects to Mr. Hinkley. Nice talking to you, Tommy. Thanks for the information."

"Yeah," said Tommy. "Later, dudes."

Chattering merrily to himself, the boy skipped down the block. "Do all kids talk that much?" asked Calvin.

"Some are worse," said Moe, speaking from experience. "Old man Hink sounds like a real charmer. I have a feeling we won't be learning much from him."

"Nobody said it was gonna be easy," replied Calvin, using one of his favorite sayings.

Together they made their way up the walk to the front door. "Nice bell," said Moe, pointing to a jumble of wire where the doorbell should be.

"Looks like someone tried to fix it," said Calvin. "Didn't make much progress."

He rapped hard on the door. Nobody answered. After waiting a few seconds, Calvin knocked harder. Again, there was no reply.

"Gone out for a while?" said Moe.

"Kid said nobody's seen the old geezer in a week," replied Calvin.

He tried the knob. Surprisingly, it turned. The door was unlocked. Carefully, the big detective eased it open.

"Mr. Hinkley!" he called, in a voice louder than most foghorns. "Police. You okay in there?"

No one answered. Calvin looked at Moe. "As police officers, it's our duty to check on this man's well-being."

"I agree," said Moe solemnly. It never hurt to have just cause before doing any snooping. As veteran cops, they were experts at bending the rules to fit the situation.

"Mr. Hinkley!" Moe shouted, opening the door and stepping inside the house. "We're the police. Where are you?"

The inside of the building matched the outside. The furniture was old and threadbare. Only the TV set in the corner looked new. The faded blue carpet was stained with beer, and there were empty cans everywhere. A half-empty bowl of potato chips rested on the sofa. Calvin picked one up and broke it between his fingers.

"Stale. Nobody's touched this junk for days."

They found Joe Hinkley in the larger of two bedrooms. He lay stomach down on the bed. His head was twisted completely around, leaving his dead eyes staring up at the ceiling. The sharp smell of rotting flesh indicated he had been dead for quite some time.

"Number two," said Moe grimly. He wondered how many more corpses would turn up before they solved this case.

"I'll notify the district commander there's been a homicide in his area," said Calvin. "Better check for clues before the local evidence team arrives. I'll request a bunch of regular cops to seal off the area and interview the neighbors. You think of anything else we need?"

Moe shook his head. Calvin tramped out to their car to

radio in the call to the local district commander and then their own supervisor. In the meantime, as primary investigator, it was his job to search for leads.

Sirens wailed in the distance when Calvin finally returned. "Uniforms are on the way. Evidence team and the medical examiner should arrive soon after."

"Take a look at this," said Moe, leading his partner into a second bedroom.

Huge posters covered the walls. Most were black-and-white reproductions of Nazi soldiers in full battle gear. Others showed KKK members complete with white sheets and burning crosses. A huge blow-up of Adolf Hitler's face dominated one whole corner. Beneath the picture on a small table was a mock altar, complete with white candles and a steel swastika.

"Oscar's room," said Moe, stating the obvious.

"So I gather," said Calvin. "I recognize most of these charmers, but not all of them." He pointed to one poster in particular. "You recognize that sucker?"

The picture was a blown-up photo of a slender, pleasant-looking young man garbed in survivalist gear, cradling an automatic rifle in both arms. At his feet were several large stacks of dollar bills. Running across the bottom of the poster were the words "America Will Be Free" in bold black letters.

"That's Carl Garrett," said Moe. "He's the leader of Blood and Iron, the most dangerous lunatic fringe group in the country. They're the ones responsible for that major crime wave on the West Coast. Garrett's the brains of the operation. His friend George Slater supplies the muscle."

Moe paused. "Slater's a huge man," he said slowly. "According to what I've read, he's six-foot-six or so and built like a football lineman."

"Or," said Calvin, catching on quickly, "a giant. I think we should talk to our friend Tommy again."

By the time they located the young boy, the local police had sealed off Hinkley's yard and were questioning the neighbors. The district's evidence team and photographer were busy at work inside, as was the medical examiner. They questioned Tommy on the front steps of the house. He seemed unimpressed by all the excitement.

"Some geek wasted Mr. Hinkley, huh?" he asked, calmly chewing a huge wad of bubble gum.

"Right," said Moe. "We think the giant you mentioned could be involved in the crime. Can you describe him to me?"

"Sure," replied the boy. "He was humongous—like the Big Boss Man or Akeem." Moe recognized the names as pro wrestlers featured on TV. His son watched those shows also.

"He had black hair and a big thick beard," continued Tommy. "And he always wore flannel shirts." The boy grinned. "Mom tries to make me wear that stuff, too, but I never do. It itches like crazy."

"*Always?*" repeated Calvin, picking up on the word. "Did you see the guy more than once?"

"Yeah, two or three times," said Tommy. "He and his friends visited old man Hink a lot."

The two detectives exchanged glances. Most cases required long, tedious hours of investigating to turn up clues. It was a novelty to be fed information by a ten-year-old.

"You remember his friends as well?" asked Moe.

"Of course," said the boy, wrinkling his nose as if insulted. "You think I'm dumb? There was this short guy, who was smiling all the time. He even said hello to me once. And a lady with bright yellow hair. She was weird."

"In what way?" asked Moe. He didn't recall any female members of Blood and Iron, but he wasn't an expert on the group.

"She wore long white dresses with a big iron cross around her neck," said Tommy. "And she had this strange expression on her face all the time." He lowered his voice to a whisper. "Like she was on drugs or something."

"Excuse me, sir," a member of the evidence crew

interrupted. He stood in the doorway of the house, holding a thick looseleaf notebook under one arm. "We found this scrapbook hidden under the bed. It looks important."

"Time for you to leave, Tommy," said Moe. He stuck out his hand. "Shake, partner. You've really helped. Maybe, if you like, one day soon Detective Lane and I can take you on a tour of police headquarters. It would be our way of saying thanks for cooperating with the police."

"Could I bring a friend?" asked Tommy cautiously.

"I don't see why not," said Moe.

He waved over one of the uniformed patrolmen watching the house. "Do me a favor and escort Mr. Gleason home. You can tell his parents he's been our star witness on this case."

"Later, dudes," said Tommy as he skipped up the front walk, policeman tagging alone.

"You check out that notebook," said Calvin, stretching his huge arms over his head. "I need some exercise. I'll inform the officers questioning the neighbors about our suspicions. If the kid saw these strangers, you can bet a few nosy neighbors did, too."

Moe entered the house. The evidence technician who had come to the door sat on the sofa in the living room. The notebook rested on a cheap coffee table a few inches away from his knees. Seeing Moe, the officer spread the book open. Carefully, they examined the contents.

Stories cut from Chicago newspapers filled the pages. Each article was pasted flat on one side of the paper. In many of the pieces, Oscar had underlined certain passages or paragraphs in pencil. In a few cases, he had written notations in the margin. Usually, the messages were brief and to the point.

Pencil scratches riddled a long article describing the growth of skinhead gangs on Chicago's south side. Alongside the story, Hinkley had scribbled "LIES" in red marker. Other critical pieces received similar comments.

Every clipping dealt in some way with the rising tide of right-wing hate groups in Chicago. In several cases, Hinkley had proudly circled his name when it appeared in a story. Nearly a dozen pages dealt with his arrest for operating a bomb factory. Several companion pieces told the story of his escapade at the Petrie Institute.

Along with the material on Midwest extremists, Hinkley had also preserved every story, news brief, or mention of Blood and Iron. There were detailed histories of the group, coverage of all their major crimes, even feature stories on Garrett and his accomplices. Moe noted that there was no mention of a woman belonging to the gang.

"We found boxes and boxes in the closet filled with privately printed pamphlets from all these hate groups," said the evidence technician, barely glancing at the pages as he turned them. "He must have spent a fortune on the stuff. The guy was sick, real sick. I'm not surprised somebody bumped him off. Hey, what's this?"

Pasted down securely to a page of the notebook was a short typed letter. Hinkley had even saved the envelope in which it had come, gluing it to the opposite side of the sheet. Moe stared down at the note, then smiled.

The letter was dated less than a month earlier. It proposed a meeting between Oscar Hinkley and Blood and Iron. There was no mistaking Carl Garrett's bold signature at the bottom of the page.

18

▲ "Have you discovered anything?" asked Jambres, looking up from his book.

"No," answered Sarah. "None of these articles mentions any unusual Egyptian talismans or charms in midwestern museums."

"They must be wrong," said Jambres. "The energy from that source revitalized my spirit as soon as the statue of Anubis was shipped to the Petrie Institute. It has to be located somewhere in this area. Without the power it contains, my mission will end in failure."

Jambres pushed the stack of books off his lap and stood up. The two of them were alone in his room in the basement. Outside the house, Carl and his troops sweated through their exercises. Garrett worried that the past few weeks of idleness had made his men soft. So three times a week he led them in several hours' worth of grueling maneuvers. The thunderstorms this morning had forced them to wait till afternoon before starting. Jambres planned to put his time alone with Sarah to good use.

"You're growing stronger all the time," said the seeress. "You told me so the other day."

"Little by little, my powers return," he replied. "Today I can perform magic that was impossible for me to control a week ago. Still, it could be many months before I once again master the necessary skills for raising . . ."

"For raising what?" asked Sarah.

"The elements," said Jambres hastily, realizing he had almost revealed too much. He doubted if Sarah believed his lie, but he elaborated on it nonetheless. "Even your modern weapons pale before the wrath of a fire elemental. A being that only you and I will command."

Sarah smiled at his words.

"What about Carl and George?" she asked slyly. Jambres knew what she wanted to hear and told her exactly that. He would say anything to keep her happy.

"They are little men, obsessed with their grandiose schemes of conquest. Their plans need not worry us. Once they have served their purpose, we will dispose of them."

"Why not kill them now?" said Sarah, trying to mask the eagerness in her voice.

"Patience," said Jambres, walking over to her. He placed one hand on her bare arm. She shivered at the touch of his cold fingers. Despite her fears, his presence still excited her. "When they cease to be useful, I will snuff out their lives in an instant."

"They're dangerous."

"So am I," said Jambres. "Of course, there is a way . . ."

He hesitated, as if afraid to continue. The trap was baited. The rest depended on her.

"A way?" she asked.

"To find the talisman in a moment. With your help, I can mentally search the entire Midwest in a few seconds. Once I discover the relic's location, we can steal it. After that, Carl and his friends become expendable."

Jambres saw no reason to mention that she also fell into that same category. None of these people meant anything to him. They were game tokens, to be discarded when the time came.

"Tell me what to do," said Sarah.

"Remove all of your clothing."

"What?"

"You heard me correctly. Not all magic requires sacrifice. Some entails pleasure. You, of all people, should know that sex is bound to sorcery with ties equal to those of hatred. Enough talking. Undress, while we are alone and undisturbed."

Sarah did as she was told. First, she removed the ever-present metal cross she wore around her neck. The symbol of her faith, she called it, though she mocked Christianity. Next, she reached down and grabbed her long white dress by the hem and lifted. In one smooth motion, she peeled the garment up and over her head. She wore nothing else. Sarah enjoyed attracting attention. Women rarely noticed her lack of undergarments. Men always did.

"You are a beautiful woman," said Jambres. He meant every word. The memories of two modern men, Oscar Hinkley and Tom Darrow, offered ample testimony that Sarah was a beauty by any standards. She had large, firm breasts, well-rounded hips, and long, trim legs. A creature of the night hours, Sarah had skin as white as wax, contrasted only by the darkness of her nipples. There was not a hair on her body. As part of her magic rituals, she routinely shaved her limbs and torso every few weeks. A special cream did the rest.

Sarah licked her lips nervously. "Now what do I do?"

Jambres didn't bother to answer. Instead, he swiftly removed his own clothes. It took only a few seconds before he was also nude. Sarah's eyes nearly bulged out of their sockets when she saw his erection.

"You're not planning . . . ," she said, shocked.

"But I am," he replied. "Only by joining our bodies can we join our minds."

Sarah moaned. Trembling, she reached up and cupped her breasts with both hands. She pushed them hard together until her fingers touched. Jambres could see her nipples hardening.

"How?"

"Whatever way you wish," said Jambres. From Darrow's thoughts, he knew exactly what positions aroused her the most. Better, though, to let her dwell on the answer. The more excited she became, the better.

Inhabiting the body of a corpse, Jambres experienced no physical desire. He never ate or slept, breathed or cried. His dead eyes never wavered, never blinked. He was equally divorced from all biological and emotional cravings—including lust.

Fortunately, his command of his host body was absolute. It didn't matter that sex no longer excited him. He could maintain an erection for hours.

"Let's do it sitting up," said Sarah, her voice slurred with emotion. She pointed to the solitary chair. With a high back and no arms, it was perfect for their needs.

Jambres sat, pressing his legs together. Eyes wild, Sarah straddled him, her feet planted firmly on the floor. She leaned forward so that her breasts rubbed against his unmoving chest.

Her breath coming in ragged gasps, Sarah reached down to guide them together. Slowly, she eased herself onto his erection. She was wet with passion. He entered her without the least amount of resistance.

"Cold," she gasped, "so very cold."

Wrapping her arms around his neck, Sarah drew his head between her breasts. Slowly, she rocked back and forth, forcing his erection deeper inside her. "Oh, oh, oh," she whispered as she increased speed.

Jambres let Darrow's memories guide him. With both hands, he massaged the taut skin of her breasts, rubbing her nipples with the roughness of his palms. She moaned with excitement and thrust her hips ever harder against him.

Concentrating, the sorcerer tried to match his movements with Sarah's rhythm. The effort required all of his attention. He derived no pleasure from the task. It was a meaningless charade, done entirely for Sarah's benefit. In some ways, it was a depressing task.

During his lifetime, Jambres had been a bold, passionate man. As second only to Pharaoh, he enjoyed the attentions of many beautiful women of the court. Many of them submitted eagerly to his embraces. And, like most of his countrymen, he looked forward to similar entertainments in the afterlife. Jambres fully expected to enjoy sex for all eternity.

According to the basic tenets of Egyptian religion, the dead engaged in the same activities as the living. As they acted in life, so they continued in death. But that only took place in the Underworld. And he could not enter the mystic region unless his spirit and soul were reunited once more.

Anxiously, he dropped his hands from her breasts to the chair beneath him. His feet firmly planted on the floor, he pushed upward with all of his strength. Inch by inch, his hips and thighs rose off the chair. Sarah's toes dangled inches off the ground, her body supported entirely by his.

Hot sweat ran in rivulets between Sarah's breasts as she continued to force her hips against his. She rode him like a wild horse, bouncing up and down, her breath coming in short, ragged gasps.

"Yes!" she cried as she thrust down with all of her strength. Jambres could feel her muscles tense as she screamed again. "Oh God, yes!"

A tidal wave of passion engulfed Sarah's senses as her body exploded with pleasure. Now was the instant for which Jambres had been waiting. As Sarah climaxed, the sorcerer linked their minds together.

Under normal circumstances, he was only able to observe her surface thoughts. Lust served to break down her mental defenses. For an instant, he controlled her magical powers. Casting out a psychic net, he searched for the mysterious talisman. And found it.

The charm throbbed with incredible energy. It was more powerful than he had ever imagined. Jambres rejoiced. Once he obtained the relic, all things were possible. Reaching out with their linked minds, he mentally touched the talisman. And recoiled in shock.

Sarah screamed in pain as his surprise slashed through her thoughts like a knife. She collapsed onto his chest, unconscious.

Frustrated, Jambres lifted Sarah off his legs and carried her to his cot. He knew the general direction of the talisman, but not its precise location. And he doubted if he could harness Sarah's psychic powers again. Such tricks depended on the novelty of the experience. Continued sex with Sarah would stimulate her, but not to the peak she'd reached today. Finding the talisman would have to be done by purely physical means.

Pulling on his clothes, Jambres pondered the vagaries of fate. Only one object in the world contained the power he had just touched—the mystic talisman used by his son more than three thousand years ago. His hope of resurrection rested with the cause of his downfall.

The irony of the situation struck him as deliberate. He sensed the involvement of the unseen gods. Time and distance meant nothing to them. Their schemes encompassed centuries. Only now did he realize the extent of their plan.

Using him as their tool, they planned to shatter three thousand years of history. But once the talisman was his, no one in the world would stop him.

19

▲ The two hours went by quickly. Ellen and David munched on taco chips while sipping sangria. Ellen told David about growing up in New York and her childhood obsession with things Egyptian. He dutifully taped their conversation, prompting her whenever necessary with a question or comment.

They progressed from chips to steak and chicken fajitas. And more sangria. Ellen spoke of college and trips to Egypt and then graduate school. Finally, talk turned to the present and her hopes and ambitions at the Petrie Institute.

Flan and cinnamon-flavored coffee ended the meal. The wine with dinner made David a little woozy. As did the company. He was captivated by his companion. It was impossible for him to believe she was mixed up in murder or terrorist conspiracies.

Reaching across the table, Ellen shut off the recorder. "Enough about me. Turnabout time. How about a little information on David Ross?"

"I'm a pretty normal guy," he answered, falling back on lies used many times before. "There's nothing the least bit unusual about me. Besides, it's not fair changing the subject."

"All's fair in love and war," replied Ellen, smiling enigmatically. "You're too polite to be a journalist. I've met a few over the years. They're all so pushy. What are you really, a spy?"

David sobered instantly. "What makes you say that?" he asked sharply.

Ellen laughed, dispelling his momentary panic. "Hey. Don't get so bent out of shape. I didn't mean it."

"Sorry," he said, deciding a little truth would work easier than a big lie. "You caught me by surprise. Actually, the truth hurt. I worked for the CIA for three years after college."

"What?"

He grinned at the surprised expression on Ellen's face. "My father and mother both taught linguistics at the university for many years. I spent my formative years hearing five different languages used around the house. Fortunately, I inherited my parents' gifts for tongues. By the time I graduated with my bachelor's degree, I spoke seven languages fluently and could make myself understood in five others."

"That's incredible," said Ellen, sounding impressed.

"Nothing special," said David with a shrug. "Anyhow, during my senior year, the CIA spent a week on campus recruiting interested students for office jobs. They offered me double what any import-export company paid. So I spent the next three years of my life as a translator for the government, keeping tabs on our overseas friends."

He left unsaid the fact that much of that time was spent working undercover for the agency in trouble spots around the globe. Excited at first by the danger, he soon grew disillusioned by the cynicism he encountered at every level of the organization. After three years, he'd had enough. It was a part of his life David preferred to forget.

"After I left the government, I taught martial arts and self-defense for a few years. I earned my black belt in karate in college, where I studied several of the other disciplines as well. Teaching offered me a chance to further perfect my skills as well as earn a living."

"When does journalism enter the picture?" asked Ellen.

"After a few years of bumps and bruises, I decided to try something else. I minored in English in school. Writing always appealed to me. So I started plugging away, sending pieces to the major magazines, hoping for a lucky break. *Voila,* here I am five years later, a successful free-lance author."

"You strike me as the type who engineers his own lucky breaks," said Ellen. "No mention in that entire recital of any female companions or steady girl."

"There have been a few," said David, without much enthusiasm. "Nothing that lasted very long. A close friend recently suggested I was dating the wrong type of women." He looked directly into Ellen's emerald eyes. "I think he made a good point."

Ellen blushed but said nothing.

"What about you?" David asked. "I don't recall hearing about Mr. Right in the story of your rise to fame and fortune."

"I spent the past fifteen years of my life chasing a dream," said Ellen wistfully. "I dated but never very seriously. My career meant more to me than romance or marriage. Now I'm not so sure I made the right choice."

"Why the sudden change of heart?" asked David gently. "Problems at work? A new boyfriend making you miserable?"

Ellen shook her head. "You're sweet, David, and very charming. I'm flattered by your concern."

Pausing, she took a deep breath, as if calming her nerves. "A dear friend of mine died last night. It made me realize just how fragile our lives really are. My job means a great deal to me, but there's more to life than working. If I died tomorrow, who would miss me? Just my parents, a few relatives, maybe some friends. Poor Andy. He's gone, and nobody knows or cares."

Ellen looked ready to burst out crying. David touched her cheek and brushed away a solitary tear. "That's not true," he said quietly. She raised her eyes to his. "You know. You care."

Sniffling, she pulled out a lace handkerchief and dried her face. "I'm sorry for getting so worked up," she said. "Too much wine makes me act silly. Could you take me home now? Please?"

Ellen remained silent all the way back to her apartment building. It wasn't until he pulled the car up in front of the high-rise that she spoke again.

"Pretty rotten way to end an evening, huh?" she asked, not expecting an answer.

"Not at all," said David. "The death of a close friend can drain you emotionally. If you want to talk about it, I'd be glad to listen."

Ellen shook her head. "I can't. Not yet." She patted his arm. "I'm okay. Really."

"I still need to interview you at least two more times," said David. "How does dinner tomorrow night sound?"

"I hope so," Ellen answered oddly. "Call me in the afternoon."

She opened the car door, then stopped. Leaning over, she circled his neck with her left hand and pulled him close. Gently, she kissed him on the lips.

"Thank you for a wonderful evening, David Ross," she whispered. "You're very special."

Then, before he could react, she was out of the car and into the foyer.

David sat there for a long time afterward before finally driving away.

20

▲ "You're telling me the absolute truth?" asked Carl, feeling sick to his stomach. "You actually saw Jambres and Sarah . . . having sex?"

Carl was a prude. A product of small-town life and a puritanical mother, he considered sex dirty and disgusting. He was a loner for most of his life, and his own experiences numbered less than a dozen.

As the most charismatic leader of the right-wing underground, Carl rarely spoke at any secret conclave without being propositioned by one or more of the female attendees. Unlike his less dedicated compatriots, he turned down all such offers. But he quickly discovered that some women refused to take no for an answer.

The most cunning and resourceful ones usually found a way to trap him alone. Incapable of dealing with sexually aggressive women, he usually submitted to their desires. Not a spectacular lover, he left most of his partners unsatisfied.

A few women demanded more, much more. Unable to resist, he found himself several times engaged in what he considered unnatural acts of passion. Though terrible feelings of guilt wracked his psyche afterward, those encounters were the only times he achieved total sexual fulfillment. Carl comforted himself with the belief that supposedly Adolf Hitler relied on the same forbidden pleasures.

Still, the thought of a living woman having sexual intercourse with a corpse ripped at his guts. Necrophilia violated all natural laws. It took all of Carl's self-control to hold down his supper.

George suffered from no such niceties. "They screwed like rabbits. I watched the whole thing, from the beginning to the end. Neither of them guessed I was there. Nobody knows about the peephole I drilled in the wall. It's too high for anybody but me to use."

The big man laughed, a crude, obscene sound that set Carl's nerves on edge. "Didn't take no genius to figure out what they were doing. That Sarah worked up a real sweat, humping and bumping for fifteen or twenty minutes at least. When she finally popped, she screamed bloody murder."

"What about Jambres?" asked Carl, forcing the words out. Though he tried to banish the thought from his mind, he found himself visualizing Sarah naked, riding the dead man's erection. The notion both repelled and fascinated him.

"He sure the hell satisfied her," said George. "Damn corpse kept it up with no trouble." He laughed again. "For a dead man, he stayed stiff as a board."

"I've heard enough," said Carl.

"She ain't a bad-lookin' woman," continued George, as if thinking aloud. "Kinda nice seeing her naked, all white like that, no hair anywhere. She didn't waste a lot of time on kissing and stroking and all that stuff. She was wet and willing right away. And hot enough to melt butter."

"I've heard *enough,*" repeated Carl angrily.

He licked his lips, trying to stay calm. Perhaps he had misjudged Sarah. If he spared her life, she could redeem herself in many ways. The thought of a grateful Sarah twisting and turning as she performed his secret perversions caused Carl to squirm uncomfortably in his seat. It had been too long since his last encounter with sin. Silently, he vowed to turn his daydreams into reality.

"I'll handle this whole thing," he said to George. "Meanwhile, don't mention it to any of the others. No reason to upset them with this latest incident."

"Sure, Carl," said George, smirking. "Don't want them all grossed out. Ain't healthy knowing a dead man is getting more sex than you can manage."

"What's Jambres doing now?" said Carl, trying to change the subject. He dared not let sex distract him from his mission.

"He's preparing more wax for tonight," replied George. "Spooks the hell out of me the way he kills people by black magic."

Carl grimaced. He disliked Jambres's use of sorcery, but for different reasons. It was an unnecessary waste of time. But there was no reasoning with the sorcerer.

According to the magician, the practice of imprisoning a magician's soul in a statue was described in detail in *The Book of the Dead*. Any well-read Egyptologist would be familiar with the concept. Jambres worried that the wrong person at the Petrie Institute might discover the missing statue of Anubis. Using that theft as a starting point, they could possibly deduce his true identity.

It was a one-in-a-million chance, but Jambres insisted on dealing with it in his own way. Carl argued without success that he was making a terrible mistake. The series of gruesome murders would draw attention to the museum. The magician refused to bend. If he killed the experts, it didn't matter what the police thought. His only concern was protecting his secrets.

In some ways, Jambres was even more ruthless than Carl. Blood and Iron struggled for a cause. Jambres fought only for himself.

"Better a thousand deaths," he told Carl before he attempted the first killing, "than one live enemy."

Carl stood up, walked over to the window, and looked outside. Despite constant reassurance from Jambres that they fought for the same cause, Carl had his doubts. The magician refused to answer too many important questions.

"Two more murders," said Carl. "Then our guest lays his plans on the table. Or we refuse to cooperate further." He swung back around and stared at George. "Who's on the list for tonight?"

"A geek named Thomas Grainger," said George. "One of the museum board members."

"And then tomorrow?"

"He kills the last one," said George, sounding relieved. "She works as the chief archivist for the museum. A woman called Ellen Harper."

21

▲ In huge letters, the headline screamed, "The Killer Corpse!"

Putting down the Sunday paper, Moe stared across his desk at his partner. "At least they spelled my name right."

"Big deal," said Calvin. Scanning the article until he came to the right line, he read, "Detective Maurice Kaufman assured reporters that police expected a quick arrest in the puzzling case."

"It's better than nothing," said Moe. "Which is what you got. I think you're jealous."

Calvin snorted. "The only time a black cop gets his name in the paper is when he's convicted of taking a bribe—or he makes the obituary page. I'll settle for anonymity."

"What time those pictures due here?" asked Calvin,

shifting restlessly in his seat. "It's bad enough working on Sunday. Sticking around the station, when we should be on the street asking questions, adds insult to injury."

"That FBI bozo, Anderson, promised them by noon." Moe glanced at his watch. "He's only a half hour late. What did you expect from the same people who run the post office?"

Neither detective admired the FBI. Most cops considered the government agents glory hounds interested only in furthering their own careers. Most of the time, they allowed the police to do all the work, then arrived at the scene to claim the credit.

Yesterday evening, the two detectives had spent most of an hour listening to the local bureau chief, Rufus Anderson, explain how it was impossible for Blood and Iron to be in the Midwest. The FBI, he assured them, was hot on the gang's trail in Washington State.

Anderson dismissed Oscar's scrapbook and reports of his visitors as "purely circumstantial evidence." Moe knew better than to mention the source of most of their information. The FBI man would have laughed them out of his office in a second.

The letter from Carl Garrett to Hinkley caused a raised eyebrow but nothing more. According to Anderson, such letters were not uncommon. Most of them came from right-wing fundraisers hoping to cash in on Garrett's name. The promised meeting was nothing more than a scam. A dozen or more gullible patrons assembled at a secret location. In near darkness, a man posing as Garrett solicited donations for Blood and Iron. All of the funds, of course, disappeared into the pockets of local extremist groups.

Still, Anderson took the letter and promised to check the signature. He even admitted the handwriting appeared to be an excellent copy.

After much coaxing, Moe extracted a promise for recent photos of both Garrett and his notorious henchman, George Slater. The FBI chief was positive that no women belonged to the terrorist band. He halfheartedly agreed to run a check for blondes with known ties to the extreme right who matched their vague description.

That was Saturday night. It was now Sunday afternoon, and they were still waiting for Anderson's report and their photos.

"Hey, look who's here," said Calvin, spotting a well-dressed individual making his way across the room. "It's Anderson."

Moe grinned. "Now, that's service. The boss delivering the mail. I take back all my unkind words about the Bureau. Or at least some of them."

"Wait till we see what he brought before you make rash statements like that," said Calvin, chuckling.

He held out a hand. "Mr. Anderson. Surprised to see you here this afternoon."

The FBI chief shook hands with both of them, then dropped into a nearby chair. Dressed in the same suit he wore last night, he appeared exhausted. There were bags under his eyes, and dark worry lines creased his forehead.

"Excuse me if I sound tired, but I've been up all night. The two of you stirred up a real hornet's nest." He smiled faintly. "Probably earned me a commendation as well."

"Damn," said Calvin. "My car really needs that tune-up. And I could almost taste those potato pancakes."

"Miriam can hold supper," said Moe. He turned to the FBI chief. "You brought us those pictures?"

Laying his briefcase across his lap, Anderson popped open the latches. Reaching inside, he pulled out two manila portfolios. "Better than that. There's a set of documents for each of you. Compliments of the FBI."

"You checked on the signature," said Moe, comprehension slowly dawning.

"It looked like a forgery," said Anderson, "but I promised to run it through our files. So we did a computer scan, checking it against a known sample of Garrett's signature. They matched perfectly. Still not convinced, we checked the sheet for prints. Special photography turned up a few shadows. We faxed those along to Washington. An hour later they confirmed your claim. That letter was written by Carl Garrett."

Anderson grinned. "The contents of the letter upset some very important people at headquarters. Heads are rolling in the Pacific Northwest. Local agents swore that Garrett was holed up in the Canadian woods. Now they're not so sure. Especially when I reported the rest of your story to D.C."

The FBI chief pointed to the folders. "In those, you'll find a comprehensive report on Blood and Iron. One fact the Bureau doesn't publicize is George Slater's gruesome habit of killing people by twisting their heads around on their shoulders."

"This guy sounds like a cross between Frankenstein and a Nazi storm trooper," said Moe, quickly skimming the report on Slater. "How do you propose stopping this ape? Kryptonite?"

"You find him. We'll stop him," said Anderson, no longer smiling. "The best we can determine, that monster is responsible for over forty murders. That total, for your information, includes three of our agents and seven cops. I promise you"—and there was no mistaking the meaning of Anderson's words—"he will not be taken alive if I have anything to do with it."

"His friends don't sound too precious, either," said Calvin, leafing through the papers. Stopping, he pulled out a black-and-white glossy photo. "Who's this babe? I thought you said these geeks didn't mess with women."

"My gift to you," said Anderson, beaming. "I ran your description of the mystery woman through the national data files. Took three hours to toss out seven possibilities. Further cross-referencing eliminated four of them. One died last week, and number six is pregnant and out of action. That left one suspect. That's her picture. Sarah Walsh."

Moe studied the picture carefully. "Not a bad-looking woman. I take it Sarah is no ordinary flake?"

"She worked as a fortuneteller on the north side up until a few weeks ago," said Anderson. "According to her shill, Sarah drove off in her van one day and hasn't been seen since. Blondie had quite a reputation for being a tough customer. Her politics placed her just to the right of Attila the Hun. She'd fit right in with Blood and Iron."

"It doesn't make any sense, though," said Calvin. "These dudes been playing the macho scene for years. Why would they suddenly recruit a woman? There must be another reason than just wanting new blood."

Anderson shrugged. "According to our sources, Sarah's a pretty hot number. Maybe Garrett wants to get laid. That's for you to find out."

Closing his briefcase, he stood up, preparing to leave. "Officially, the case is still yours. If you turn up any hot leads, call me immediately. I'll provide you with all the backup you want. Remember, these lunatics aren't your typical run-of-the-mill psychos. They're armed with enough weaponry to start World War III, and they're not afraid to use it. Bringing them down won't be easy."

"It's never easy," said Moe, expressing a truism of the violent crimes division. "Every case is tough."

"Almost forgot," said Anderson, reaching into his coat pocket. "This ID came in right before I headed over here."

He smoothed out a crumpled piece of paper and dropped it onto Moe's desk. "It's the make and model of Sarah Walsh's van. You might check it out with your witnesses at the scene of the crime. Who knows? She's probably escorting Garrett and his friends around town in it. Crazy people sometimes do crazy things."

Moe sighed. "Tell me about it. That's the trouble with these murders. Anything's possible."

22

▲ Ellen didn't rise until noon on Sunday. After returning to her apartment the night before, she went through the rituals of protection as described in *The Coffin Texts.* She still considered it a probable waste of time, but better to be safe than sorry. Too keyed up to sleep, she stayed awake, mentally reviewing her dinner date.

She couldn't remember ever meeting a man as fascinating as David Ross. There was something about him that defied ordinary description. With his curly, dark hair and bushy eyebrows, he was pleasant-looking but definitely not handsome. Nor did he seem particularly muscular. He impressed her as the quiet, laid-back type of guy who stayed out of trouble.

He spoke quietly, but with a self-assurance she found appealing. David was confident without being conceited. Most of all, he appeared genuinely interested in everything she said. The look on his face after she kissed him caused Ellen to smile more than once through the long night.

Nothing the least bit unusual took place during her vigil. Finally, around five A.M., she drifted off to sleep. Images of David softly caressing her fingers haunted her dreams. When she awoke, her first thoughts were whether the reporter would call that afternoon as he promised.

Both papers waited at her front door. She sorted through them as she nibbled on toast and eggs.

She barely glanced at the lead story, something about a weird murder on the north side. Instead, she spent five minutes flipping through local and state news looking for some mention of Andy's death. She found the report mixed in with a dozen other crimes taken from the police blotter.

Nothing in the few bare paragraphs suggested anything unusual about the death. The official cause of death was listed as a stroke. No mention was made of the condition of the body. Ellen shivered when she read the last line of the story. "Police are investigating several similar deaths in the suburbs."

The phone rang as she was reading the article for the third time. She wondered if it might be David. Trying to stay cool, she picked up the receiver.

"Ellen, it's Tammy Williams. Have you seen the paper this morning?"

Tammy was a junior archivist working in the prehistoric section. She and Ellen often ate lunch together in the Institute cafeteria.

Ellen hesitated before answering. Tammy lived for gossip. Telling her a secret was the same as broadcasting it to the world. If Ellen mentioned one word about Andy Yates, the entire museum staff would know the details in an hour. For now, she preferred to keep her involvement a secret.

"I just walked in the door," she lied. "The newspaper arrived while I was out. What's up?"

"Remember that Oscar Hinkley who asked you for a date last year? The guy we voted most likely to end up in jail for life? Well, he's dead. Killed in some bizarre murder on the north side. And so is his uncle, the night watchman at the Institute."

Ellen gagged, caught completely by surprise. "Joe Hinkley? Murdered?"

"Yeah. It's really a weird story. I thought of you right away. Figured you would want to know. Spooky, huh? But that isn't all. I heard that Sheila Parsons died over the weekend, too."

"What?" said Ellen, feeling faint. Sheila Parsons

worked in publications and publicity. "How did she die?"

"I'm not sure," said Tammy. "Gloria Carter told me, and she didn't have all of the details. She heard it secondhand. Somebody mentioned something about Sheila dying in her sleep from a heart attack."

Ellen swayed in her chair, her head spinning. "Did you call Dr. Henderson with the news? He'd want to know."

"Funny thing about that," said Tammy, her voice sinking as always when she had something juicy to reveal. "After I heard the story from Gloria, I tried dialing the old man's private number. But he didn't answer."

Tammy and the museum curator had been a hot item a few years ago, and she was one of the few staff members who knew how to reach him on the weekends. "Another man picked up the phone. He said Henderson couldn't talk to me. Then he started grilling me with all sorts of personal questions. Naturally, I hung up."

Her voice dropped to a whisper. "He sounded like a cop. Maybe the police are questioning the old man about Hinkley's murder."

"Maybe," said Ellen, presuming much worse. Henderson, she felt quite sure, wouldn't be talking to anyone ever again.

"Tammy, I gotta go. I'm late for an appointment already. If you hear anything else, give me a buzz later. 'Bye."

Ellen placed the receiver on the hook before Tammy could squeeze in another word. She hated being abrupt, but she wanted to read that newspaper account immediately.

It took only a few minutes for her to finish the story. Afterward, she had no idea if Joe Hinkley's murder was related to the nightmare killings or not. The newspaper was not very clear on how the watchman's death tied in with Oscar Hinkley's murder. She guessed no one knew the answer to that question.

Oscar's death frightened her. Too many weird things were happening to museum staff or their relatives. She was sure there was a common factor linking all the murders. But she had no idea what.

Mentally, Ellen compared the three victims. She left Oscar and his uncle off her list, since neither man had died in his sleep. Except for their association with the Petrie Institute, the trio shared no other common bonds. Andy Yates, Albert Henderson, and Sheila Parsons were as disparate a group as could be assembled. Only their ties to the museum bound them together. And their most recent project.

Ellen paused, turning numb as the truth overwhelmed her. Getting the Rivington collection of Egyptian rarities for the museum had been old man Henderson's goal for years. Recently, with the financial backing of board member Thomas Grainger, he'd finally realized his dream. Andy Yates worked as purchasing agent on the deal. Sheila Parsons reviewed the collection for publicity. And Ellen had done all of the cataloging.

Other people were responsible for the actual displays and exhibits. But only the five of them were familiar with the entire contents of the collection. With them all dead, wholesale looting of the huge accumulation could take place without anyone being the wiser. Especially if one of the gang worked as a night watchman in the museum.

Anxiously, Ellen looked up Thomas Grainger's phone number. If her theory were correct, the millionaire's life was in deadly peril.

Listening to the phone ring, she reviewed her ideas. Someone was intent on plundering the Rivington collection. He was using ancient Egyptian sorcery to kill anyone who might realize pieces were missing. Aiding him in his operation were several museum guards. When Joe Hinkley had either discovered his plan or refused to cooperate, he had been killed. Oscar's death tied in as well, though Ellen had no idea how. Details would fall into place once the killer was unmasked.

"Grainger residence."

"May I speak to Mr. Grainger, please? It's quite important."

"Mr. Grainger can't come to the phone at the moment," replied the voice on the other end of the line. "Who's calling, please? And what's the problem?"

Ellen broke the connection. Grainger was dead. The mysterious killer had struck again. She was the only one of the five still alive. And Ellen knew beyond any doubt that she was the murderer's next target.

Last night she had gone through the ancient rites of protection more to satisfy her own mild anxiety. Faced with today's evidence, she no longer doubted the truth. Horrible death waited in the night. One mistake in her preparations, and she was dead.

The telephone rang, breaking into her thoughts. Ellen stared at the receiver, wondering if she should pick it up. Her two calls so far had brought only bad news. The telephone kept on ringing.

Finally, she answered.

It was David.

23

▲ David spent most of the night listening to dead air. Earlier, during dinner, he had dropped his knife on the floor. Bending over to retrieve it, he managed to slip several tiny electronic devices into Ellen's purse. They were designed to work in tandem with the high-tech relay he planted at her apartment building.

Together, the incredibly powerful miniature microphone and transmitting device, powered by several wafer-thin lithium batteries, enabled an agent to eavesdrop on conversations taking place just about anywhere. David monitored Ellen's apartment from the comfort of his own office. Except for a few odd moments when she recited an oddball chant, nothing happened. For which David was quite thankful.

He liked Ellen Harper. She combined good looks with sharp wits. David rarely trusted quick judgments, but he was quite positive about Ellen's innocence. A warm, vibrant person, she was definitely not the type to be involved in mysterious murders. He tried never to become involved in his assignments, but he could see already that staying objective with Ellen would be difficult.

He turned off the microphones at sunrise. According to Eli, the deaths took place only at night. Ellen was safe for another day. With a sigh of relief, he headed to bed.

Yawning, he turned on his answering machine. His body needed rest. The world could survive without him for a few hours. It took him only a few seconds to fall asleep.

He awoke around noon, feeling refreshed. One of the benefits of years of training was his ability to manage on only three or four hours of sleep a night. After a little brunch, he turned his recorder to playback. There was only one message.

"David, it's Eli. Call me back as soon as possible. It's quite important."

The old man sounded worried. It wasn't like him to call about an assignment, or to leave a message on an answering machine. Too many people could tap into such devices with the right tools.

David dialed Eli's unlisted number. The intelligence officer answered on the first ring.

"It's David. What's up?"

"The girl?" Eli asked, his voice shaky. "She's okay?"

"She was fine when I ended surveillance early this morning. Sleeping like a baby from the sound of things. Why do you ask?"

"There was another murder last night. One of the museum trustees died. That makes five."

David frowned. "Five? The other morning, you only mentioned three deaths to me. One more brings the total up to four."

"Remember how I told you yesterday I covered all bets? This time, the gamble blew up in my face. I assigned Saul Shransky to watch this Thomas Grainger. Saul was one of my brightest stringers, nearly in your class—smart, resourceful, full of ideas."

"Was?" asked David, already suspecting what followed.

"Saul approached Grainger in the guise of a professional bodyguard. Talking fast, he convinced the millionaire he needed protection from an unknown killer who had the police baffled. Grainger hired him to watch his back. They spent every minute together."

"Eli," said David, growing impatient. "No more stalling. Tell me what happened."

"Since all of the murders occurred late at night, after the victims fell asleep, Grainger and Saul decided to sleep during the day and stay awake after dark. They rented a bunch of movies to watch on the VCR. Old horror films, no less, like *The Mummy* and *Frankenstein Meets the Wolfman*.

"They remained downstairs while everyone else went to bed. Nothing happened until a little after two in the morning. Their screams roused the household. By the time Grainger's wife and the servants descended the stairs, both Saul and her husband were dead."

"Fell asleep watching the flicks?"

"No," said Eli, his voice shaky. "Whatever killed them struck while they were awake. Their eyes were wide open, and so were their insides! The killer savaged their bodies. Bits and pieces of their intestines were splattered all over the walls and floor. According to the servants, the place resembled a slaughterhouse. And smelled like a cesspool."

"Nobody seen fleeing?"

"Doors were locked and protected with alarm systems," said Eli. "Attack dogs patrolled the outside grounds. Not a sign of disturbance there. And, by all accounts, both murders took place in an instant. Impossible, yet two men are dead."

"What did the police say?"

"What do you think? They're completely baffled by the crimes. Any clues on your end?"

"You can rule out Ellen as the killer," said David. "She's not the type. And she was home all night. I can vouch for that."

"Anybody's the type," said Eli, "if the motive is right."

David said nothing. Years of espionage assignments had taught him that same difficult lesson. Only a novice trusted a stranger. Even one as attractive as Ellen Harper.

"I take it you find Ms. Harper interesting?" asked Eli, sounding a bit more like himself. "She's a good deal different from your usual blond bimbos."

"Spare me the 'I told you so's,'" said David with a groan. "You were right, and I was wrong."

"As usual," said Eli. "David, be careful. You're my best, but this time I'm worried about you."

"That makes two of us," said David. "Time for me to hang up. I want to call Ellen. Talk to you tomorrow."

"Tomorrow," said Eli in return. David only wished it sounded less like an obituary.

He hung up and spent the next half hour organizing his thoughts. A brave man, he knew the difference between courage and stupidity. Spending the night with Ellen Harper tended toward the latter choice. Still, it appeared his only way of learning the truth behind these mysterious deaths.

The odd chant Ellen had recited the night before bothered him. She didn't strike him as the type to utter prayers before bedtime. David wondered how much Ellen really knew about the killings. There was only one way to find out. He dialed her number.

"David." Ellen's voice sounded strained. "I'm glad

you called." She paused for a second, then blurted out, "Do you mind if I ask you a personal question?"

"It depends on the question," said David truthfully. This conversation was not proceeding as planned. He wanted to pump her for information, not the other way around. Cautiously, he asked, "What do you want to know?"

"The story you told me last night about working for the CIA—it wasn't all BS you concocted one day at the office. There was some truth in it, right?"

David snorted in disgust. "I'm not in the habit of fabricating stories merely to impress the women I interview."

"Please," she said quickly. "I didn't mean to insult you. It's just that I never encountered a secret agent before."

"That's stretching my role with the Company a bit," said David, sticking to his cover story. "I worked as a translator over a three-year period. Not the most romantic of jobs."

Ellen rushed on, ignoring most of what he said. "I need help. You're the only person I know with any experience in this type of situation. Remember the friend I mentioned last night? The one whose death started me brooding about my own mortality? Well, there's more to the story than that. Three other people died the same way this week. That makes four so far. And I'm positive that my name is next on the list."

"Huh?" said David. It was the only thing he could think to say. "Want to back up a little and explain things—from the beginning?"

"Not on the phone," said Ellen. "Come over to my place, and I'll tell you everything."

"Be there in a half hour," said David.

Five minutes later, David locked his front door and headed down the sidewalk to his car. His body bristled with concealed weapons. Along with his pocket gun, David carried two knives, a length of wire in his belt, and several small but very deadly mechanical devices. He doubted their efficiency in this matter, but the feel of cold steel always boosted his morale.

Again, David sensed hidden eyes watching his every move. Getting into his automobile, he tried without success to spot his nemesis. He wondered if it might be a Mossad agent. What better way to find a killer than trail his next victim?

He promised to ask Eli about the tail tomorrow. Assuming that he made it safely through the night.

24

▲ Moe loved Clint Eastwood films. He especially liked the "Dirty Harry" movies and had watched them all four or five times each. The action never stopped, and the dialogue snapped like a whip. Eastwood made a great cop. The only problem with the flicks was that they never showed Clint handling any of the tedious, time-consuming busy work that filled a detective's life.

Not everyone ran around busting up robberies during lunch breaks. Nor did most cops constantly argue with their superiors. They were too busy handling the routine paperwork that took much of their time each week. Most police work relied on Edison's formula for success: ninety-nine percent perspiration, one percent inspiration.

Sunday afternoon, Moe and Calvin put that maxim to the test. Armed with pictures of Carl Garrett, George Slater, and Sarah Walsh, they canvassed Joe Hinkley's neighbors for leads. Unfortunately, their luck, so good before, turned sour. All of the elderly people in the section refused even to look at the photos. They treated the two police detectives with undisguised hostility.

"What drives me nuts," said Moe after the fifth door in a row slammed shut in his face, "is that these are the people who scream the loudest about not enough police protection. They want cops on the street, but not asking them questions."

"No surprise," said Calvin, undaunted by their cool reception. "These folks saw what happened to Hinkley. Probably a good number of them saw Slater. They know he's still at large. Would you want to be the one who fingered him?"

Moe shrugged. "You think they're afraid?"

"I don't think it," said Calvin, with a short laugh. "I know it. Damned monster scares the hell out of me. If push comes to shove, I aim to shoot first and talk later."

"Anderson wants him," said Moe.

"He can have him," said Calvin.

"Witnesses always cooperate with Clint Eastwood," said Moe, still annoyed, as they walked up the path leading to the next house on the block.

"Amazing how a .44 Magnum inspires confidence," said Calvin. One of his big fists pounded on the front door. "Anybody home? Police officers."

The door opened immediately. They were expected. "Whadda you want?" asked an elderly man dressed in a pair of bermuda shorts and an undershirt. Skinny to the point of starvation, he clutched a pipe between his teeth. A string of tattoos ran up and down both arms. Short, bald, and bowlegged, he resembled Popeye without muscles.

"Police officers, sir," said Calvin, showing his badge.

"Ya told me that already," said the old man, removing the pipe and shaking it like a pointer. "I'm not deaf."

"No sir," said Calvin, with infinite patience. "We're investigating the Hinkley murder. Trying to identify some possible suspects."

Moe braced himself for the slammed door. Nothing

happened. "So," said the old man. "I heard you brought some pictures. Let's take a look-see."

"You heard?" said Moe.

"Hedda Bronski called the whole block," said the old man with a chuckle. "She warned the rest of those cowards to keep quiet. I'm the only one not afraid to talk."

"Why not?" asked Calvin, pulling the glossies out of their envelopes.

"Nick Kowalski ain't scared of nothin'," said the old man proudly. "Besides, I'm dying of cancer. It's been eating away at me for months. My doc gave me six weeks four months ago. The way I see it, maybe I lasted this long for a reason. Divine retribution and all that crap. Joe Hinkley treated me to a good share of brews over the years. Maybe it's time for me to pay him back for the favor. Gimme those pictures."

Kowalski stared at each blow-up carefully. Neither Carl Garrett nor George Slater provoked any response. But his face broke into a huge smile when he spotted Sarah Walsh.

"My kinda woman," he stated, holding the photo up close to his eyes for a better look. "Good knockers. She never wore a bra. Old Joe claimed she didn't wear no panties, either."

"Probably not," said Moe. "You recognize all three?"

"Yeah. They visited Joe's nephew, Oscar, two, three times during the past month. Joe never talked much about them other than teasing me about the blond fox."

Kowalski chuckled. "Last time I went in the hospital, they cut me up pretty bad. Took the starch out of my sails, if you get my drift. Otherwise, I woulda made a play for the lady myself. You'd be surprised how many of these young babes enjoy boffing old coots." He winked. "Bimbo charity, I called it."

"Did you ever hear any names mentioned?" asked Moe, grinning. Cancer or not, Kowalski looked good for another twenty years or more.

"Oscar called the short, pleasant-looking geek Carl. The guy smiled a lot, but he had the eyes of a snake. Cold, real cold. The big dude's name was George. He looked like a football player gone to seed. Joe was scared of him." Kowalski paused. "Guess he had good reason."

He passed the pictures back to Calvin. "Never did catch the girl's name. She never said nothing."

"You didn't happen to notice their car?" asked Calvin.

"Of course I did," said Kowalski, sounding insulted. "They drove a big black van. 'Eighty-eight Chevy, I think, with an out-of-state license. Vanity plate, no less. Some Jap word."

"Japanese?" said Moe, puzzled.

"Yeah," said Kowalski. "Bandi."

"Bandi?" repeated Moe. "Do you mean Banzai?"

"You heard me right the first time," said Kowalski. He spelled it out. "B-A-N-D-I, Bandi."

"Not Bandi," said Calvin, with a shake of his head. "You're pronouncing it wrong. Try B and I. For Blood and Iron."

"Fancy that," said Kowalski.

"Arrogant bastards," said Moe.

25

▲ "Her name is Ellen Harper," said Sarah as Jambres put the finishing touches on the substitute body. "She cataloged the Rivington collection for the exhibit."

"An unfortunate mistake," said Jambres, carving the proper runes into the white wax. "For her, a fatal one."

The sorcerer held the doll up to the light. He examined

it closely, carefully checking his work. Satisfied, he handed it to Sarah. Unfurling the linen cloth, he recited the spell against nightmares over it.

Supremely confident, he sat down on the floor. Sarah passed him the substitute body, then wrapped the bandage around his neck.

"What next?" she asked. "When do we finish off Carl and George?"

"Soon," said Jambres. "Very soon."

Sarah nodded, expecting nothing more. The sorcerer refused to discuss his future plans other than in vague generalities. His schemes, she suspected, ran deeper than any of them suspected.

Finished whispering to the doll, Jambres waved Sarah back. She huddled in the far corner, close to the door, as he summoned Shakek.

For the fifth time, the demon materialized in the room. The overwhelming odor of long-decayed human waste assaulted Sarah's nostrils. Breathing shallowly, she forced herself to ignore the smell.

She kept careful watch on the black smoke that curled around the dead man. Despite Jambres's assurances of her safety, she was prepared to make a quick exit if Shakek ever drifted away from the sorcerer. According to Jambres, once summoned, the demon required a human life before departing.

Around and around the demon circled, searching for entry into the sorcerer's body. Each night, the creature followed the same routine. A mindless entity from the outer dark, it never learned from past experiences.

Finally, Shakek settled on the substitute body. Sarah breathed a sigh of relief. Swiftly, the demon forced itself into the white wax. Black tar smothered the tiny figure.

Sarah shivered as she watched Shakek disappear. In a few minutes, the obscene thing would be gone. Then Ellen Harper—and anyone with her—would die.

26

▲ Yawning, David glanced down at his watch. It was twenty after two in the morning. Five minutes later than the last time he'd checked.

He looked up, his gaze latching onto Ellen, sitting quietly on the floor a few feet away. Lost in her book, she seemed totally unaware of his attention. Or so he thought, until he noticed the slightest trace of a smile develop. Otherwise, she kept on reading.

They sat in the center of the living-room floor, surrounded by stacks and stacks of books. Trying to stay awake, they were hunting for more information on Egyptian black magic. Actually, Ellen was doing most of the work. David tried his best, but his attention constantly wandered. Waiting patiently for death to strike was not his idea of a night's entertainment.

When he arrived at Ellen's apartment hours before, she had greeted him with a hug, more from desperation than desire. Haunted eyes stared straight into his as she anxiously recited her story for the next twenty minutes.

"Well, do you think I'm crazy?" she asked him after finishing the tale.

"Under normal circumstances, I'd say yes," he answered truthfully. "But these are definitely not normal circumstances. Four unexplained deaths stretch coincidence beyond acceptable limits. Let's say I'm willing to be convinced."

He saw no reason to mention his own knowledge of the events. Halfway through her account of the facts, he suddenly realized how alone and vulnerable Ellen felt. A hardworking single woman, she had numerous acquaintances but few really close friends. Faced with a threat the police could not handle, she turned to a stranger for assistance. Telling her about Eli now would be a terrible mistake.

"Then you'll help?" she continued, her voice cracking with emotion.

"Of course." Reaching out, he patted her on the hand. "Though the CIA never taught me anything about dealing with black magic."

Laughing, she grabbed him by the shoulders and hugged him again. This time the embrace lasted a little longer, and when she pulled back, it was with a certain reluctance to let go.

"I know exactly what to do. It's all spelled out in *The Düsseldorf Papyrus.* All I need from you is moral support. I can't ace this mess on my own. One more night, and I'd be ready for the nuthouse."

They ordered a pizza for dinner. Afterward, Ellen insisted they perform the ritual of purification as part of their protection.

"Pure of body, pure of spirit," said Ellen, handing him a piece of paper. "Memorize these lines. After I'm finished with my shower, it's your turn. Try to recite the prayer while you're washing."

She emerged from the bathroom twenty minutes later, clad in a pair of bright red silk pajamas. She laughed at the expression on his face. "What do you say?" she asked, twirling around for his inspection. "I bought this outfit for myself last Christmas but never wore it."

David whistled. "Now I need that shower. An ice-cold one."

Ellen giggled. Then her expression turned serious.

"David," she said, her voice soft, almost apologetic. "It's strictly platonic tonight. Okay?"

"No arguments from me," he answered. "Staying alive takes precedence over romance anytime. But," he added, "when this mess is all cleared up, we've got a date."

"You bet," said Ellen. "I'll hold you to it. Now, go

shower. Don't forget to recite the prayer. Unfortunately, I don't have any men's clothes around. Just put what you're wearing back on."

"I prefer it that way," said David, thinking about his concealed weapons. "And I'm not the least bit disappointed you don't keep extra clothing on hand."

They both smiled, as if sharing a secret thought. He was pleased she was unattached. And she was pleased that he was pleased.

A short while later, showered and dressed, he returned to the living room. He found Ellen on her knees, mixing a number of ingredients in a small pot on the floor.

"Funny," he said, bending over and sniffing. "That stuff smells like beer."

"Probably because it consists of beer, myrrh, and herbs," said Ellen. "I discovered the formula in *The Düsseldorf Papyrus.*"

"Not your average best-seller," said David. "Don't tell me we drink this gunk."

"No," said Ellen cheerfully. She dipped a hand into the thickening paste and raised it to her forehead. "We rub it on our faces to protect us from night gaunts."

"Glad I washed up," said David.

All that took place five hours earlier. Since then, they had watched a wretched comedy show on TV, played Scrabble, and discussed Chicago politics. They finally settled on searching Ellen's library for accounts of Egyptian sorcery.

"Two-thirty," said David, stretching his arms. "Maybe we're safe for tonight."

"I don't know," said Ellen. She yawned and stretched also. The movement pulled the red silk of her pajama top tight across her breasts. "I hope so."

David swallowed, squeezed his eyes tightly shut, and shook his head.

"Is something wrong?" Ellen asked, sounding concerned.

"Do me a favor," said David. "Don't do that again."

"Huh?" asked Ellen, puzzled. Then, realizing what he

meant, she chuckled. The deep, throaty sound of her laughter sent chills running down David's spine. "Sorry."

"No need to apologize," said David. "In other circumstances, it would be a pleasure."

"According to von Gelb, night gaunts only prowl the Earth for a few days each month. If we survive tonight, we should be safe for the next three weeks."

"Hopefully giving us enough time to discover who is behind these murders," said David. "Though how to find a killer who uses black magic has me stumped."

"I'm sure you . . ." Ellen stopped in mid-sentence. "Do you smell something funny?"

David inhaled deeply.

"Pretty rancid odor," he said, struggling to his feet. After sitting on the floor for hours, he felt stiff as a board. His joints creaked in protest. "I don't see anything."

"Shakek," said Ellen, then screamed.

David recoiled in horror. A thick cloud of oily black smoke poured out of Ellen's body. It swirled around her, enveloping her in darkness, pulsating like a living thing.

"Ellen, Ellen," he cried, catching a glimpse of her panic-stricken face inside the demonic haze. She screamed again. And yet again.

Desperately, David reached into the darkness, trying to grab hold of the girl. He howled in shocked surprise. The black cloud was cold, terribly cold. But he refused to retreat. With a lunge, he caught Ellen by one shoulder. Her skin felt like ice. Stumbling back and away, he wrenched her free from the smoke.

She crashed into him, knocking them both to the floor. David's head slammed hard into the leg of the sofa, sending a spasm of pain shooting through his skull. No time to check for damage. Blood dripping down his neck, he pushed Ellen off to the side. Already, Shakek coiled above them in the air, like a gigantic bird of prey ready to strike.

Ellen knew the banishing spell by memory, but he

didn't. It was scribbled on a piece of paper he had thrust into his jeans pocket earlier that evening. Hurriedly, he pulled out the sheet. But before he could read a word, the demon struck.

Tentacles of black fog whipped around his face. David gagged as the overpowering stench of the demon filled his nostrils. Icy fingers tore at his skin, as if trying to slash through the flesh, down to the bone. Like some gigantic python, the cloud creature coiled around his torso, its frigid blackness flattening against his flesh.

Gasping for air, David realized the truth. The paste on his face prevented Shakek from entering his body. Unable to rip him apart from within, the demon sought to tear him to bits from without. If he couldn't pull loose from its paralyzing grip, he was a dead man.

All of his combat training, his martial arts experience, meant nothing now. His fingers tore helplessly at the fetid air as black smoke drifted through his fists. Sensing victory, the demon tightened its invisible hold around his body. The numbing cold made him groggy.

David staggered blindly across the room. Tiring fast, he careened back and forth like a madman. Completely unexpectedly, he crashed into the big TV set in the corner. At the same time, both of his knees smashed against the oak display stand. Bellowing in pain, David collapsed to the floor. The sudden action caught the demon by surprise. For a second, he was free from the black smoke.

Frantically, David searched his pockets for the spell of banishment. Cursing, he remembered dropping it when the demon attacked. Whirling around, he spotted the sheet on the floor five feet away. With a cry of despair, he flung himself forward.

For all of David's speed, Shakek moved faster. Tendrils of smoke lashed down at his back. A thousand knives sliced into his nervous system. Writhing in agony, David fell to the carpet, only a few inches away from the spell.

Rolling over, he stared up at the descending darkness. This time, he knew, there was no escape.

"Ra maketh thee to turn back, O thou that art hateful to him." The words, ringing loud and clear through the room, tore into Shakek like bullets. The demon flashed yellow, then red, as the litany continued.

"He looketh upon thee, get thee back. He pierceth thy head, he cutteth through thy face, and it is crushed in his land. Thy bones are smashed in pieces. Thy members are hacked off from thee. The god Aker hath condemned thee, O Shakek, thou enemy of Ra."

David rubbed his eyes in astonishment. The spell worked. Shakek was being forced to return to its master. The demon disappeared much the same way it originally appeared. The dense black smoke curled back in on itself and vanished. Slow at first, then faster and faster. In seconds, Shakek shrank down to the size of a basketball. Then to a baseball. Then to the head of a pin. Then nothing. Carefully, Ellen continued to recite the spell until all traces of the thing were gone.

Then she ran over to David and helped him to his feet. "You saved my life," she said, holding him close.

"You returned the favor," said David, savoring the warmth of her body. He'd never felt so cold before. "I'd call it even. Damn, I'm freezing."

David glanced down at his watch. Incredibly, it was still running. He shook his head in disbelief. It was a few minutes before three o'clock. The whole fight had taken less than twenty minutes.

"What happens next?"

"We sent Shakek back to its master. The creature still required a human sacrifice before returning to the outer dark. Hopefully, it caught the one who summoned it by surprise."

"I doubt it," said David. "People that dangerous always prepare for the worst."

"Agreed," said Ellen. "At least, we've won some time. Want some hot coffee?"

"Sounds good," he answered. "After which I plan to take a scalding hot shower. Care to join me?"

Ellen laughed. "I'll think about it."

David shivered, but this time not from the cold.

27

▲ The ether vibrated.

Jambres, still weak from summoning Shakek, immediately sensed the disturbance. Unable to sit up, he waved weakly at Sarah. Unaware of what was happening, she took her time coming over.

"You need something?" she asked.

"Shakek," he managed to whisper, barely able to speak. Drawing air into his useless lungs took energy he did not possess. "The demon returns."

A few seconds passed for his message to register. Then, horror-struck, Sarah swiveled to stare at the white wax doll. Already a thin black slime was forming on its surface.

"Flee this place," said Jambres. Marshaling all of his remaining strength, he forced his body erect. "The woman used a spell of banishment. Shakek will not depart without a sacrifice. Escape while you can."

Sarah needed no further prompting. She flew out of the room, slamming the door behind her. Jambres faced the demon alone.

The black sludge around the substitute body grew thicker and thicker. Drops of it fell to the floor, hissing like steam as they touched the ground.

Then, as if boiling in the air, the dark slime melted into

black smoke. A cloud of absolute darkness rose in the center of the room, hovering over the white wax doll. Flashing red and yellow, the angry demon confronted Jambres.

Shakily, the sorcerer stood up. Still terribly weak, he swayed like a sapling in the wind as he raised his hands in defense. The demon ignored him. Shakek wanted living, breathing prey, not a walking corpse.

Under normal circumstances, Shakek was no match for Jambres. An Egyptian magician possessed power equal to those of the gods. He feared nothing, not even demons from the outer dark. But now Jambres possessed only a small measure of his magical skill. He could only stand by and watch helplessly as Shakek rose to the ceiling. Effortlessly, the demon sank into the plaster ceiling boards. In seconds, only a black stain marked its passage. The demon was loose in the house.

Upstairs, men screamed. Jambres cursed in a language five thousand years old.

The screams continued, mixed now with curses. Pushing his host body to the limit, Jambres shuffled out of the basement room and made his way up the steps to the first floor. Five pairs of eyes swung around and stared at him as he entered the living room.

Garrett and three of his followers were on their knees, clustered around a fifth man lying on the floor. Only George Slater, sitting on the sofa cracking his knuckles, seemed unconcerned.

The fallen man moaned in pain. Both of his hands clutched the area directly over his groin. His wide-open eyes stared at the ceiling, seeing nothing.

"Ice in my gut," he groaned. "Colder than hell."

Garrett glared at Jambres.

"You caused this," he said angrily.

"An accident," said Jambres. "What happened?"

"We were sitting around, discussing our routine for the next few days," said Garrett, "when out of nowhere, this cloud of black smoke filled the room."

"It came from the floor boards," said George Slater, done with his knuckles. He appeared totally unconcerned by the excitement. "I saw it. Stuff appeared like magic."

"Shocked the hell out of me," said Garrett. "Before anyone could move, the stuff settled on Sam. I couldn't believe my eyes. One second, it hovered around his face. The next, it poured down his throat and nostrils and disappeared. It was as if he sucked it all in with one breath. He started screaming right after."

As if in response, Sam moaned again, his hands pressing even harder against his abdomen. "God, the pain. The pain!"

Garrett's hands clenched into fists. "Can't you do something?"

"Too late," said Jambres. "His life is . . ."

Sam shrieked. His body jackknifed as he thrust his knees up against his chest. "My guts!" he screamed. "It's tearing out my guts!"

Horrified, the others fell back. Sam screamed again. Like missiles, his legs shot straight out. For a second, he was flat on the floor. His whole body quivered, as if being pulled apart. He howled, the sound rising to a high-pitched shriek of mortal agony.

With a ripping sound of tearing flesh, Sam's abdomen exploded. Hot blood and bits and pieces of still-quivering intestine pelted the faces of everyone present. Men screamed as a cloud of blood-red smoke rose out of Sam's guts and into the air. The cloud hovered overhead for a second, pulsating with life, then disappeared.

"He ain't dead yet," said George calmly, peering closely into Sam's eyes. Gathered around the dying man, his comrades gagged in disgust and heaved up their dinner. Drawing back one huge fist, George slammed it into Sam's face, crushing his features into bloody pulp. "Now he is."

White-faced, Carl Garrett grabbed Jambres by the shoulders. "Sam died because of you!" he exclaimed passionately. "Give me one good reason I shouldn't send you back to Hell right now."

Calmly, Jambres bent close and whispered into Carl's ear. And told him some of the truth.

28

▲ They buried Sam in the backyard. An old piece of plastic sheeting served as his shroud. A solitary cross hastily assembled from wood scraps marked the spot.

Carl spoke a few words, then dismissed the men. Nobody felt much like talking. Silently, he trudged back to his room, pondering their next move.

A surprise visitor awaited him when he opened the door. Sarah sat on the edge of his bed, toying with the hem of her dress. George's story immediately flashed through his mind. He wondered what she wanted. Softly, he closed the door behind him.

"Sarah," he said, approaching her. "It's very late."

"I know," she replied. "But I need to talk to you. Now."

Carl stopped only a few feet from the edge of the bed. Sarah leaned toward him, causing her large breasts to rub against the thin material of her shift. Carl couldn't help but notice her dark nipples pressing into the thin cotton. Restlessly, he shifted back and forth on his heels.

"I'm listening."

"Jambres frightens me," she said, shivering slightly as if to emphasize her point. The motion set her breasts bouncing against her top, threatening to burst through the fabric. Carl's throat suddenly felt very dry. He couldn't take his eyes off her.

"He's meddling with powers beyond his control," she continued. "Tonight, you witnessed the results firsthand. Sooner or later, he's going to release something much more deadly. And then all of us will pay the price."

Carl shrugged. "What do you suggest?"

"You're the leader," said Sarah, rising to her feet. She stood only inches away from him. "You can make him stop."

She inched closer, her breasts pressing up against his chest. "I've heard stories," she murmured softly, "about your special . . . desires. Maybe we can reach an understanding. You help me, and I'll repay the favor. Like this."

Her hands worked swiftly with his belt. Undoing the buckle, she slid her fingers inside his pants and down across his stomach to his groin. Carl tensed at her touch.

"Relax," she said, her body melting into his. "You'll enjoy it more."

Unexpectedly, the bedroom door rattled with a series of sharp knocks. "Carl, you inside?" asked George Slater.

"Go away, George," said Carl angrily. "I'm busy."

"It's important, Carl. I gotta talk to you."

Carl cursed in frustration. Sarah seemed reluctant to stop but finally withdrew her hands. "Another time," she said as he adjusted his clothing. "Think of your wildest fantasy. Give me a chance, and I'll make it come true."

Without another word, she opened the door and exited. Caught off guard, George stood absolutely still as she walked past him and out into the hall. He entered, a puzzled expression on his face.

"What was she doing in here with you, Carl?" he asked suspiciously. "You ain't fooling around with that bitch, are you?"

Carl reacted instinctively. He lashed out furiously, slapping George in the face with the back of his left hand. "Watch what you say," he declared, his voice deadly cold. "No man insults my virtue. Not even you, George."

"Gosh," said the big man, raising his hands and

backing away quickly. "I didn't mean nothing bad, Carl. I just thought . . ."

"You fight," said Carl, pressing his advantage. *"I* think. Never forget that."

George nodded, eager to please. Only then did Carl offer an explanation. "I asked Sarah to come to my room and explain what happened tonight. You interrupted before I could learn anything important."

"I'm sorry," said George. He appeared ready to burst into tears. "But the men are getting awfully restless. I thought you oughta know. Sam's death scared 'em bad. Real bad. Keeping them in line won't be easy. We need some action to stir things up."

"I appreciate your concern," said Carl, calming down as his passions diminished. "In the morning, tell everyone to start packing. We're leaving this place tomorrow night."

George clenched his huge hands into fists. "We're going out on a raid?"

"Perhaps. Jambres knows the approximate location of the talisman he requires to defeat our enemies. I aim to obtain it. No matter where it is or what the cost."

"I don't like it," said George, shaking his head. "What guarantees him not turning on us once we find this talisman?"

"Trust me," replied Carl. "Jambres hates our enemies with a passion even greater than mine. He won't betray us. In different ways, we fight for the same cause."

"I hope you're right," said George. "But I still plan to keep a close watch on him. Along with that bitch, Sarah. G'night, Carl."

The big man departed, leaving Carl alone. Wearily, he sat down on the bed and pulled off his shoes. It was nearly four A.M. By the time he fell asleep, it would be time to wake up.

As he fumbled with the buttons of his shirt, the door opened. Moving without a sound, Jambres slipped into the room.

"What do you want?" asked Carl with a yawn.

"My apologies for disturbing you at this late hour," said Jambres. "I waited quietly for your other company to depart."

"I appreciate your thoughtfulness," said Carl sarcastically. "I'm dog tired. Make your point, then leave."

"I want a new body."

Carl blinked. "Something wrong with this one? You only acquired it a few days ago."

"It functions well enough," said Jambres. "However, with your help, I plan to acquire a much more useful one. Remember, I can tap into the memory of any body I occupy. Consider the possibilities that raises.

"One of the foremost authorities on ancient Egypt lives in Chicago. Tomorrow afternoon, I plan to telephone Professor Ivan Short. After I reveal a few secrets lost for three thousand years, he will demand, even beg, to meet me. We will arrange a meeting at a location favorable to our purposes. Following the blood offering to Anubis, all of Short's thoughts belong to me. Including, I believe, the location of the talisman."

"Very slick," said Carl. "What if he refuses to see you?"

"Men like Short hunger for knowledge," said Jambres. "Or so they claim. However, most of them desire fame as well. If he hesitates, I shall threaten to disclose my information to one of his rivals. As with any trap, the right bait makes it work."

Carl laughed. "It sounds foolproof." Then he frowned. "So did your plan to eliminate the museum personnel."

"The fault lies with me," said Jambres. "I never expected anyone living to be knowledgeable enough to resist Shakek. Thus, I did not take the necessary precautions in case it returned. This woman, Ellen Harper, caught me unprepared. It will not happen a second time."

"You plan on attacking her a second time?"

"Of course. She evidently possesses a bit of the dark lore. That makes her a dangerous foe, and a threat to our plans—she must die."

"You want me to send my men after her?"

"I prefer dealing with this woman in my own way," said Jambres. "I feel certain that tomorrow she will investigate the artifacts at the museum. My curse rests on the forgery Hinkley left. Possessing it means death. She will not escape again."

29

▲ "Pull over to that phone booth," said Moe, disgusted with life in general. "I want to call Miriam."

"Need a shoulder to cry on?" asked Calvin, steering their car over to the curb. "You won't get much sympathy from her. Can't sing the blues to your wife. She's too positive."

"Tell me about it," said Moe. "Sometimes I swear she takes uppers after I leave for work. Anyway, I'll tell her to hold dinner for us. No reason we should work till midnight. It's our day off. So far we've been wasting our time."

Much of their enthusiasm from the day before had disappeared in Monday's steady drizzle. Nick Kowalski proved to be the only bright spot in two days of monotonous investigation. And while the old man provided some new information, his story added little toward solving the case.

Their first big disappointment came when they learned that the van Kowalski described had been found, burned and gutted, on Chicago's west side several days ago. A fingerprint check of the vehicle hadn't turned up one identifiable print. Carl Garrett was a careful man.

Hoping to find other neighbors willing to cooperate, Calvin and Moe had returned to Hinkley's block. That whole morning turned out to be a long, frustrating washout. Nothing had changed from the day before. All of the residents refused to say a word. They treated the two detectives like escaped criminals. A few old women even made threatening and obscene gestures at them as they trudged from house to house. Meanwhile, the constant, numbing drizzle soaked them down to the skin. Their clothes, their shoes, even their socks dripped water.

Finally, around noon they decided to abandon the operation and break for a quick lunch. On the way to the nearest McDonald's, Moe yielded to the urge to call his wife. Always cheerful, Miriam managed to lift his spirits on the worst of days.

She answered on the first ring. "Hello, dearest. Having one of those days?"

"How did you know it was me?" he asked. "It could have been an insurance salesman calling."

Miriam laughed. "Shows what you know about telephone sales. They only call in the evening, when the gentleman of the house is home. Besides, I recognized your ring. What's bothering you today? Other than this miserable weather."

Moe ignored the line about the telephone ring. He knew better than to argue metaphysics with his wife. Miriam used a special brand of logic that only women understood.

"Those old geezers still refuse to open up," he answered, toning down his expressions. Cursing upset his wife.

"You expected them to change overnight?" she replied, making the question into a statement. Miriam liked to speak obliquely. She thought it made her sound like a lawyer. It was an old Yeshiva teaching method that drove Moe crazy. But it often resulted in positive feedback.

"Not really," he admitted. "But they might know why Slater killed Hinkley. We're still shuffling around in the dark without a motive."

"Wasting valuable time, you mean," said Miriam. "One motive won't solve this case. You need two reasons. Instead of focusing all of your attention on one killing, shouldn't you try to link the two deaths together? When the kids are stumped with their homework, don't you always tell them to explore all the possibilities? Maybe you should listen to your own advice."

Moe frowned. "We never found a common bond between Joe's murder and Oscar's weird death. You think they're related?"

"It seems likely," said Miriam. "You tell me how."

"Maybe, just maybe," said Moe, muttering to himself. Then, remembering his wife, he added, "I gotta go. Calvin's waiting for me in the car. Thanks, honey. As usual, you started me thinking straight. By the way, we're not working a whole shift today. I'm bringing Calvin back with me for dinner around six. That okay with you?"

"Of course," she answered. "Maybe by then you'll have some better news. Good luck."

"Love you lots," he said in return. Hanging up quickly, he ran back to the car.

Calvin gunned the engine as soon as Moe jumped in. "I recognize that look," he said, grinning. "Your wife hit the right nerve."

"There's a McD's up ahead," said Moe, not answering the unspoken question. "Pull through the drive-in. We can eat while driving."

"Yeah," said Calvin, not overly enthused with the notion. "Where we heading?"

"Back to Darrow's apartment building. Remember Mrs. Wronski's tirade about his sexual escapades? She recited a whole string of names—a partial list of Darrow's ex-girlfriends."

"Yeah," said Calvin, studying the menu though he

knew it by heart. They ate too often at McDonald's when working on a case.

"Her list of floozies included a woman named Sarah," said Moe. "From what we've heard about a certain Miss Walsh, she sounds like Tom Darrow's type of girl."

"Neat," said Calvin, "very neat. What do you want to order?"

Munching on cheeseburgers and fries, they made it to Mrs. Wronski's apartment in thirty minutes. Though the drizzle continued unabated, Moe felt much more relaxed. The two officers rang Mrs. Wronski's bell and discovered she was at home watching the soaps.

The feisty old woman was not surprised to see them. "I figured you boys would return sooner or later after all the hype in the papers. Damned rags made me sound crazier than a loon. Wish I'd learned to keep my mouth shut when I was younger. Too late now. That's what I get for being so damned curious. No matter. What brings you back?"

Calvin pulled out the picture of Sarah Walsh. "You recognize this young lady?"

"Sure," said Mrs. Wronski. "That's Madame Sarah, the fortuneteller. I visited her establishment once or twice. Best damned reader I ever met. Stupid about men, though. She supported Darrow for a while last year. Until he dumped her for another tramp."

"You didn't happen to notice her in the building the night of Darrow's disappearance?" asked Moe.

"No," said Mrs. Wronski firmly. "I told you exactly who and what I saw. I will admit that if anyone plotted to kill Darrow, Sarah would make a perfect candidate. She hated the guy with a passion. The last time she came by, things turned pretty nasty. Darrow threw her out of his place. She screamed curses in the hallway for fifteen minutes before leaving. That girl was missing a few screws, if you know what I mean."

"I believe so," said Moe. "I suspect Miss Walsh could clear up this mystery if we could find her. If we only knew if she were here the night of Darrow's disappearance."

Mrs. Wronski pursed her lips together, wrinkle lines appearing on her forehead. "Let me make a quick call," she said, reaching for the telephone. "I know someone who might help."

She stayed on the line for less than a minute. Hanging up, she said, "It's all arranged. Come with me."

Not exactly sure what to expect, the two detectives escorted Mrs. Wronski down to an apartment on the first floor. She knocked loudly on the door.

"It's open," a man's voice called from inside. "Come on in."

They entered a room exactly like the one upstairs, except here the windows were not sealed shut. A cool breeze blew in from the street. Sitting in front of the open window was a short, squat man in a wheelchair. Balding, with a neatly trimmed mustache, he appeared around fifty years old. On a small nightstand by his side was a small telescope and two pairs of binoculars.

"Greetings," said their host, swiveling his chair around to face them. "Pardon me if I don't stand up, but my legs don't work too well."

"Lou Hudzik, meet detectives Lane and Kaufman," said Mrs. Wronski. "Show Lou your picture, boys."

Calvin smiled at Mrs. Wronski's familiarity. Without a word, he passed over the photo of Sarah Walsh to Hudzik.

"I spend most of my time at the window watching the world go by," said Lou, staring at the glossy print. "An accident at work a few years ago paralyzed me from the waist down. I manage okay on workers comp and social security, but it gets pretty boring here after a while. So I keep track of the street with my trusty binoculars. You'd be surprised at what I see out my window."

"No I wouldn't," said Moe. "Nothing surprises me anymore. You recognize the young lady?"

Lou closed his eyes in concentration. Biting his lower lip, he nodded gently to himself.

"Friday night," he announced after a minute. He grinned, obviously pleased with himself. "She drove up to the building around ten o'clock and parked right out in front. I caught a glimpse of her when her passenger opened his door. Rest of the time she sat in darkness."

"Time checks out right," said Calvin. "You get a good look at her companion?"

"Nah," said Lou, shaking his head. "He ducked right in the door. Besides, I hardly noticed the dude."

"How long before she left?" asked Moe.

"Fifteen, twenty minutes, tops," said Lou. "Until another guy, taller than the first, came running out and they zoomed off."

Lou squinted. "Cops arrived a short time later. Any connection?"

"Possibly," said Moe. Mrs. Wronski remained silent. "Thanks for your help. We'll send an officer by later to take your statement."

Back in the hall, they said good-bye to Mrs. Wronski. The old lady seemed disturbed.

"You heard Lou. Darrow drove away with Sarah Walsh. It makes no sense. They hated each other."

Moe shrugged. "People change," he said.

"Not that woman," said Mrs. Wronski. "She wanted him dead. Hate like that never changes. Never."

30

▲ Ellen awoke to the smell of french toast frying in the kitchen. Smiling, she rolled over, intent on a few more seconds of sleep. Despite the worst of intentions, nothing had taken place last night. Exhaustion overrode any thoughts of passion. They slept separately—Ellen in her bed, David on the sofa.

Yawning, Ellen stretched, then giggled, remembering David's reaction only hours earlier. Then, suddenly fully conscious, she looked over at the clock—it was nearly eleven.

Throwing on her robe, she rushed out to the kitchen. David, fully dressed, was sprinkling powdered sugar on the french toast. "Just in time for breakfast," he said cheerfully.

"I forgot to call in sick," said Ellen, grabbing the phone. "With all these deaths, who knows what . . ."

"No problem," said David, setting one of the two plates in front of her. Sliced strawberries accompanied the french toast, and he poured freshly brewed coffee as he spoke.

"I phoned the Institute earlier this morning and told one of the girls there you wouldn't be in today." He chuckled. "She never even asked if you were okay. Instead, she only wanted to know who I was. Not wanting to arouse any suspicions, I told her I was your boyfriend. Hope that won't cause any problems?"

Ellen sighed. "That had to be Tammy Williams."

"Talks pretty fast?" asked David. "With a trace of a Southern accent?"

"That's her," said Ellen. She bit into a piece of french toast. "The biggest blabbermouth imaginable. There goes my reputation. Hey, this stuff tastes great."

"It comes from years of cooking for myself," said David. "You either learn a how to prepare food or you starve to death."

"I tend to eat out a lot," said Ellen, busily devouring everything on her plate. "That and TV dinners keep me going."

"Flavored cardboard on a tray," said David. "Real food requires time and effort."

Ellen finished her portion and held up the plate. "More?"

"Of course," said David, dishing out another piece.

"Time for me to put on some clothes," said Ellen,

finishing the last bites of french toast. She paused for an instant, then continued. "Any time you want to head off, it's okay with me. I don't want to monopolize your time."

David laughed. "Trying to dump me already? After I saved your life?"

"No, no, no," said Ellen, her cheeks turning red. "Please. Don't take it that way."

She stammered, trying to find the proper way to express her emotions. Unable to cloak her feelings, she instead stated exactly what she felt.

"Listen, Mr. Ross," she said slowly, staring him directly in the eyes. "I'm crazy about you. Though I suspect you've heard lines like that before. You're handsome, intelligent, funny, and very, very brave. Not to mention the fact that you cook and probably clean better than I do."

By now, David was turning colors also. But his gaze never wavered from hers. "Most of all," Ellen continued, "you risked your life for me for no reason other than I asked for help. And you almost died in the process. Which is why I can't ask you to put your life in jeopardy for me again. It just isn't right."

David shook his head. "You worry too much. I'm a big boy. I fully accept all responsibility for my actions. It's as simple as that. Besides, did it ever occur to you that maybe I'm crazy about you, too?"

Tears blurred Ellen's vision. "You don't mean it," she said, her heart pounding so hard she could hardly hear her own voice.

"Wanna bet?" he replied, and pulled her close.

They kissed. A long, passionate kiss that left her gasping for breath. Then they kissed again. And suddenly all of her doubts melted away.

"So much for that argument," said David ten minutes later, when some semblance of reason caused them finally to break apart.

Ellen smiled, feeling quite content. She sat curled up

on David's lap, her fingers gently running through his curly dark hair. At least for now, the world seemed a wonderful place.

"Actually, I need to take care of some business today," he said, nibbling on her neck. "It should only take me an hour or two. Then I'm free for the rest of the day."

"That works out fine for me," said Ellen, trying to regain her composure. David's fingers casually stroked her arm through her silk nightshirt, making serious thought difficult. "Let's meet at the museum late in the afternoon. Once the Institute closes for the night, we can do some snooping in the Egyptian section. If someone has been looting the exhibit, it won't take me long to discover what's missing."

"Sounds perfect," said David. "If we present the police with hard evidence of theft, they'll take action. No reason to mention black magic at all. They can tie in the murders one way or another."

David gently removed her from his lap, making ready to leave. "Uh, Ellen," he said, sounding contrite. "I have a minor confession to make."

She smiled. "You don't actually work for *Nineties Woman* magazine. You're actually employed by the CIA."

"Make that another intelligence agency with similar goals," he said, looking uncomfortable. "I guess I wasn't a very convincing journalist?"

Ellen laughed. "Not in the least."

"My boss wanted me to check on the deaths," said David. "For reasons entirely unrelated to the actual cause. Once I report the facts to him, we're on our own."

"Too bad."

"I meant everything I said," continued David. "About you and me, I mean."

"I know, silly," said Ellen, reaching out and pinching him on the cheek. "You're awfully transparent. How do you manage as a secret agent?"

"Fortunately, I rarely deal with women," he said with a smile. "Industrial espionage and Russian agents don't faze me. But beautiful girls cause me all sorts of problems."

He retrieved his coat from the parlor. "Time for me to get going. Meet you around five at the Institute?"

"Okay. Do you carry a gun?"

"Sometimes. Why do you ask?"

"Our mysterious foe wants me dead," said Ellen. "He struck once, using black magic, and failed. That doesn't mean it's all over. Unless I'm wrong, he'll try again. Either we stop him, or he stops us. Permanently."

31

▲ Quietly, Sarah wedged the chair from her desk under the doorknob, effectively sealing her room from the inside. She trusted that arrangement much more than the flimsy lock—especially against a brute like George Slater. Several times this last week, she sensed the big goon lurking outside her door. He always left after a few minutes, leaving her shaking and covered with sweat.

She knew he planned to kill her. Sarah planned to be ready when he tried. The chair would slow him down just enough for her to thrust a steel darning needle through one eye and into the brain. She kept several of the deadly rods hidden throughout the room. In a way, she looked forward to the moment.

Stretching out on her bed, Sarah cleared her mind of disruptive thoughts. A faint smile crossed her lips as she recited her mantras. Not even Jambres comprehended the fullness of her occult training.

Sarah possessed the power to read minds. She could skim surface thoughts from anyone within a range of several hundred feet. Using her gift carefully, she had established herself as the most reliable medium in the Midwest. Her powers served equally well in these perilous times.

During her first few weeks with Blood and Iron, she refrained from scanning her companions' minds, but as her trust turned to suspicion and then fear, Sarah began carefully monitoring both Carl's and George's thoughts.

Her talent revealed their deadly schemes and kept her safe. She was able to stay one step ahead of George Slater and his murderous plans. She discovered Carl's unnatural passions and desires. Sensing his growing lust for her body, she acted to bind him to her will. He proved to be a willing subject. Like most deep thinkers, Carl found it impossible to deal with his animal instincts. A few nights of passion, and he would be her willing slave.

Only Jambres's mind defied her probing. She dared not search too deeply for fear of alerting him to her power. Instead, she monitored his actions through the eyes of the others. She knew Jambres's history but not his plans for revenge.

Earlier this afternoon, the sorcerer left their compound with Garrett. Neither of them said a word to anyone about their mission, but Sarah knew all the details from reading Carl's mind. They'd returned only a little while ago. She caught only a glimpse of them as they entered Carl's room, but it answered her silent question. Jambres inhabited a new body. Ivan Short had suffered the Dead Man's Kiss.

Closing her eyes, Sarah reached out with her mind, searching for Carl's thoughts. It took only a second for her to make contact. Effortlessly, she melded her perceptions with his. Like a silent partner, she observed the world through Carl's senses—it took a moment to regain her orientation. The world looked very different from a man's perspective.

The other night she had been tempted to leapfrog into his mind as she performed sex on him. Now, the thought of experiencing her own seduction caught and held her fancy. She swore to try it as soon as possible. The decision made, she turned her attention to what Jambres was saying.

"Locating the information I needed proved extremely difficult," said the sorcerer. He spoke in the same flat, unemotional monotone he used in his previous incarnations. Instead of Darrow's handsome body, this time he inhabited the corpse of a fat old man with thick white hair and a bushy beard. Even his eyebrows were white. Except for the sallowness of skin and the dullness of eye, he resembled Santa Claus.

"Why was that?" asked Carl. "I thought you had access to all of your victims' memories."

"I do, but Short buried many facts he thought unimportant deep in the recesses of his brain. Summoning the correct information took time and patience. But after reviewing what he observed several years ago, I feel confident about the success of our expedition."

"Where did you say we're going? Someplace in Iowa?"

"Gibson, Illinois," said Jambres, pronouncing the name carefully. "According to Short, it is a small town on the banks of the Mississippi River. In the center of town stands a small museum housing a unique collection of artifacts. These ancient relics come from a burial mound excavated in the 1850s. Among them is the Staff of Fire."

"The talisman you want," said Carl, recognizing the name. "How the hell did it end up in Illinois?"

"That adventure is an incredible story," replied Jambres. "Or at least Professor Short thought so. Along with a number of other archaeologists, he studied the Gibson collection several years ago. At the time, he expressed grave doubts about its authenticity. Too bad I wasn't there to tell them that the relics were exactly what they seemed. The artifacts came from the wreckage of a warship from Kamt that sailed up the Mississippi River thirty centuries before."

"Egyptians in America three thousand years ago?" said Carl. Sarah could sense his astonishment. "That's crazy."

"Your disbelief springs from the arrogance of the uninformed. Your archaeologists are skeptics, too. They refuse to acknowledge the facts because the facts contradict beliefs they hold sacred."

Jambres laughed with a terrible barking sound that made Carl cringe. "These men of learning are not so different from the sages of my lifetime. What they cannot understand, they ignore.

"My people were great sailors. The pharaohs sent huge fleets of ships, manned by many hundreds of men, around the tip of Africa. They hunted for gold for the temples of the god-king. Your scientists accepted these voyages without question. Yet the much shorter trips to this continent the same scientists considered impossible. Thus, with their minds already closed, they examined the artifacts and labeled them fakes."

"All the better for us," said Carl. "Assuming what you said about Egyptian sea voyagers is true, why did they sail all the way up the Mississippi to Illinois? It seems a pretty far distance to travel to establish a colony."

"Several tablets inscribed with hieroglyphics tell their tale. The sailors traveled here on a mission for Pharaoh. They carried with them a cursed object, with instructions to bury it at the end of the world.

"Sifting through Short's knowledge of Egyptian history, I placed this expedition approximately four hundred years after my death. At that time, powerful invaders threatened Kamt from the east. According to the tablets, the Staff of Fire had been recovered many decades earlier. Fearing what would happen if it fell into the hands of his enemies, Pharaoh ordered the indestructible rod hidden for all eternity.

"The crew brought it this far north when a sudden storm swamped their craft. They judged their shipwreck to be a sign from the gods. The survivors buried the talisman on the banks of the river, thinking they had obeyed their pharaoh.

"Thus it remained, hidden for ages. In the nineteenth century, its discoverers mistook it for an Indian ceremonial spear. The museum labeled it such, and it remained there undisturbed for nearly a hundred years. Until my *ka*, trapped in the statue of Anubis, was moved close enough to absorb some of the incredible power it contained."

"The whole story reeks," said Carl. "Why didn't Pharaoh destroy the staff instead of wasting his money on a boat trip? Or use it himself on his enemies?"

"Only the most powerful of sorcerers knew the secrets of the talisman," said Jambres, answering the second question first. "My son was one. I was another. Perhaps, after centuries, the knowledge was lost. Ships and sailors meant nothing to the god-king. Better to send them all to their deaths than let his enemies obtain the talisman."

Jambres hesitated. "Pharaoh ordered the talisman hidden because he knew it could not be destroyed. The Staff of Fire cannot be damaged by mortal means. It is indestructible."

"Indestructible?" echoed Carl, doubt edging into his voice.

"Fool," said Jambres. "You sneer at what you do not comprehend. How old is this nation of yours? A little more than two centuries, correct? Your religion dates back to the birth of a man two thousand years ago. I served as a priest of Anubis more than a thousand years before then. And, remember, at that time the history of my nation stretched back for another two thousand years.

"Fifty centuries ago, the earliest god-kings of Kamt set down their stories for all those who followed. The earliest written records in the world dealt with the history of my nation. In my youth, I studied those tales extremely carefully. As did all those interested in the black arts. The ancient writings discussed a period two thousand years previous to my lifetime. And several of them described the talisman we seek, the Staff of Fire.

"Even five thousand years ago, legends shrouded the talisman in mystery. It dated from a much earlier time, when gods walked the Earth and men were little more than beasts. According to the ancient texts, the staff was originally a branch of the Tree of Life. Growing too heavy, it broke and fell to the ground. One of the mystic protectors of the sacred tree shaped the piece into a walking stick and inscribed on it the secret names of the Most High God.

"Later, that nameless demigod gave the staff to the first true man as protection from the wild beasts that roamed the world. Since the material was a direct creation of the Most High, it was ageless, unbreakable, and indestructible. Inscribed with the secret names of eternity, the staff controlled the basic elements of the universe and became known as the Staff of Fire, because though it burned, it was not consumed by the flames.

"Magic follows magic. Thus, art imitates life. Since the creation of that first magic staff, all magicians have relied on their wands and staffs as the sources of their powers. Without his rod, a sorcerer cannot perform great acts of magic. With it, nothing can stand before him. Once I hold the Staff of Fire in my hands, the modern world will shake. My might will rival that of a god."

"Sure," said Carl, sounding skeptical. Sarah could sense his disbelief, tinged with a trace of fear. "I instructed George to spread the word. Tonight we leave for Gibson. I hope we will find the staff late tomorrow afternoon."

"Good," said Jambres. "As we discussed earlier, once I finally possess the staff, all the others must die. You and I alone shall direct its power."

"No problem," said Carl. "They're excess baggage anyway. George gets more difficult to control every day."

"His body will replace this worthless shell," said Jambres. "As I planned from the very beginning."

"What about Sarah?" asked Carl. "You including her in this massacre?"

"Of course," said Jambres. "She serves me well, but I cannot take any chances. She dies with the rest."

Sarah broke contact. Licking her lips, she quickly reviewed her options. Death stared her in the face. In a few seconds, she reached a decision.

Swinging off the bed, she hurried over to the door and removed the chair. Mentally, she scanned the hallway. Nearly dinnertime; no one was about. Except for Carl and Jambres, the men were all outside preparing the vans for the trip.

Moving quickly, she headed for the kitchen. The phone was in the corner of the room. Calmly, she dialed 911.

32

▲ David called Eli as soon as he arrived home. Dialing the Mossad director's private number, he rehearsed what he would say to his old friend. Not struck with any brilliant deceptions, David settled for the truth.

Eli picked up the phone on the third ring. "Yes?" he answered, as always, with a question.

"It's David. Alive and reasonably well."

"David." Eli's voice trembled with emotion. "Shalom. It makes me feel good to hear your voice again. What happened last night?"

"You're not going to believe this story," said David, and launched into a concise but complete account of his adventures over the past twelve hours. The only detail he edited out was his growing emotional attachment to Ellen Harper.

After he finished, David waited anxiously for Eli's reaction. Usually, he knew what to expect. Most of his assignments ran like clockwork, and results tallied exactly as planned. This case broke all the rules.

As seconds turned to minutes, David started wondering if perhaps his days as a stringer were over. Little beads of sweat formed on his brow. A few choice words from Eli could ruin his reputation in the intelligence community in a matter of hours.

He enjoyed working in the espionage field. Spying was a dangerous way to make a living, but it paid extremely well, and the hours were good. David hoped he wasn't scheduled for an early retirement.

Finally, Eli spoke. "This wild story you just told me," he said quietly. "It's the truth?"

"I never lied to you before," said David. "And I didn't lie to you today. It's all true."

"Most people would say you're crazy," continued Eli, "but fortunately for you, I'm not most people. In the course of my life, I witnessed several events that defied logical explanations. While I remained the skeptic, I also recognized the fact that not everything in this world is as cut and dried as we like to think."

Eli paused. "I accept your report as stated. However, it resolves nothing. You still must discover the identity of the person behind this demonic attack. Until then, the possibility of a plot against Israel still exists."

"I'm scheduled to meet Ellen at the museum in an hour," said David. "She wants to examine the Rivington collection after the place closes for the night. What she expects to find, I don't know. But so far, she's been right on the money with this whole affair."

"A very sharp young woman," said Eli, "with both brains and beauty."

"No need for the hard sell," said David, laughing. "I'm hooked already. Though she thinks I work for the CIA, which might cause a problem sooner or later."

"Tell her you're on loan from them to us," said Eli. "That only bends the truth a little."

"I'm off," said David. "I prefer not to be late when meeting this lady. I'll call again when I know more."

"Take care," said Eli.

Driving away, David had the distinct impression of being watched. He carefully checked his surroundings but spotted nothing out of the ordinary. Putting it down to jumpy nerves, he climbed into his car and headed downtown to meet Ellen.

They met in front of the large cement lions that guarded the front doors of the Institute. Ellen's face lit up as she saw him coming down the street. She bustled over, eyes twinkling in the growing twilight.

"Perfect timing," she said, sliding one of her arms through his. "I arrived only a couple of minutes ago."

"Was your day okay?" David asked as they mounted the wide steps leading up to the entrance.

"Smooth as silk," answered Ellen. "I talked to Lionel Vanderbeek a few hours ago. He's the one temporarily in charge of things. I cleared everything with him. Lionel promised to alert the guards to our presence. We can stay as long as we like."

"I always wanted to camp out in a museum," said David.

"See if you feel that way once they turn down the lights," said Ellen. "It gets pretty spooky in the dark."

A few hours later, David had to admit she was right. As they moved from exhibit to exhibit, Ellen switched on the lamps as needed. Except for a small patch of illumination, they were surrounded by a sea of darkness. David felt distinctly uneasy as he tried to concentrate on their mission. He kept glancing over his shoulder at the ancient mummy cases that dotted the chamber. Any minute, he expected one of them to swing open and Boris Karloff to pop out.

In the meantime, Ellen worked while David worried. She shut down the alarm system and, equipped with a master key, opened one long display case after another, examining each relic, then closing and locking the case. The six-foot-long, two-foot-wide tables formed narrow aisles throughout the chamber. David noted the pressure-sensitive tabs beneath each item, and he wondered about the glass enclosures.

"Seems to me that a clever crook could smash the top of one of these displays and steal a valuable artifact before any of the guards responded to the alarm," he said as Ellen finished studying another exhibit.

"Not really," said Ellen as she opened the next case. "These units are manufactured specially for museums. The glass is bullet-proof and shock-resistant. It's reinforced with thousands of fiberglass cables. The case itself is strong enough to support a thousand pounds or more. Your thief could dance a jig on top of these exhibits without disturbing the contents. I know. I tried doing exactly that before I authorized buying them."

"Then how did our thieves steal things?"

"They shut off the alarms and took what they wanted," said Ellen. "But to do so they needed a master key. And only museum personnel and night watchmen have those."

"Now I understand why they killed Joe Hinkley," said David.

"Exactly," said Ellen, and continued to work. Patiently, she examined each piece in the latest exhibit, studiously comparing it to a thick batch of notes and photos from her files. Watching her, David shook his head in bewilderment. All of the relics looked ancient to him. He marveled at the fact that anyone could tell one from another.

"How much longer do you think it will take?" he asked, anxious to break the stillness of the room. "Find anything yet?"

"Not a thing," said Ellen, sounding annoyed. Putting her notes down on the floor, she stretched her arms high over her head. "I really thought we'd notice major gaps. I can't find any evidence of anything missing or replaced so far. Of course, I've only gone through about a third of the collection, but still, that covers many of the most valuable pieces."

David started to say something, then stopped. Footsteps echoed in a hallway leading to the exhibit room. Nervously, he reached for his gun.

"That you in there, Miss Harper?" asked a voice from the darkness.

"Yes, Gus," said Ellen, grinning at David. He relaxed as she continued. "Expecting other visitors?"

"No ma'am," said the security guard as he came into sight. He raised a hand in greeting to David. "Glad to meet you, sir. Nice to see Miss Harper with a young man for a change. She spends too much time working and not enough time socializing.

Ellen blushed and pretended to throw a pencil at Gus.

"I agree," said David. "And I plan to limit her time in the Institute to a bare minimum for the foreseeable future."

"That's the best news of the day," said Gus, smiling briefly. "The only good news, for that matter."

"Problems, Gus?" asked Ellen.

The security guard grimaced. "Sorry. I forgot you missed work today, Miss Harper. Two homicide detectives came snooping around, asking all sorts of questions about Joe Hinkley. They wasted a half hour of my time. And me, an ex-cop at that."

"Detectives investigating Joe's death?" repeated Ellen. "Did they mention who they suspect killed him, or why?"

"Nah. Why should they? The newspapers carried all the details this morning. Remember Joe's dopey nephew, Oscar? Well, he got mixed up with this bunch of neo-Nazi fanatics. I always thought that Oscar had a few screws loose. Anyway, they're the ones who killed Joe—and Oscar, too. None of the stories explained why. That's still a mystery.

"One funny thing those detectives discovered," said

Gus as he shuffled off. "According to the records, the last time Joe worked was on the second of this month. But nobody recalls seeing him that night, and it wasn't his handwriting in the log book. The signature was forged by that dumb nephew of his. Kaufman, one of the detectives, figured Oscar dressed up like Joe and bluffed his way inside, pulling the same trick he did years ago."

"You wouldn't happen to know what area Joe was assigned to patrol first that night?" asked David, playing a hunch.

"Sure," said Gus from the doorway. "He always followed the same routine. After making all his door checks, Joe walked through this room next. He loved this section of the museum."

"David," said Ellen, growing excited. "The last time Oscar broke into the museum, he stole a mummy."

"He didn't take one this time," said Gus. "Those detectives made us check the whole display. Not a thing was missing. Damn waste of time, took most of the afternoon."

Gus looked around the room as if trying to spot something amiss. Shrugging, he stepped into the dark hall. "See you folks later. I gotta visit the dinosaurs."

Gus wandered off, leaving them alone again.

Once the guard disappeared, David threw up his hands in frustration. "There goes your theory shot to hell. We've been wasting our time, rechecking work that was done this afternoon."

"Not really," said Ellen. "A good forgery can't be detected so easily. The guards aren't qualified to do that type of work. They only looked to see if anything was missing. Given the information about Oscar, I feel certain he stole something from the exhibit and replaced it with a fake."

"At least that narrows down the field a little," said David. "To make the exchange, he needed the replica on hand. Which means he smuggled it into the museum that night. I can't imagine him doing that with a two-by-four."

Ellen nodded. "I vote for a statue. They're easy to hide, and even a small one is worth a fortune."

"I'm beginning to think there's more to this case than mere money," said David. "Even if it involves millions."

Twenty minutes later, Ellen's victory cry rang through the chamber. "I've found it, I've found it!"

Faced flushed with excitement, she waved David close. As he drew near, she shut a display case and locked it. She held up the twelve-inch-high figurine of Anubis.

David stared at the worn statue of the jackal-headed god and then up at Ellen. "You're positive this idol isn't the real thing? It looks pretty authentic to me."

Ellen grinned. "You should know better than to argue with an expert. As soon as I laid eyes on this piece, I knew it was the fake. It's a decent copy, but no more than that. According to my notes, the original dates back a little over thirty-two hundred years ago. This copy was made in the mid-1980s when a factory in Cairo started producing cheap imitation relics by the hundreds for the tourist trade."

David gingerly examined the fake as Ellen quickly thumbed through her notes. It looked thousands of years old to him. Completely out of his element, he placed the statue on top of the nearest display case.

"Now what do we do?" he asked.

"I'm not sure," said Ellen, flipping page after page, searching for the correct entry. "Frankly, I'm puzzled why anyone would want this particular statue. It's a rare piece, but not anything unique. The Institute would never agree to pay a huge ransom for its return. And once it's listed as stolen merchandise, no collector in the world would dare buy it."

Finally, she found the desired papers. David waited silently as she scanned the information. The darkness made him feel uneasy. Senses alert, he caught the muffled sound of footsteps in the distance heading their way. Gus was probably on his way to check out Ellen's screams.

"Very curious," said Ellen, pulling out a photograph of the real statue. "According to my notes, this figurine contained a number of unusual hieroglyphics on the base. I wrote a note to myself to reference them further in *The Coffin Texts Decoded,* but I never did."

"Any idea what made them special?" asked David.

"Statues like this one served many different purposes," said Ellen, folding the photo and putting it in her purse. "Most of them were used in religious rites involving the transfer of souls after death. But others were worshiped in homes as household gods. The markings probably described the idol's actual purpose."

Ellen looked around, her eyes narrowing as she peered into the dark corridors. "Did you hear something?" she asked.

"Probably Gus coming to investigate your screams," said David, smiling to calm her fears.

"Bad guess, shitface," said a voice directly behind him.

David whirled. Less than six feet away stood the orange-haired hoodlum from the park. His eyes gleamed wildly in the dim light. In one hand, he held a two-foot-long tire iron.

"Payback time," said the punk, and he swung the bar in a roundhouse blow from the hip. Caught totally off guard, David tried to block the blow with his arms. He succeeded in deflecting it only slightly. The steel slammed into his forehead with devastating effect. Searing pain exploded in his skull.

Collapsing backward, the last thing he heard was Ellen screaming. Then darkness claimed him.

33

▲ Resting his weary feet on the coffee table, Moe settled back and listened to his wife unravel the secrets of Jewish cooking for Calvin.

"I tried again last week to fry a batch of latkes," his partner declared, looking despondent. "As always, they turned out terrible. Mine fall apart when you lift them. The ones you made tonight crunched. Where did I go wrong?"

"Your oil isn't hot enough," said Miriam. A short, dark-haired woman with shining black eyes and an ever-present smile, she glowed with unrestrained energy. Moe often joked that his wife's energy could fuel a nuclear power plant if they ran out of uranium.

"How can you tell the right temperature?" asked Calvin. "I'm afraid of setting the kitchen on fire."

Miriam patted Calvin on the arm, in her most motherly fashion. "You need a good wife to take care of you, Calvin. Didn't your mother ever tell you how to test oil to see if it's hot enough? You dip your fingers in a little cold water. Then you turn the flame on under your pan. When the thin layer of oil coating the bottom starts to bubble, you flick a few drops of water onto it. If the oil crackles, it's ready for the batter. Otherwise you wait."

"Splash water on the oil," said Calvin, his voice serious, as if reciting the facts in a murder case. "Any other hints I should remember?"

"Grate your potatoes by hand," said Miriam. "Don't ever use one of those blender things. They chop the poor potatoes to shreds. Good latkes need body. These modern food processors turn the ingredients into mush. Use one of them, and you'll end up with soft pancakes instead of nice, crispy ones."

"She makes it sound too easy," said Moe, unable to resist butting in. "It takes a lot of elbow grease. Plus your fingers take a lot of punishment. Once Miriam asked me to grate the potatoes. In five minutes, I scraped my knuckles blood red. First and last time I helped prepare the latkes."

"Hey, Dad, want to play some video games?" asked Kevin, his ten-year-old son, turning on the TV set. "How about two-player Double Dragon?"

Moe shrugged. "Why not? I feel pretty sharp today. Maybe I'll survive till the third level."

A passionate devotee of all types of electronic devices, Moe had bought the video game system when it first came out. For several years, he played the games while his son watched. At four and five years old, Kevin did not understand the games, but by the time he turned six, he was playing along with his father. At eight, he was beating games that gave Moe problems. Now he routinely defeated the most difficult cartridges with ease.

They played Double Dragon for the next fifteen minutes. Moe managed to reach the third level before his player was permanently erased.

"Better luck next time, Dad," said Kevin, trying to sound encouraging as Moe laid down his joy stick. "You're improving. I can tell."

"Thanks, son," said Moe. Playing with his son reminded him too much of a scene out of *The Hustler*. Happily, his eleven-year-old daughter, Esther, was not nearly as accomplished a player as Kevin. Moe preferred testing his skill against her.

"Any luck on your new case, Dad?" asked Kevin as he performed a triple head butt on a particularly stubborn enemy. "The newsman on channel nine said the police were baffled by the crime. What does baffled mean, Dad?"

"Baffled means puzzled, Kevin," said Miriam. "It's

time for me to pick up your sister from Hebrew school. Want to go with me for the ride?"

"Nah," said Kevin. "I'll stay home and bother Dad and Calvin. I want to hear all about this dead dude."

"Let your poor father rest for a little while. We can stop for frozen yogurt on the way back."

Kevin contemplated the offer for a second, then switched off the game. "I've changed my mind. I'll come along. This game is too easy. It's not enough of a challenge. I need new worlds to conquer." Moe grinned at his son's choice of words.

"Off we go," said Miriam, handing Kevin a windbreaker and slipping into her own coat. "We should be back in a half hour or so. Calvin, you'll stay for a while more? Esther always enjoys saying hello. And she wants to invite you to a special event at Hebrew school."

"I'm yours for the evening," said Calvin. "Besides, I'm too stuffed with good food to move for at least another hour."

Mother and child departed, with Kevin nailing aliens with his ray gun as they went out the front door.

"Want to try the video game?" asked Moe.

"No thanks," said Calvin. "I recognize my limitations, brother."

Moe looked at the game controller and shook his head in dismay. "It's amazing the reflexes a little kid possesses. His reaction time is incredible."

"It improves his hand-eye coordination," said Calvin with a smile. "I read that in the newspaper."

"Too bad it doesn't work for adults," said Moe.

"What's this about Esther being in a special event?" asked Calvin, shifting subjects.

"Each year, one class at the Hebrew school holds a traditional seder on the first night of Passover. Each student invites one or more non-Jewish friends to attend. The kids explain all of the rituals and customs that take place during the ceremony and run through the entire service. Even an old hand like you should find it informative."

"It sounds like fun," said Calvin. "They'll ask the four questions?"

"And drink the four cups of wine," said Moe, smiling. "Though I believe they plan to use soda pop instead of Mogen David."

"It's nice the way you keep tradition in your lives," said Calvin. "Not many people seem to care anymore."

"Passover is more than tradition," said Moe seriously. "The word *seder* means 'order of occurrence.' That's because all of the happenings in Jewish history begin with the Exodus from Egypt. Without it, there is no Judaism. The true history of the Jews starts with the events of Passover."

"You know quite a bit about religion for a cop," said Calvin.

"I wanted to be a rabbi when I was a kid," said Moe. "I spent years studying at the Yeshiva. Then one day I lost interest. I shifted gears and became a detective instead."

"Which makes no sense at all," said Calvin. He sighed. "I wanted to be an actor on the stage. So much for ambition."

"We made the right choices," said Moe. "We're good cops. Probably the best detectives in the whole department."

"Maybe," said Calvin. "Though after today, I'm not so sure. We spun our wheels, going nowhere fast."

"What did you think about the museum?" asked Moe. "Those records show that Hinkley snuck in there the night he disappeared. He probably went there under orders from Carl Garrett."

"Blood and Iron wanted Oscar to steal something," said Calvin. "That's why they went to the trouble of recruiting him. More than likely, they killed his uncle afterward to keep the old man from talking. But what were they after? Nobody at the place appeared aware of anything valuable being taken."

"The bigger question is *why?*" said Moe. "I can see that group raiding an arsenal or a bank. But a museum?

What item in the Petrie Institute is worth the lives of two men? Answer that one question, and we solve our mystery."

"And explain how a corpse rode an elevator to a guy's apartment and then stabbed him ten or twenty times?" said Calvin, sounding slightly sarcastic. "I'm all ears if you care to elucidate."

"I'm working on a theory," said Moe. "Just give me a little more time to iron out all the details."

"Better find a way to tie in those unexplained deaths at the Institute, too," said Calvin. "Too many people died there over the past week for my liking. It boggles the mind to think the two cases aren't related. I'm sorry we didn't contact Dr. Harper today; she might know something important."

"Tomorrow," said Moe, heading for the kitchen. "We earned an evening off. You want a piece of mandelbrot?"

They were both munching on thin strips of the wafer-style cake when the phone rang. Moe glanced over at his partner. "You expecting a call?"

"No. How about you?"

"Not that I remember. Maybe it's for Miriam. Or one of the kids."

He picked up the receiver. "Moe Kaufman here."

"It's Rufus Anderson." The FBI chief sounded excited. "Some of my boys tracked down your lady friend. And her buddies. We're planning a big party for them. You and Lane want to tag along?"

"I thought you said *we* made the bust?" said Moe.

"Be my guest," said Anderson, chuckling. "According to my last reports, Blood and Iron travels with enough heavy artillery to take Fort Knox. They're equipped with Skorpion machine gun pistols, M79 grenade launchers, a few boxes of hand grenades, and plenty of the right ammo. We suspect they robbed an armory last year, but nobody knows for sure. If you two boys want the honors of taking them down, I won't object."

Moe covered the receiver with one hand and told

Calvin the news. "You willing to let the glory hounds run the show?"

"No problem for me," said Calvin. "I never cared much for the clay pigeon routine. Especially when you're talking SWAT stuff. If Anderson and his boys want to do the dirty work, they can claim all the credit."

"We're free to question the girl once she's in custody," said Moe into the phone.

"All you want," said Anderson. "She wasn't involved in the crime spree on the West Coast. I'm after Garrett and Slater."

"Okay, then," said Moe. "Send a car."

"It's already on the way," said Anderson. "I knew you'd agree. See you soon."

"Yeah," said Moe, and hung up. "They'll pick us up in a few minutes. I'd better write a note for Miriam."

"Make it short and sweet," said Calvin, standing up. "I just heard a car pull up in front of your house. Knowing the way Anderson works, that's his men already. That dude doesn't waste any time."

Moe scribbled a quick note and left it folded on the dining-room table. Before leaving, he grabbed a fistful of mandelbrot wedges.

"Supplies," he said, handing several to Calvin. "I don't think Garrett will surrender without a fight. Which is exactly the way Anderson wants it. He's anxious to even a few scores. If I'm correct, we're heading straight into his version of the Gunfight at the O.K. Corral."

34

"Working through the computer network," said Carl, "I rented a large estate about twenty miles outside of Gibson. According to the printout, it used to be an old farmhouse that once served as a bootleggers' headquarters. I checked out the area on the population index. Nobody lived for miles in any direction—it sounded perfect for our purposes."

Jambres nodded, barely listening. He sensed important events taking place somewhere else. Concentrating, he tried to conjure up a vision but his efforts yielded nothing.

Reaching into his pocket, he pulled out the small, smooth stone he always carried with him. The rock tingled beneath his cold, dead fingers. Holding it to one eye, he whispered the name Osiris three times.

His eyes blurred, and for an instant he caught a glimpse of three people. Two men and a woman, they stood in the center of a large room filled with Egyptian artifacts. The vision disappeared before he could make out any details.

"I must return to my room at once," he said, rising to his feet. "At this very moment, several people at the museum are handling the counterfeit statue Hinkley left in place of the original. Once moved, the idol calls down the Curse of the Vermin on the possessor. With Sarah's help and the Eye of Osiris, I shall observe Miss Harper's very painful end."

Carl's expression turned sour. "The Curse of the

Vermin?" he repeated with a shudder. "There's no chance of that spell backfiring on us, I hope?"

"The curse affects only the person holding the statue," said Jambres testily. "And the spell cannot be reversed."

Carl's constant references to the mishap of the night before annoyed Jambres. The sorcerer believed that great plans called for great sacrifices and good soldiers fought and died without question for their superiors. Carl worried too much about the well-being of his men; he lacked the true ruthlessness of a great leader.

"Continue with the preparations for our departure," said Jambres, opening the door to the room. "The sooner I obtain the Staff of Life, the better."

Jambres walked swiftly to Sarah's room. He knocked and without waiting for an answer, entered. To his annoyance, the seeress was not there.

He wondered where she could be. Sarah rarely left her room other than when she worked with him in the basement. Deciding she must be looking for him there, he started for the stairs to the lower level.

Halfway down, Jambres halted. He heard Sarah's voice coming from the kitchen. Who was she speaking to? He was positive no one else was in the house with them. She spoke in whispers, all of her words merging together into a meaningless jumble. Suddenly suspicious, Jambres crept silently down the passage to the far door.

Sarah stood huddled in one corner, shielding the phone with her body. "How many times must I repeat myself?" she asked, her voice muted but filled with anger. "Send the police here immediately. Blood and Iron plan to abandon this base tonight. If Jambres recovers the Staff of Fire . . ."

Jambres couldn't believe what he was hearing. "Enough!" he cried, mindless rage overwhelming his usual caution.

Without thinking, he rushed forward, intent on stopping her.

Dropping the receiver, Sarah whirled and faced Jambres. In her right hand she held a large meat cleaver.

The heavy-duty carving knife gleamed brightly in the lights. Jambres tried to stop, but his momentum carried him ahead. He was only a few feet away from Sarah when she slammed the heavy blade down into his skull. Cold steel smashed deep through bone and brain, splattering gore across the room.

The force of the blow knocked Jambres to his knees. Desperately, he jerked his head to the side, wrenching the blade out of her grip. Thrusting hard with both legs, he forced himself back. He collapsed to the floor, a few feet away from where Sarah stood motionless with fear. Smashed bone blurred his vision, but he could still see out of one eye. The long wood handle of the chopping knife, sticking out of his forehead like a unicorn's horn, dominated his field of sight. Reaching up, he tried to tug the cleaver loose. Wedged tightly in his skull, it refused to budge.

"You can't kill the dead, Sarah," he said, letting go of the knife. The barely audible words tumbled out of the wreckage of his mouth. He staggered to his feet. "This body is worthless now. I need another. Yours."

The sorcerer's threat galvanized Sarah into action. With a shriek of rage, she darted past him, running for the hall. Jambres, grabbing an ice pick from the kitchen counter, stumbled after her.

"What the hell is going on?" asked Carl Garrett, emerging from his bedroom into the hall where he blocked Sarah's escape route.

Sarah, caught completely by surprise, crashed into him, sending them both tumbling to the floor. Her legs trapped beneath Carl, she struggled to pull free.

"Stop her!" cried Jambres. "She betrayed us to the police."

Growling like a wild beast, Carl grabbed Sarah by the hair. He yanked hard, causing her to scream. Viciously, he punched her in the chest. Moaning, Sarah collapsed to the floor. Feeling her body go limp, Carl released Sarah's hair and grabbed her by the neck, leaving his face exposed.

Striking with the speed of a snake, Sarah jabbed her fingers into Carl's eyes. Shrieking in agony, he tumbled back to the wall, his hands clutching his face. Sarah drove an elbow into his stomach, and Carl doubled over, gagging. Shoving him aside, Sarah stood up.

"This is the end of the line for you, Sarah," said Jambres as he thrust the ice pick at her exposed back.

The cleaver wedged in his skull betrayed him. Working with only one eye, Jambres badly misjudged his target. The sharp point of the ice pick merely grazed Sarah on the arm, and he didn't get a second chance.

Whirling, she knocked the kitchen tool from his hand. Reaching down, she grabbed it off the floor. "I should have chopped off your head," she declared, waving the ice pick around like a knife. "Come any closer and I'll finish the job."

Keeping a close watch on Jambres, she began backing out of the hallway. Carl groaned once, and Sarah kicked him in the head.

The sorcerer stood by silently, his body a wreck, and watched her escape. He did not dare try anything else. Sarah knew his weakness. If his face became so badly damaged he could not perform the Dead Man's Kiss, he was doomed to remain in this body forever. The blow from the cleaver had nearly split his head in two. A few more inches would have sealed his fate. He couldn't risk any further injury to his shattered face.

Jambres seethed with impotent rage as Sarah edged over to the door leading outside. She knew too much about his plans to be allowed to live. But he could do nothing to stop her.

Reaching behind herself, Sarah pushed open the door. In one hand, she still held the ice pick, its point aimed right at Jambres's middle. Preoccupied with him, she never noticed the huge figure framed in the doorway behind her. The first inkling of her peril came when two massive arms wrapped themselves around her chest and shoulders, pinning her arms against her sides.

"Gotcha," said George Slater.

Sarah screamed and tried to pull free. She thrashed about wildly, trying to break George's iron grip. The giant laughed and tightened his arms. Sarah's face turned white. Her breath came in deep, ragged gasps.

Savagely, she ground her left heel into the arch of his foot. George grunted in sudden shock as Sarah shifted all of her weight onto the bone. Angrily, he flung her face forward to the ground. Sarah struck the floor hard and lay still.

"You'll pay for that," he said, his face red with fury. He bent down and grabbed Sarah by the back of the neck. Raising the seeress to her feet with one hand, he shook her like a rag doll.

"Watch out!" shouted Carl, still on his knees. "She has a knife."

George ignored him. "I'm gonna break your neck," he declared, tightening his grip. The huge fingers of his other hand wrapped around the back part of her head. Slowly, he started to twist.

Bone grated on bone. Sarah screamed and lashed out with her feet. George laughed. "You ain't gonna make a fool of me twice," he said, and continued to apply pressure.

"Don't damage her body, fool," said Jambres, hobbling up close to the giant. "I can't use it if you break her neck."

George turned and stared at Jambres. "What the hell happened to you?" he asked, distracted for an instant by the bizarre appearance of the sorcerer.

Seizing the opportunity, Sarah reacted with blinding speed. She swung the ice pick in a short, deadly arc aimed at George's midsection. Only luck and his heavy clothing saved the big man from being gutted.

The point of the ice pick caught in the thick folds of George's flannel shirt. Deflected by the material, the steel tip missed all of his major organs. Instead, the blade dug inches deep into the fleshy part of George's side. The sudden, intense pain caught the big man by surprise. Shocked, he released his hold on Sarah.

Yanking the pick free, Sarah leapt past George and out the door. Blood spurting from his wound, the giant clutched his side with both hands, desperately trying to stop the bleeding. Moaning in pain, he dropped helplessly to the floor.

Jambres maneuvered carefully past George's outstretched legs and peered outside into the darkness. He caught a fleeting glimpse of Sarah racing for the surrounding forest. The night swallowed her, and she was gone.

Behind him, Carl ripped away the blood-soaked flannel clinging to George's skin. "Keep your hands pressed firmly against the wound," he said to the white-faced giant. "That'll slow the bleeding. I'll go get the first aid kit."

Angrily, Jambres grabbed Carl by an arm. "We cannot waste much time. Sarah called the police. I heard her. They are probably already on their way here. Gather the men. We must escape before they arrive."

"Shit," said Carl. "Where the hell are the others?"

He darted off, hunting for the rest of the members of Blood and Iron. In less than a minute, he returned, followed by his three underlings. "The damned fools were still outside waiting for George," said Carl angrily. "They never heard a thing."

Eyes blazing, Carl swiftly made plans. "Luther will drive the van. Jasper, Otis—the two of you help George into the back. You can patch him up after you're safely away from here. Use the first aid kit we stashed under the seat. Anybody tries to stop you, blast them off the road.

"Jambres and I will take the car. We rendezvous at the new hideout. Once you hit the open highway, change plates and vehicles as often as possible. Take no prisoners. Dead men tell no tales. Tonight, Blood and Iron strikes."

"What about that bitch Sarah?" asked George, struggling to stand. Blood oozed from the wound in his side. "She knows all of our plans."

"It's too dangerous to search for her in the woods," said Carl. "She's gone."

"Leave her to my magic," said Jambres. He touched the handle of the cleaver with one hand, as if reminding himself of the damage done to his body. "No matter where she hides, my thoughts will find her. The police don't matter. Let them surround her with a thousand men. They will not save her from my vengeance. No one can."

The sorcerer's pudgy short fingers tightened into fists. "Tonight Sarah dies—strangled to death by these hands."

35

▲ "Come any closer, and I'll smash in your worthless skull," Ellen screamed, her voice shaking.

"You and what army, bitch?" The screaming brought David back to consciousness. He immediately recognized the orange-haired punk's voice. "That dumb statue don't scare me none. It ain't no weapon," the young thug shouted menacingly.

David lightly touched the wound on his scalp—it throbbed painfully, but the bleeding had stopped. He had deflected the tire iron so that it struck him at an angle and not straight on. The glancing blow had ripped the skin off his temple and knocked him unconscious. His arms ached, but nothing felt broken.

Ellen shouted something at the punk that David missed. The hoodlum laughed.

"I'm gonna give it to you good," he said. "I'll teach you

and your boyfriend a lesson neither of you will ever forget."

Then his voice turned syrupy sweet. "Why don't you put down that hunk of stone, and I'll show you what a real man can do?"

"Why don't you get the hell out of here before the police show up?" said Ellen. "I'm sure the night watchman already turned on the alarm. You're already guilty of breaking and entering, attempted murder, and all sorts of other offenses. Those crimes sound good enough for around a hundred years in prison."

"Nah," said the punk. "You ain't so smart, bitch. I'm not twenty-one. I'd pull three, four months tops. Maybe even serve probation if the right lawyer takes my case. And that old geezer of a night watchman didn't phone the police, either. I knocked him cold before I swatted your boyfriend. We're all alone, babe. Ain't nobody around to interfere with my fun."

David knew he didn't have much time. The punk planned to rape Ellen, and all of her threats and warnings meant nothing to him. David was convinced the hoodlum planned to murder both of them, too.

Drawing in a deep breath, David forced himself to sit up. The sudden motion set the wound on his head bleeding again. Warm drops of blood trickled down his cheek as he leaned his weight on his hands and tried to push himself up. He grimaced as the palm of his right hand rested on a hard shell.

Shuddering, David shifted his fingers over a few inches. He wondered how this insect had gotten into the museum.

Head spinning, he grabbed hold of one of the exhibit tables with his right hand. Using the table as a fulcrum, he managed to stand erect. A dozen feet away, Ellen gasped, both surprised and concerned. David looked like a dead man rising up from the grave.

"Well, well, well," said the orange-haired punk, turning to look at David. He still held the tire iron, tipped red with David's blood, in his right hand. He gently tapped the end of it into his other palm. "Ain't this a big surprise. The Lone Ranger rides again."

"You should have listened to my warning," said David. He knew that escape was out of the question. His adversary wasn't going to be sacred off by words. But the punk liked to talk. The longer David delayed their fight, the better. His battered body needed the time to recuperate. "Remember what happened in the park?" David asked.

"You were lucky," said the punk. "That karate shit caught me by surprise. But I turned the tables on you quick enough. I stayed in the woods. When you left, I played boy scout and followed you home. For the last few days, me and my buddies watched your place, kept tabs on you. I figured sooner or later there would come a time when I could get even. Tonight's the night."

David gritted his teeth, angry at his own stupidity. He never once associated his feelings of being watched with the juvenile gang. He missed the obvious answer and now was paying for his mistake.

Something large and multi-legged scuttled over the counter onto his hand. David jerked the bug onto the floor. Glancing over at the table, he spotted four or five large insects crawling about in the dim light. He quickly stepped away from the display. The big bugs spooked him.

"What's wrong, shitface?" asked the punk, not realizing the source of David's concern. "Not so brave anymore?"

"David," said Ellen. "Watch out, he's carrying a knife. He threatened me with it before."

"Shut up, bitch," said the punk, his gaze never leaving David. "You'll suffer for your big mouth. Once I finish with your boyfriend, I'll shut you up for good."

Ellen stood with her back to the rear wall of the exhibit, her escape blocked by the orange-haired hoodlum. She clutched the phony statue, holding it upside down like a bludgeon. David's blood ran cold as he noticed dozens of small black shapes running across the floor toward Ellen.

"You talk a good fight," said David. "But, last time I crushed your nuts, and this time I'm going to shove them down your throat."

The punk's face turned beet red. His fingers tightened on the tire iron. David braced himself for an attack. Under normal circumstances, he would not have been worried. He had supreme confidence in his abilities. Tonight, battered and bloody, with a possible concussion, facing an enemy armed with a steel bar, he felt anything but secure. To add to his anxiety, an active horde of insects was gathering in the room.

"I'm gonna knock your fuckin' head off!" screamed the punk. Raising the tire iron over his head, he charged. Beneath his feet, the hard shells of dozens of beetles cracked like fireworks.

David waited until the punk was only a few feet away before acting. Calling on hidden reserves of strength, he darted forward and grabbed the teenager's wrist just as the punk started swinging the steel bar. Holding tightly to his attacker's arm, David dropped to the floor, pivoting and pulling as he did so. With a shriek of surprise, the punk went flying over David's head. Unable to slow down, he slammed into an exhibit table a dozen feet away.

Feeling a little more confident, David hurried toward his foe. He knew better than to wait for the punk to regain his feet. Sportsmanship had no place in street fighting. A few kicks to the head would render his opponent senseless.

Behind him, Ellen screamed. David hesitated, half turning. At the same moment, the punk struggled to his feet. Blood stained his face, but he still held the tire iron. His breath hissing like a steam engine, he swung the bar back and forth in short swings. "I'll kill you for that," he said, slowly advancing on David. "No fancy tricks for you this time."

Again, Ellen screamed, pure terror in her voice. David risked a quick look over his shoulder.

Ellen was standing on top of one of the exhibit tables. She held the statue of Anubis in one hand, and with the other, she desperately swatted as hundreds of insects swarmed at her from all directions.

The bugs covered the tabletop like a living black carpet. Ellen hopped from one foot to the other, trying to prevent them from covering her feet. Relentlessly, the beetles, ants, and roaches inched their way up her legs. A score of black shells marked her white blouse, and she bled from a dozen nicks on her arms and face.

She screamed, shaking her head violently from side to side. A half-dozen large bugs went flying from her hair. There was an edge of madness in her cry.

"Jump, jump," shouted David, the punk behind him momentarily forgotten. He rushed toward her, his hands held up shoulder high for assistance. "Get off the table."

"No-o-o," she wailed, waving the statue in the direction of his feet. David looked down and almost collapsed in shock. The white marble floor seethed with life. Thousands of black bugs covered the tile. As he stood there paralyzed with fear, hundreds of the insects crowded onto his shoes and scurried up his pants.

Behind him, the punk roared with laughter. "Bugs, bugs, bugs!" he shouted. "How you plan to stop them, Lone Ranger?"

"Throw me the statue," David cried. "It's attracting the insects."

Ellen failed to respond. David recognized the problem immediately. She was fighting for her life and sanity, and he doubted if she even heard his cries. There was only one way to get the statue away from her. He had to grab it.

Behind him, the orange-haired punk was content to laugh while the insects attacked his enemies. "Keep going, shithead," he shouted. "I'm loving every minute of this. It's better than watching TV."

David gazed down at the floor separating him from

Ellen. No white showed beneath the carpet of tens of thousands of roaches and beetles.

Whispering a silent prayer for help, David jumped. With a cry of both relief and despair, he crashed into Ellen. For a second, they tottered on the edge of the exhibit table, nearly falling. Sweating profusely, David helped Ellen regain her balance.

Heedless of the roaches attacking his feet, David wrenched the statue away from Ellen. Angrily, he flung it far across the room. The phony relic disappeared in the darkness. David no longer cared what happened to it. Moving quickly, he swept the bugs off of Ellen. Even with the idol gone, the insects showed no signs of retreating.

Big tears rolled down Ellen's cheeks. "David, David," she sobbed. "I'm so scared."

He lowered himself to the ground, then helped Ellen down from the table. With a sigh, she hugged him tight.

"How very touching," came the acid-toned voice of the orange-haired punk. "It chokes me up. I'm so-o-o impressed."

Releasing Ellen, David turned to face his nemesis. The young hoodlum stood in the center of the aisle, blocking the only path to the outside corridor. He no longer held the tire iron. Instead, in one hand he gripped an open switchblade knife. In the other, he held the fake statue of Anubis.

"I thought you might want this," said the punk, laughing nastily. "So I retrieved it from where you tossed it. Damned thing seemed the center of attraction back there."

"It's cursed," said Ellen, her voice shaking. "Someone carved on the bottom the ancient Egyptian spell known as the Curse of the Vermin. According to the texts, whoever possesses the inscribed object is doomed to be devoured by the things that crawl in darkness. Egyptologists always wondered exactly what that phrase meant. Now I know."

"Neat," said the punk. Holding the statue by the neck, he waved it around like a trophy. "So this thing draws the bugs like a magnet, huh? Then why don't you take it back?"

With a flip of the wrist, he sent the statue spinning back at them. Instinctively, David reached out and grabbed it.

"Nice catch," said the punk. "Now we'll just wait and see what happens next."

"David," said Ellen, clutching his arm. "Drop it—quick!"

"Not yet," said David. "Time for us to make an exit. Stay close behind me while I settle things with our friend."

David paced cautiously up the aisle. Fenced in on both sides by exhibit tables, he had little room for any spinning kicks or fancy moves. The orange-haired hoodlum waited, switchblade pointing directly at David's middle.

"Come on, tough guy," said the punk, his voice rising with excitement. "I'm gonna carve my initials in your face."

David said nothing. Ten feet separated them, then five. His feet squashed a score of roaches with each step. The bugs grew more aggressive with each passing second. Ahead of him, the teenager tensed, baring his teeth in an insane grin.

"Move out of our way and I won't hurt you," said David, giving the boy one last chance.

"I'll take my chances," answered the punk, sneering.

David shrugged, as if accepting the inevitable. Then, with blinding speed, he knelt to the floor, scooped up a handful of roaches in his free hand, and flung them right in the face of his opponent. A dozen of them splattered against his young opponent's forehead and cheeks. One large black beetle landed directly in his open mouth. Scuttling forward, it disappeared down his throat.

The punk gagged horribly; his eyes wild with shock, he raised both hands to his face, trying to sweep the bugs from his flesh. The knife dropped forgotten at his feet.

David crashed into the teenager shoulder first, sending

the hoodlum tumbling to the marble floor. Straddling him, David grabbed the boy by the hair and ruthlessly smashed his head again and again into the cold, hard floor. Red blood stained white stone.

"Run," he gasped to Ellen. "I'll catch up with you in the hallway."

"The curse," she started to say.

"I heard what you told him," said David. "Get going."

She hesitated for only a second, then bounded past him for the entrance. Hundreds of bugs were climbing over the punk's motionless body, searching for the idol.

Hurriedly, David pulled the boy upright. A few quick slaps brought the punk back to semiconsciousness. "You're lucky I'm no killer," said David, shaking the teenager until he could stand upright without any help.

Jerking the groggy teenager around until he faced the other way, David grabbed him by the back of his jeans. An ornate leather and silver belt encircled the punk's waist. Holding it tightly, David shoved the narrow statue down into the hoodlum's pants. Wedged tight at the small of the boy's back, the idol was impossible for him to reach without major contortions.

"If you run fast enough, the bugs won't catch you," said David. "Try stopping, even for a minute, to pull it loose, and you're dead."

Taking the boy by the shoulders, David shoved him in the general direction of the side exit. For an instant, the punk stood there, dazed. Then, as a black carpet of bugs began climbing his legs, he shrieked and started running, disappearing out the door.

Weary but satisfied, David headed out the main door, looking for Ellen. He found her nursing a bruised but otherwise unharmed Gus in the main hall of the museum.

"You okay?" he asked, brushing off the last few bugs from his clothing.

Ellen nodded. "I found Gus tied up by the fountain. We already called the police. How's your head?"

"Throbbing but otherwise still functioning. Once the police arrive, a quick trip to the hospital sounds like a good idea for both of us."

"What happened to that horrible thug?" asked Ellen.

David told her. "If he heads for Lake Michigan, he'll survive. The bugs will drown, and he can divest himself of the statue in the water. Otherwise, who knows?"

"The spell was commonly used to protect the valuables that were buried with the dead from grave robbers," said Ellen. "In ancient Egypt, it probably summoned scorpions and poisonous snakes. In our more temperate climate, it invoked beetles and roaches."

"Not nearly as deadly," said David, "but they almost scared us to death. Too bad they destroyed the photo."

Grinning, Ellen undid the first three snaps of her blouse. Reaching into her bra, she pulled out the folded but otherwise intact picture. "Better than pockets," she said as David shook his head in amazement.

36

▲ Moe and Calvin approached the old mansion on foot. Never a great fan of the outdoors, Moe felt sure they were walking into a trap. Calvin, even more of a city boy than his partner, stared at the trees with ill-concealed suspicion.

"I'll kill the first deer that moves," he muttered softly. Like Moe, he held his sidearm drawn and ready for action. No one on this mission expected Blood and Iron to surrender peacefully.

A few feet ahead of them, Rufus Anderson raised one

hand in the air, signaling stop. Shaking his head in displeasure, Moe rested against a nearby tree. He wondered when this insanity would end.

There were at least two dozen FBI men scattered throughout the woods. Anderson worried that an assault by car would enable members of the terrorist group to escape through the forest, so he decided to attack on foot, with backup units guarding the roadway in trucks. Moe didn't think it was a bad plan. He only wished he was back with the trucks.

Meanwhile, up front, Anderson conferred with another agent. Moe looked over at Calvin and raised his eyebrows in an unspoken question.

Anderson spoke quietly with the man for several minutes. His shoulders sagged as he talked. Moe suspected the other agent brought bad news.

"Move on in," said the FBI chief, not bothering to whisper. "The place appears abandoned. They left all the lights on, and the doors are wide open. No sign of either van in the drive. Somehow, the scum learned about the raid."

Moe caught up to a despondent Anderson as he mounted the front steps of the building. "How did they find out?"

"Beats me," said Anderson with a deep sigh. "I hope they rushed out of here so fast that they forgot something important. If they did, my men will find it. They're searching the house from the basement to the . . ."

"There's a lady in the kitchen, sir," interrupted a dark-haired agent. "She matches the description of Sarah Walsh."

"In the kitchen?" repeated Anderson, caught completely by surprise. "What's she doing in there?"

"Cursing, sir," said the agent, dead serious. "She's yelling curses at everyone."

"Remember our deal," said Moe, hurrying after Anderson. "You made a promise."

"I never break my word," said Anderson. "At least, not very often. I don't want Walsh. She's small potatoes. I'm after bigger game. You can ask her all the questions you like. All I need to find out is if she knows where her buddies plan to strike next."

The officers hurried to the kitchen. A steady stream of obscenities greeted them as they entered. Four FBI agents stood by helplessly as a solitary woman cursed them with the fluency of an old sailor.

Moe recognized Sarah immediately. Dressed in a loose white shift, stained in several spots with what appeared to be blood, she matched her pictures perfectly—and she definitely was not wearing a bra.

"What the hell took you so long?" she screeched, her voice as shrill as chalk on a blackboard. "I called nearly three hours ago. Carl and his buddies drove off twenty minutes later. I hid out in the forest until I was sure they weren't coming back. Then I came inside and waited for you jerks to show up."

"Call?" said Anderson. "We received no call. My men traced this place through your van. Besides, we're with the FBI, not the police department."

"I phoned 911," said Sarah with a laugh. "On TV, the cops always respond in minutes."

"Life isn't television," said Anderson. "From the sound of things, you're not working for Blood and Iron any longer. What happened?"

"You pegged me all wrong," said Sarah. "I never willingly cooperated with those creeps. They threatened to kill me if I didn't help. I'm innocent."

"As pure as newly fallen snow," said Anderson sarcastically. "Don't bother lying to me. You double-crossed the gang, and now you want protection. I'll keep you safe from Garrett and his buddies, if you make it worth the effort. For openers, perhaps you could describe the vehicles Blood and Iron used for their escape. We still might catch them."

Sarah snorted in derision. "No way. Carl knows I called the law, that's what sent him running for cover. He probably changed cars twice or three times in the past hour. And switched license plates with five others as well.

He's an expert at avoiding detection. You'll never find him."

"I plan to try," said Anderson. "Talk."

Moe wandered over to Calvin as the FBI chief interrogated Sarah. The big detective pursed his lips and shook his head slowly from side to side.

"Yeah, I feel the same way," said Moe. "She's right. A pro like Garrett won't be run down in a dragnet. He's gotten away clean. Whatcha think about her remarks on 911?"

"The lady was probably telling the truth," said Calvin. "She seemed pretty burned about our arriving so late. Mrs. Wronski was right on target about her temper.

"As to the lack of attention from the locals, I'm sure it relates to what she said over the phone. You know the dispatchers are trained to ignore crank calls."

Moe wrinkled his nose in vexation. "Wonderful the way this adventure is taking place on our day off. I'd hate to think we wasted department time. Well, at least she's on the outs with her friends; that should make our play for information a lot easier."

"Good-cop, bad-cop?" asked Calvin.

"Why not? She's looking for protection. One push in the right direction should do the trick."

Rufus Anderson tapped Moe on the shoulder. "She's all yours for the next twenty minutes. Shouldn't take us longer than that to do a quick check of the house. After that, we take her downtown. I'm not taking any chances on Garrett planting a sniper to take our prize out of the picture."

"Twenty minutes isn't very much time," said Moe.

"Tell me that after you talk with her," said Anderson with a shake of the head. "The woman is definitely not playing with a full deck."

Anderson gestured to one of his agents. "Curt's guarding the back door from any unwanted intruders. If you run into any problems with Ms. Walsh, he's around."

"I think we can handle her on our own," answered

Calvin, a little testily. "It's been at least a month since a woman beat the crap out of the two of us."

Anderson grinned. "Don't take it so personal. He's there mostly because Garrett's crazy. Call him if you need any assistance."

The FBI chief and his men filed out of the kitchen, leaving Moe and Calvin alone with Sarah Walsh. Sitting calmly on a kitchen chair, she looked them over carefully.

"Two dumb cops," she declared after a short inspection. "I knew I shoulda left when I had the chance. What now?"

"We'd like to ask you a few questions, Sarah," said Moe, sitting down across from her. Calvin, still standing, positioned himself directly behind his partner. "Strictly off the record. You answer them straight, and we'll all be friends."

"And if I don't?" she asked.

"Eyewitnesses placed you at the scenes of two recent murders," said Calvin harshly. "If the evidence was slanted a certain way, you'd be convicted for both killings. You ain't worth that much to the FBI for them to fight the verdict."

Sarah blanched. Moe waited a minute before speaking. They played good-cop, bad-cop better than any other team in the city. Though he never made it to the stage, Calvin had become quite an actor.

"Don't listen to him," said Moe. "We know you didn't commit those crimes. Help us find the real killer, and things will work out fine."

"You're lying," she said.

"Why should I?" said Moe. "We're not out to lynch anybody. Besides, Garrett knows you called the police. Do you really think Anderson can stop him? Your life won't be worth a plugged nickel unless that madman's captured. Or killed."

Sarah licked her lips nervously. "You won't believe me if I tell you the truth."

"Sure we will," said Moe. "As long as it *is* the truth."

"No you won't," she insisted. "Only those who accept the powers of darkness would understand."

Moe drew in a deep breath. His worst dreams had just come true. "Sarah," he said quietly, "Calvin and I investigated the Dark Man murders last year. Maybe you remember the circumstances? The case involved voodoo, black magic, and the occult and provided us with quite an education in the dark side of the universe. Nothing you say tonight will shock us."

"All right," said Sarah, still sounding doubtful. "You asked for it."

Taking a deep breath, she spoke quickly, the words rushing out all at once. "Two months ago, the spirit of a long-dead Egyptian sorcerer, Satni Jambres, contacted Carl Garrett in the dream world. Working together, they formed an unholy alliance linking our world and the supernatural.

"With my help—unwilling, of course," she added, not very convincingly, "we raised Jambres's spirit from a golden statue of Anubis where it had been imprisoned for centuries. The spell involved human sacrifice. After the killing, Jambres's soul assumed control of the body of the victim, Oscar Hinkley. When that body wore out, the sorcerer murdered Tom Darrow and transferred his spirit over into the fresh corpse. This afternoon, he performed the ritual, known as the Dead Man's Kiss, for the third time."

Moe glanced up at Calvin. His partner's face revealed none of his thoughts. "What about the museum deaths? How do they tie in with this resurrected Egyptian?" Moe asked.

"Jambres worried that someone at the Petrie Institute might threaten his plans. So he murdered everyone he considered dangerous." She paused. "Actually, he guessed right. His final attempt, against a woman named Ellen Harper, backfired. She evidently realized what had happened to her comrades and took the necessary precautions. The sorcery boomeranged and killed one of the members of Blood and Iron. Indirectly, it caused the gang to flee and allowed me to escape their clutches."

Moe felt sure Sarah was doctoring her story as it unfolded. She changed her participation from willing accomplice to helpless prisoner. He didn't care. Despite the incredible nature of the tale, he believed most of what she told them.

"It doesn't make much sense to me," said Calvin. "You claim that Garrett and Jambres are working together. Why? What links a modern right-wing extremist and an ancient Egyptian magician?"

"Hate," answered Sarah. "Revenge. Death and destruction."

"Pretty strong emotions," said Moe. "We all know Garrett's manias. The guy's loony. No problem there. What stirs up this Jambres character?"

"I'm not sure," said Sarah. "Carl knows a little of the truth, but he's the only one. So far, the Egyptian has obeyed Carl. But Jambres has his own secret plans that don't include Blood and Iron. Man and spirit are using each other. In the long run, only one will emerge victorious."

"When can we expect that happy occasion to take place?" asked Moe.

"I eavesdropped on a conversation earlier today," said Sarah slowly. "Jambres spoke of a legendary Staff of Fire hidden in this part of the country. Possessing it would increase his magic powers a hundredfold. That's when he'll make his split with Carl and pursue his own schemes."

"Great news," said Moe. "Do you know where this staff is located?"

Sarah hesitated, then shook her head. "I'm not sure."

Moe knew she was lying. Sarah obviously planned to use the information to bargain for her safety. For the moment, he let the question slide.

"How about motive? From what you said, this

Jambres lived thousands of years ago. What possible . . ."

Without warning, Sarah gagged violently. Her hands flew up to her neck, grabbing at emptiness. "Air, air," she sputtered, ripping feverishly at invisible bonds.

The two detectives looked at each other in astonishment. Sarah thrashed about wildly on the chair, as if she was being brutally beaten by an invisible assailant. Moe reached out and touched Sarah on the neck. An ice-cold band of air circled her throat like an invisible, intangible snake.

Sarah turned white. Her mouth was wide open, trying desperately to suck in precious oxygen. Helplessly, Moe and Calvin watched as the outlines of ghostly fingers indented the skin on her neck.

"What the hell's happening?" whispered Anderson's man, Curt. He had slipped into the room unnoticed. "She's being strangled to death. But nobody's there."

Slumped in her chair, Sarah beckoned Moe close. Breathlessly, she gasped, "Jambres . . . wants . . . revenge . . . against . . ." She collapsed. Convulsions shook her entire body. Eyes closed, her head sagged limply on her chest.

"Against who?" asked Moe, gripping her by the shoulders as if trying to pass along some of his strength. "Against who?"

For an instant, Sarah's eyes opened a crack. Her lips moved, but no sound emerged. Then, with a finality only death brings, her body shuddered and was still.

"What did she say?" asked Curt.

"I didn't hear a thing," said Moe despondently. He drew in several deep breaths. "The sorcerer killed her with black magic before she could reveal his secret."

"You're wrong," said Calvin quietly. "Jambres didn't murder her quickly enough. She said *son.* I read her lips."

"You believed her story?" Moe asked his partner as Curt rushed off to find Anderson.

"Not until a minute ago," Calvin admitted. "I thought

she invented the whole thing. But now I tend to think she told us the truth."

"Reporting her death isn't going to be easy," said Rufus Anderson, entering the room. He glanced at Sarah's body, then shook his head, looking very unhappy. "How do you explain murder by black magic to a bunch of Washington bureaucrats?"

"Don't ask me," said Moe.

"Find Garrett and nobody will care about Sarah's death," said Calvin.

"Meanwhile," said Moe, "we need to learn a lot more about a malevolent spirit named Satni Jambres. And I think I know exactly who to ask."

37

▲ Jambres tapped Carl on the shoulder. He gestured with one hand at the exit sign illuminated by the car's headlights.

"Pull off," he spat out through the remains of his mouth. During the past few hours, the heavy cleaver had sunk further into the sorcerer's decaying flesh. The steel blade had crushed most of his features into a haphazard ruin of smashed bone and fragmented strands of flesh and muscle. Nothing remained of his nose. One eye dangled uselessly on his left cheek. Most of his teeth were gone. Each time he spoke, his head quivered like a rotten apple, ready to collapse inward.

"We're still an hour away from Gibson," said Carl, slowing the car down as he spoke. "George and the others will start worrying if we don't show up soon."

"I don't care," said Jambres, trying to say as little as

possible. "The more energy I expend holding this body together, the faster corruption attacks. I need a new body. Right away."

Every time the dead man moved his head, bits of gristle and tissue dropped to the seat. In a short time, the sorcerer's entire head would dissolve in ruin, and it would be impossible for him to perform the Dead Man's Kiss. Jambres's spirit would be trapped forever in the decomposing corpse.

With a nod to himself, Carl filed away the thought for later consideration. George had once asked him how to kill a man already dead. Now Carl knew the answer. Death never entered the equation; it was preventing Jambres's further resurrections that mattered. And Carl was content to wait, at least for the time being.

The exit from the highway left them on a two-lane road in the middle of nowhere. Pulling the car up to a stop sign, Carl searched in both directions for some signs of habitation. "It looks like the glow from a gas station off to the right. I'll try that way first."

The light came from a solitary convenience store and gas station. The gas pumps stood deserted. A car, a van, and two motorcycles were parked in front of the store's huge glass picture windows. Peering inside, Carl counted five customers and a heavyset middle-aged woman who sat behind the cash register, reading a magazine.

"Peaceful scene," he declared. Reaching beneath his seat, he lifted the Skorpion pistol off the floor and placed it in the holster beneath his overcoat. The machine gun was fully loaded and ready for use.

"I'll signal for you," he told Jambres, and opened the door to the car. "Stay out of sight till then."

Casually, he strolled over to the door and stepped inside. The cashier, fat and wrinkled, looked up for a second, judged him harmless and unimportant, and went back to her magazine. Her mouth formed unfamiliar words as she scanned the pages. Nodding to himself, Carl checked out the other people in the store.

A young couple, armed with a shopping list and a half-filled metal basket, were gawking at a vending machine that offered video tapes for rent. The girl, pretty with curly brown hair, wanted to watch Elvis. Her male companion, short and stocky with darting, suspicious eyes, preferred James Bond. Carl dipped his head and smiled in greeting as the man's gaze swept across him. With a shrug of dismissal, the short man returned to his argument.

In the rear of the store, a solitary pinball machine flashed brightly. A broad-shouldered man in his early thirties, dressed in paint-splattered blue jeans and a black leather jacket, cursed loudly as he manipulated the flippers. His greased-back hair poorly disguised an obvious bald spot. His companion, dressed in a similar outfit, stood close by, thumbing through the pages of a Batman comic book. Neither biker paid any attention to Carl.

The fifth customer was a tall, lanky man with gnarled hands and skin the color of tanned leather—Carl immediately identified him as a farmer. He had seen many men just like the old-timer in his youth. An old Cubs baseball cap planted firmly on his head, the man stood motionless, examining the rows of cold beer in the store's cooler, carefully checking the prices.

Carl felt a twinge of regret. These were the true common folk of America. These were the people he fought to free from tyranny. Though they were nameless strangers, he felt a loyalty to them. He deeply regretted what he had to do next. It was an unfair world; innocents often suffered in the struggle for justice. To Carl, these unfortunates were the true martyrs in his undeclared war.

Loosening the Skorpion beneath his coat, he stepped over to the cashier. "You want somethin'?" the woman asked, not bothering to look up from her magazine.

In one smooth, practiced motion, Carl drew the machine pistol from the holster and shoved its mouth into the soft skin beneath the clerk's chin. "If you step on the alarm," he warned, his voice cool and unhurried, "I'll blow your head clean off."

The woman squawked in panic, then froze as he pressed the cold metal deeper into her warm flesh. "Ease out from behind that counter," commanded Carl. *"Now."*

Gray-faced and trembling, the fat clerk slid off her chair. "Make it quick," said Carl sharply. "I'm not a patient man."

"What the hell is goin' on?" asked the short man with suspicious eyes, coming up quickly from behind.

Calmly, Carl swung around and fired a quick burst from the Skorpion into the floor. The bullets exploded into the tiles only inches in front of his adversary. Gunfire rolled through the store like thunder. Afterward, silence blanketed the aisles like a shroud. No one dared move.

Smiling, Carl raised the machine pistol waist high. "In case you're all wondering, I'm armed with a Model 61 Skorpion machine pistol. It is quite light and easy to handle; fully loaded, it weighs less than five pounds. In the hands of an expert, which I am, it is astonishingly accurate."

Carl tilted the gun slightly and fired a short burst at the pinball machine. The glass face exploded into a thousand pieces, sending the two bikers scurrying for cover. Chuckling, Carl motioned them to the rear of the store.

"If any of you harbor wild ideas of rushing me, please forget them immediately. When set on automatic, this gun fires more than eight hundred rounds a minute. That's enough firepower to cut a man in two before he takes two steps."

"Whaddaya gonna do with us?" asked the black-haired biker. "It ain't worth the trouble robbing one of these places." He grinned nervously. "I know. Me and Butch knocked one over a month ago. There's nothing in the cashbox but loose change. All the money goes into a safe."

"I'm not here for loot," said Carl, carefully herding his prisoners in single file against the back wall. He put the young couple at the end of the line. Next to them, head nervously turning from side to side, stood the old man with the baseball cap.

Fourth was the clerk, violently chewing a wad of gum and clutching her magazine tight to her chest. The two bikers finished the group.

Carl checked his watch. Less than five minutes had passed since he first entered the store. He knew he didn't have much time. Sooner or later, a patrol car would cruise by on its local rounds.

"My friend and I need supplies," he lied. "That and gasoline. No reason for anyone to act heroic. Stay cool, and nobody gets hurt. Keep your hands up and face the wall. It should only take a few minutes. I promise."

Keeping close watch on his captives, Carl waved to the car. Jambres, moving with a lurching, unsteady gait, joined him in seconds.

The dead man looked worse. The cleaver had sunk another inch into his skull. The wood handle stood out at a right angle from his skull, nestled directly between his eyes. Cold steel rested only a half-inch above his upper lip. Carl wondered if it was already too late to perform the Dead Man's Kiss.

"Pick," he muttered softly.

"The tall one," said Jambres.

"Hey you, in the Cubs hat," said Carl. "Walk over to the pinball machine. My friend wants to ask you a few questions."

"Whatever you want, mister," said the farmer, and shuffled over to the wrecked machine. Anxiously, he peered over his shoulder at Carl. His eyes bulged when he caught sight of Jambres.

"What the . . ." he began.

The Skorpion shrieked, cutting the man off in midsentence. The wail of bullets couldn't drown out the unexpected shrieks of agony. Like grotesque, giant marionettes, the five captives jumped and jerked about in a dance of death. Bright red blood sprayed the glass doors and walls of the store.

Relentless, Carl fired at his victims long after they collapsed to the floor.

"You dirty lying bastard!" screamed the farmer, his face chalk white, his eyes brimming with horror. "You killed them in cold blood. Butcher! Madman! I hope you burn in hell!"

"They died serving their country," said Carl, lowering his gun.

Jambres, gone for an instant, stepped forward. In one hand, the sorcerer held an eight-inch-long hunting knife, liberated from one of the store's display cases. Carl shivered. He moved out of the way as the dead man advanced on the old farmer.

"There are fates worse than dying," said Carl, more to himself than the other. "I'm sure of that. Much worse."

38

▲ The figure on the cross leaned his head forward so that his eyes stared deep into Carl's. "Remember," said the man Carl knew for certain to be Jesus Christ, Christian, "that I, too, once was a Jew."

Moaning, Carl sat up in bed. Fragments of the dream clung to his mind like a spider's web. He remembered odd bits and pieces of an eerie landscape and bizarre conversations with the dead. The final words of Christ haunted him. He felt sure that his subconscious mind was warning him of something. Groggily, he tried to make sense of his nightmare.

In the corner of the room, a figure as gaunt as the one in his dream rose from the floor. Silently, Jambres eased himself into the chair across from Carl's bed. The two shared the quarters; the other men refused to let the sorcerer stay anywhere else in the house.

The battered van was parked outside the old farmhouse that now served as Blood and Iron's new hideout. It had belonged to the farmer Jambres had murdered for his body. Their old vehicle, complete with the decayed corpse of Ivan Short, rested at the bottom of a small lake. The exchange guaranteed them a few days of anonymity. Which was all the time Jambres claimed he needed.

Swinging off the bed, Carl walked over to his suitcase and pulled out a pair of jeans and a rumpled shirt. He dressed in silence, trying to ignore the dead man who watched his every move.

"You been staring at me the whole night?" he asked, turning to face Jambres.

"Of course," said the sorcerer. His flat, lifeless tones could not hide the bitterness of his words. "I never sleep."

"Tough," said Carl. He felt no sympathy for Jambres. "I guess that comes with the territory. It's part of being dead. What do you say to that?"

"I thought it wise to remind you of Sarah's demise," said the sorcerer. "There is no reason to worry about her any longer. She perished during our trip west, soon after I switched bodies."

Jambres opened his clenched hands and dropped a small wax doll to the floor. Carl stared at the misshapen figure and shuddered. The sorcerer had squeezed the substitute body's neck so hard that only a wafer-thin strand of paraffin held the head and torso together.

"She died in terrible agony," said Jambres, his unblinking eyes looking straight at Carl. "The same end destined for all those who betray my trust."

"All?" repeated Carl, unable to resist baiting the Egyptian. "I recall your tale of a wayward son. But that was thousands of years ago, wasn't it?"

A stray thought struck him before Jambres could say anything in return. "Your most recent attempt at murder didn't work very well. Why didn't you strangle that Harper woman, like you did Sarah, instead of raising that demon?"

"This spell only works between those . . ." Jambres paused, searching his new mind for the correct words. ". . . sharing intimate sexual knowledge of each other."

Carl frowned. He disliked being reminded of the obscene coupling of the living and the dead.

"Did the slut tell the cops about our plans?" he asked, seeking to change the subject. "How much do they know?"

"I cannot say for sure. I broke the mind link several minutes before I strangled her. Until then, she had revealed little of importance."

The sorcerer stood up and walked over to a window. "While you slept, I examined our surroundings."

"The place meets with your approval?" asked Carl. For all of his sarcasm, he still feared the dead man.

"In most respects," replied Jambres. "Please instruct your men to clear away the debris in the backyard. To work my greatest spell, I need a large open space."

"I'll supervise the job myself," said Carl. "As soon as I eat my breakfast."

"No," said Jambres. "Let George Slater handle it. His wound makes him too weak to do much else. I want you to drive me into town. The power of the staff calls out to me. I must find it."

"You can sense it nearby?"

"It burns like a beacon, blazing with incredible energy," said Jambres. "When I close my eyes, it shines like a flame in my mind. Finding it will be easy—by searching through Short's memories. . . . It is located in a small local museum on the other side of town."

"Nothing is easy," said Carl. He headed for the door. "We can't just walk in the place and blast everyone away. Not if we expect to return here afterward."

"I understand," said Jambres. "There is no need to

repeat the slaughter of last night. I merely want to locate the staff this afternoon. Tonight, when the museum is closed, we can return and steal it. My powers, amplified by my nearness to the talisman, will shield us in darkness. It could not be any simpler."

"Yeah," said Carl, unconvinced. "We grab the staff. Then what happens?"

"Great sorcery requires much blood," said Jambres, cryptically. "When I obtain the staff, I will finally possess the power necessary for the greatest feat of sorcery in the past three thousand years. In that hour, all your questions will be answered."

"Tonight?" asked Carl.

"Tomorrow evening," said Jambres. "That is when the moon and stars are right. The ancient gods of Kamt will again walk the Earth, and thirty centuries of history shall be ripped asunder."

Carl frowned. "What about your promise?"

The dead man smiled. "Your enemies will die by the thousands." His voice grew louder. "There will be deaths by the tens of thousands." Then louder yet. "By the millions."

39

▲ Moe stared at the books scattered all across the floor of the parlor, then glanced over at Ellen Harper. "You sure you don't have any kids?"

She giggled. "I'm not married. Why do you ask?"

"Your apartment looks exactly like my house," said Moe. "My children don't believe in shelves. At least, not as long as there is an inch of space free on the floor."

"You interrupted my research," Ellen replied. "I was trying to locate some obscure information in one of those volumes when the two of you disturbed me."

"Ellen didn't have to answer your questions," said David, sounding defensive. "She only agreed because of her abiding belief in law and order."

"Yeah, yeah," said Calvin Lane, only slightly sarcastic. "We appreciate the cooperation."

Moe sighed. His one attempt at small talk had fallen flat. Ellen Harper and her boyfriend were definitely not in the mood to chat.

The young woman refused to allow them into her apartment until Ross showed up. It then took fifteen minutes of explanations and assurances before the couple finally relented and allowed the officers upstairs. Moe suspected that Ellen knew quite a bit about this weird case. The only problem was ferreting the information out of her. Fortunately, he had an idea.

"His name," Moe said, speaking slowly, "is Satni Jambres."

"What?" asked Ellen, caught by surprise. "Whose name?"

"The ancient Egyptian sorcerer behind the two attempts on your life," said Moe. He was risking everything on one roll of the dice. If they rebuffed this attempt, Moe had nothing else to offer for their secrets. "Now, are you willing to talk?"

"How much do you know?" asked David cautiously. Next to him, Ellen quickly thumbed through a thick hardcover, searching for something.

"Enough to understand your reluctance to talk to the police," said Moe. "We heard all about your adventure in the museum last night. Plus, we saw the squashed remains of a lot of bugs. The two of us know you aren't crazy. This case will never make it into the official records. Calvin and I want to bring a killer to justice. The only way we can do it is with your help."

Ellen tossed one book onto the couch and grasped

another. Again, she turned pages quickly, hunting for a specific reference. "You're positive on his name?" she asked. "You did say *Satni* Jambres?"

"I'm a cop, miss," said Moe. "I don't forget names or faces. Even Egyptian ones. I gather Jambres is a pretty common moniker among magicians?"

Ellen nodded, slamming the book closed with a loud thunk. "A surprising number of sorcerers bore that title," she said, her eyes unfocused, seeing far-off things. "But there was only one Satni Jambres."

"I propose we trade facts," said David. "You tell us what you know, and then we'll follow suit. Maybe by pooling our information, we can make some sense out of this mess."

"That sounds fine to me," said Moe. Calvin shrugged and nodded his agreement. "We better sit down, though. It's a long story."

Starting with the discovery of Oscar Hinkley's body, Moe sketched in everything they knew about the strange murder case. It took nearly a half hour to tell his story.

"Early this morning," said Moe, finishing up, "a cleaning woman discovered Tom Darrow's body. She found the corpse in the basement of the home of her client, a Professor Ivan Short. Needless to say, the professor was missing. Perhaps you knew him? He was an expert on ancient Egypt."

"We met at the museum a few times," said Ellen, drawing in a deep breath. "I liked him. He loved his work."

"You think he's dead?" asked David.

"If we take Sarah at her word, Jambres changes bodies the way we switch clothes," said Moe. "I suspect Short won't turn up alive."

"Then you believe in all of these stories about black magic and changing bodies?" asked David. "That doesn't jibe with the usual no-nonsense police treatment of satanism and black magic crimes. Most cops consider sorcery a fraud."

"I saw Sarah Walsh strangled to death by invisible hands," said Moe. "I smelled Oscar Hinkley's rotting corpse and knew without a doubt he died a week before he attacked Tom Darrow. It's difficult to argue with the facts, no matter how bizarre they appear."

He shrugged. "I might be skeptical, but I'm not that hardheaded. Calvin and I have dealt with the supernatural before. We don't need to be convinced. Jambres exists and is out there plotting his next killing. Unless we stop him first."

"The ritual he used to return to life was called the Dead Man's Kiss," said Ellen. "Most scholars assumed it was just a variation of the Opening of the Mouth ceremony performed during the mummification process. Like most black magic practices, the ritual was never committed to papyrus. No one ever realized it served any actual purpose."

"Well, the evidence on hand definitely indicates otherwise," said Moe. "It's unbelievable but real. A long-dead Egyptian magician walks the streets of modern Chicago. And he's murdering anybody who suspects the truth."

"Which explains the attacks on all of the people connected with the Rivington exhibit," said Ellen. "Jambres wanted to cover any possible loose ends. I guessed right after all. My only mistake was with the motive. I thought criminals were stealing valuable artifacts and trying to cover up their crimes."

"Maybe Ellen should tell you what took place here," said David. "It should fill in some of the blanks in your story."

Ellen proceeded to describe the events of the past several days. David interrupted from time to time to elaborate on certain points. Moe noticed several hastily contrived jumps in the narration, but they all seemed to cover personal information. When Ellen finished speaking, he felt certain that she had not left out anything of import.

"Everything ties together nicely," said Moe. "Except

for the one big unanswered question. Why did Carl Garrett raise this Egyptian sorcerer from the dead? We need motives. What did he stand to gain? And equally important, why did Jambres specifically contact Garrett? Why him and not any of a dozen other people?"

"Sarah Walsh claimed that Jambres spoke to Garrett in his dreams," said David slowly. "That meant the Egyptian initiated the whole string of events. For some reason, he wanted to return to life. Garrett and his group provided the bridge between our realm and the hereafter."

Calvin grunted. "Hate. Revenge. Death and destruction. Sarah said those were the passions that brought Jambres back."

"What heinous crime could spark a hate for three thousand years?" asked David. "Can an overwhelming desire for revenge revive the dead?"

"The whole mystery centers on Jambres's identity," said Moe. "If we knew who he was and what he wants to accomplish, then the entire puzzle would lock together."

"Great," said Calvin. "How do you propose answering the sixty-four-thousand-dollar question?"

Ellen stood up and walked over to the bookshelves. "Sarah Walsh provided the necessary clue," she said. "As soon as I heard her last words, I knew all that I needed to solve the mystery. She probably never understood the significance of what Jambres told her. Nor did you."

"Enough bragging," said Moe impatiently. "Explain yourself."

"Don't deny me my one moment of glory," said Ellen, grinning. Then her face turned serious. "Tell me, Mr. Kaufman," she said, "what Jewish holiday starts tomorrow evening?"

Moe's face wrinkled in confusion. "Why, Passover, of course." He hesitated for an instant, eyes narrowing. "You aren't implying . . ."

"Passover," repeated Ellen, ignoring Moe's question.

"God passed over the homes of the Jews while striking down the first-born of the Egyptians. Afterward came the Exodus. Then the giving of the Ten Commandments at Mount Sinai. And the belief in one God instead of many." She paused. "The course of history changed dramatically that one night."

"I'm not sure how this explanation ties in with our case," said Calvin. "You are leading up to that, I hope."

"Patience," said Ellen. "It will all make sense shortly. I promise."

Hesitating for only a second, she continued speaking. "As children, we all heard the story of Moses, a Hebrew boy raised as a prince of Egypt, who led his people out of bondage. Surprisingly, though, archaeologists never found any record of his existence in the chronicles of that period. Some scholars therefore concluded that he never really existed. Those same few claimed that the Exodus was no more than a legend.

"Other, wiser men theorized that Moses was not actually a prince of Egypt, and that any mention of his name was obliterated from the scrolls and temple walls by order of Pharaoh. That was the usual sentence for all those who rebelled against the god-king."

"Who?" asked Moe.

"In ancient Egypt," said Ellen, "the pharaoh was much more than the hereditary ruler of the land. He was a living god, on the same level as Horus, Osiris, and the other immortals. Standing against him was tantamount to defying the very lords of creation. In a land where religion permeated every aspect of daily life, it was the most terrible crime imaginable."

"Punishable by . . . ?" asked David, leaving the question open for her answer.

"Eternal oblivion," said Ellen, "along with denial of passage to the Underworld. A sentence considered by the Egyptians to be a fate worse than death. Life on Earth lasted only for a set number of years, but in the Underworld your soul continued forever."

Ellen held up a photo of the cursed statue. "Unless it was imprisoned in a golden idol like this one. Many centuries later, Arab storytellers told tales of genii trapped forever in bottles. The names reflected the times, but the facts remained the same."

"I'm still lost," said Calvin. "What does all this stuff have to do with Jambres?"

"When a man committed a crime against Pharaoh, not only was he punished, but his family suffered the same penalty as well. Moses escaped the wrath of the god-king. But his father did not."

"His father?" asked Calvin.

"The early Greek translations of the Bible, from which our English versions are taken, often added the letter *s* to the end of names. One of these was Mose, who became Moses."

"Mose," repeated Moe, knowing what she was going to say next.

"The Egyptian word for *son,"* said Ellen. "Jambres seeks vengeance against his son—against Moses."

No one said anything for a minute. David glanced at the two detectives. Moe Kaufman appeared shocked, and Calvin Lane sat unmoving, his eyes half-closed, like a sleeping black Buddha.

"What about this Staff of Fire that Sarah mentioned?" Moe asked. "She said it would increase Jambres's powers a hundred times over. He struck me as being pretty dangerous already."

"We live in a different age," replied Ellen. While the magic used by Jambres seems impressive, his spells are actually minor ones, the type cast by rank-and-file conjurers. Truly great magic requires a rigid physical discipline, not a very easy task for a dead man."

"So he wants the staff to help him regain his original strength?"

"Exactly. In ancient Egypt, a magician's power rivaled that of the gods. A number of mystical chants, for example, called upon Osiris to help the user or suffer the consequences. Jambres served as chief sorcerer to Pharaoh. That meant his skill was second to none."

"Hey, clue me in," said Calvin Lane. "What is this Staff of Fire? You keep talking about it, and I still don't know a thing about it."

"Fire and Moses," said David.

Calvin grimaced, trying to wrestle the association out from the back of his mind. "Does that have anything to do with the Burning Bush?"

Ellen smiled. "Not a bad guess. Not bad at all."

Stretching, she snagged the top book from the nearby end table. Swiftly turning the pages, she finally arrived at her destination. "I'm not an expert on the occult, but I recognized the description of the staff right away. Especially in association with Jambres."

Ellen turned the volume around, showing them all a painting of Moses extending his staff over the Nile. Beneath his sandals, the water ran red as blood. Nearby, Pharaoh and his court attendants watched in awe.

"According to the great Hebrew mystics, Moses worked wonders using a rod given to him by God. As it was written, 'And thou shalt take this rod in thy hand, wherewith thou shalt do the signs.' Nowhere in the Bible or the Hagadah, the Book of Passover, was there any mention of the origin of this rod.

"However, other apocrypha described a walking stick carried from the Garden of Eden by Adam, a branch from the Tree of Knowledge. Carved on it were the secrets of the universe. As this staff originated as part of a direct creation of God, it was unchangeable and indestructible. It could be neither cut nor burned.

"These same books tell how Moses discovered the staff in the midst of a patch of thorn bushes on Mount Sinai. The grove had been struck by lightning, and while the thorn bushes burned, the staff at the center remained untouched. Seeing this miracle, Moses realized his destiny. Taking the Staff of Fire, he returned to Egypt and freed the Hebrews from slavery."

"Okay," said Calvin. "I can accept that story. It isn't very different from the one in the Bible. And I understand why Jambres wants that rod—seeing how his son bested him using it. Just explain to me how it ended up in the United States."

Ellen shook her head. "The rod disappeared in the vastness of history. Biblical scholars assumed it was buried with Moses or given to Joshua. In either case, no one gave it much thought.

"I assume it turned up in an archaeological dig in the Mideast and made its way into a museum. To be perfectly honest, I don't know the contents of all the collections of pre-Christian artifacts in this area. And the staff is probably cataloged wrong anyway."

"Great," said David. "Then all we can do is sit on our hands and wait for Jambres to strike."

"Unfortunately, I don't have any better suggestions," said Ellen.

"Let the professionals handle it," said Calvin. "There's an intensive five-state manhunt for Carl Garrett and his friends taking place right now. Chances are decent that the FBI dragnet will locate them. Police work relies a lot more on old-fashioned foot power than on brain work. In the meanwhile, what do you remember about Ivan Short?"

"Ivan?" said Ellen. "Not much, I'm afraid. As I told you, we only met two or three times. He wrote popular nonfiction books about ancient civilizations. I never read any of his work, but another woman at the Institute said he liked to sensationalize history. You think he knew something about the staff?"

"The notion crossed my mind," said Calvin. "Jambres singled out Short for the Dead Man's Kiss. I'm not sure why. But it seems logical to assume the Egyptian selected him for a reason. Any ideas?"

"No. However, that friend I mentioned owns copies of Short's five books. I'll borrow them. David and I can read through them for clues."

"Good," said Calvin. He turned to his partner. "You've been quiet too long, Moe. That isn't like you at all. What's the story?"

"Tomorrow evening," said Moe, his hands clenched together in a fist. "That's when Jambres will strike."

"Huh?" said his partner. "You sure?"

"Yes," replied Moe. "Don't ask me how I know. I'll explain when the time comes. My daughter is in a play at her Hebrew School at six P.M. tomorrow. Here's the address. Meet me there. And come ready for action."

"What about the FBI and your department?" asked David.

"Try telling them this story and see if they act," said Moe. "The only ones who can stop Satni Jambres are sitting in this room. Like it or not, we're the right people for the job."

"Ellen and I won't feel safe until the Egyptian's sent back to the spirit world," said David. He glanced over at her, and she nodded. "You can count on us."

The two detectives headed for the door. "I'll call if anything happens," said Moe. "Otherwise, try not to be late tomorrow. They start the program promptly on the hour."

40

▲ Alone with David, Ellen breathed a sigh of relief. She instinctively liked both of the detectives, but she was happy to see them leave. Talking about Jambres made her nervous.

"It's nearly lunchtime," said David. "Want to take a break for a bite to eat? I'll take you out to a nice restaurant. Afterward, you can call that friend about those Short books. I want to see a man about some equipment."

"What kind of equipment?" asked Ellen.

David grinned, the smile lighting up his face. "Up to now, we've played the game strictly by Jambres's rules. Only your knowledge of Egyptian sorcery has kept us alive. Our luck can't hold out forever. I plan to fight back using a little modern sorcery of our own. Say an Uzi machine gun and a few hand grenades."

She shrugged. Despite David's confidence, Ellen suspected that once Jambres obtained the Staff of Fire, defeating him would require supernatural assistance. She planned to consult von Gelb's book for help. At present, there were more pressing matters.

"I'll change my clothes in a minute," she declared. "How about a hug first?"

"Sure," said David. "My pleasure. Lunch can wait for a few minutes."

Ellen cuddled up close to David on the sofa. Burrowing her head into his shoulder, she gently caressed the back of his neck with her fingertips. He shivered and held her closer.

"Dream of me last night?" she asked, pressing her body hard against his.

"Of course," he answered, his hands massaging her back. "In technicolor."

She giggled. "Nobody dreams in technicolor. That's only in the movies."

"Tell my subconscious," he said. His hands slipped under the back of her sweatshirt. She wore nothing beneath the fleecy garment. Caught by surprise, David hesitated for a second. Sensing his indecision, Ellen raised her face and nibbled on his earlobe.

Slowly, he slid his hands around and cupped her breasts beneath his fingers. Ellen could feel her nipples harden as he rubbed them back and forth with the inside of his palms. Her body quivered beneath his touch.

Urgently, she pulled his mouth to hers. Their lips met

and fused in a long, passionate kiss. Her breath came in short, hot bursts.

Breaking for air, she pulled out of his grasp. Raising her arms, she tugged off her sweatshirt. Passionately, David pressed his hot mouth between her breasts. Ellen gasped. She could feel the wetness growing between her legs.

"Not here," she whispered, tugging at his shirt. "In the bedroom."

Reluctantly, he let her go. Shakily, they both stood up. "I love you, Ellen Harper," he said, looking deep into her eyes.

"I love you, too, David Ross," she replied. She saw no reason to mention the definite possibility that neither of them might live beyond tomorrow.

41

▲ Carl handed George the Skorpion machine pistol. "Keep your eyes open," he said grimly. "I'm counting on you."

"Don't worry, Carl," said the giant, cradling the deadly gun in his huge hands. "That dead man ain't gonna pull any of his tricks with me watching."

"Remember to stay hidden in the park," said Carl. "Luther and Jambres head off for the museum in fifteen minutes. I want you there, off to the side, when they arrive. Keep out of sight unless something drastic goes wrong—like the Egyptian decides to wipe out Luther or he tries to run off with the staff once they steal it from the exhibit. Otherwise, you just follow the two of them back here. Right?"

"Right," repeated George.

"In the event that Jambres leaves the building with the stick and without Luther . . ." began Carl.

"He won't go far," said George, smiling. His eyes narrowed as he spoke. "Nobody crosses Blood and Iron."

The giant raised the machine pistol in one immense hand. "I shove this gun down his throat and squeeze the trigger. No more kissing for the dead man. He won't do nothing without a face."

"Make sure you catch him unaware," said Carl. The memory of flames spurting from Jambres's fingers haunted his dreams. "One chance is all you'll get."

George clenched his free hand. Muscles tightened as his fingers turned blood red. It was a grip that could crush bones to powder. "One chance is all I need," said George.

Carl nodded. "You're the only one I trust with a mission this important. The fate of Blood and Iron—of white Christian America—turns on what happens tonight. You must not fail."

"You can depend on me," said George.

"I know I can. Now move. You don't have much time."

George headed for the door. Pulling it open, he stepped into the hall. "I'll be back in an hour."

"I hope so," Carl muttered under his breath as the big man walked away. "But I doubt it."

Alone, Carl rested his head in his hands. Softly, he cursed unyielding fortune. He had cooperated with Jambres because the Egyptian promised him revenge for past injustices. But it had become increasingly clear that the sorcerer planned a much wider slaughter than he ever envisioned. Unless they stopped Jambres, the elite membership of Blood and Iron would be remembered as the greatest mass murderers in history.

Scant minutes following George's departure, two faint knocks signaled the arrival of Carl's backup team. Not making a sound, Jasper and Otis slipped into the chamber. Dressed in heavy coats, they waited impatiently for Carl to speak. Wearily, he stared at his insurance policy.

"You heard my instructions to George?" he asked after several minutes of silent contemplation.

"Every word," said Jasper. Tall and thin, he had the face of a vulture. His pinpoint black eyes betrayed no hint of emotion. "The big guy hates the dead man. He'll attack Jambres no matter what takes place at the museum."

"I know," said Carl with a heavy sigh. "That's why I want both of you there. The sorcerer is completely helpless during the Dead Man's Kiss. You strike then. Blow his head off, the same way I instructed George. It's the one chance to end his existence without any risk."

"What about George?" asked Otis. Almost as tall as Jasper, he had a pleasant, open face that reflected none of the brutality that lurked right below the surface. His cheerful smile concealed the heart of a madman.

"A trap only works with the right bait," replied Carl. "Jambres wants George's body. Not much we can do to stop him."

Jasper laughed. "Who cares?"

Otis nodded in agreement. "The big oaf gives me the shakes. The way he looks at people sometimes. Like he's measuring them for a coffin. I won't miss him a bit."

"The two of you all set?" asked Carl. He felt depressed. He was witnessing the last gasps of his band of freedom fighters. They were being destroyed by the monster he had released in their midst.

"No problem," said Jasper. "I stole a car this afternoon. It's parked down the road a bit. Me and Otis will arrive at the museum in plenty of time for the fireworks."

Otis reached beneath his coat and pulled out a .45 automatic. "This baby can stop a bear dead in his tracks. I don't expect no trouble putting that slimeball Jambres out of his misery."

Jasper grunted his agreement. "We'll blast him to bits in a crossfire. I'm gonna enjoy blowing that mother away. Pay him back for what he did to poor Sam."

"Get going," said Carl. "And don't forget. Aim for his head."

"Sure, sure," said Otis, with his choirboy smile. "We'll take care of business, Carl. Don't you worry none. See you later."

Alone for a second time, Carl carefully checked his spare Skorpion. The gun was fully loaded and ready for action. He was tempted to fire away the second Jambres stepped through the door. Almost, but not enough to risk failure. Carl suspected the dead man could not be defeated so easily.

"Hey, boss," called a voice from the other side of the door. "We're ready to head off."

Hastily, Carl shoved the machine gun beneath his chair. Luther, followed by Jambres, entered the room just as Carl sat down. "Any last-minute words of advice?" asked the final member of Blood and Iron.

"Nothing beyond the usual stuff," said Carl. "Be careful. Stay alert. Don't attract attention. The museum lock shouldn't cause you any difficulty. In case of trouble, don't lead the police back to our hideout. You've heard me say it a hundred times before."

Luther chuckled. "You treat us all like little kids, Carl. I won't make any dumb mistakes."

"Jambres knows the location of the staff," said Carl. "Just listen to his instructions, and everything will work out fine."

"Sounds okay with me," said Luther.

"The gods of Egypt accompany us tonight," said Jambres. "We cannot fail. Come. I grow tired of waiting."

Luther grinned. "I never broke into a museum before. Especially not with gods on my side. It should be a kick."

"No tricks," said Carl. Luther nodded his head in return, not realizing the remark was not aimed at him.

"Of course not," said Jambres, his cold dead eyes unwavering. "We remain partners in this endeavor. I need you as much as you need me."

Alone again a few minutes later, Carl wondered what the sorcerer meant by those last words. Increasingly nervous, he lifted the Skorpion onto his lap. If all the others failed, he would stop Jambres—or die trying.

42

▲ Jambres reached out and touched the Staff of Fire. Instantly, a burst of psychic energy surged through his body. For the first time since his resurrection, he experienced something akin to pain. He felt as if he had thrust his hand into the center of an oven. Carefully, he uncurled his fingers from the ancient wood.

"Is it the right one?" whispered Luther, his voice echoing through the deserted room. "Or is it a fake?"

"There is no question of its authenticity," said Jambres.

Gingerly, he stretched out his hands. As he expected, his second contact with the staff was not nearly as shocking. The initial jolt insulated his system from future discomfort. Stepping away from the open display case, he lifted the nearly six-foot-long stick free from its supports. For such a large piece of wood, it weighed surprisingly little. Jambres managed it easily with one hand.

"What does the writing mean?" asked Luther, peering at the long serpentine column of figures that ran along the entire length of the staff. "They look like gibberish to me."

Jambres examined the staff in the bright moonlight that illuminated the entire chamber. Memories of his earlier life, thousands of years before this night, flooded his mind. He recalled staring at the same staff, clutched in the hands of his son, and wondering the same thing. The words were inscribed in no language known to man. They dated from a time before Kamt, when the first men walked the Earth.

"This staff is indestructible," said Luther, rubbing one hand along the rough wood. "Then how did somebody carve those letters in it?"

Jambres had pondered that same question many times in the past. Then, as now, he arrived at no conclusion.

"Enough questions," he replied. "It is time to leave. We must not keep our friends outside waiting too long."

"Huh?" said Luther, caught by surprise. "What are you talking about?"

"Carl doesn't trust me," said Jambres. "And with good reason."

As if sensing the underlying menace in the Egyptian's words, Luther released the staff and stepped backward. But it was already too late.

Jambres swung the hunter's knife he clutched in his left hand on a short, deadly arc. The sharp blade caught Luther square in the belly. He shrieked as Jambres methodically ripped the knife across his abdomen, tearing his intestines to shreds.

Desperately, Luther grabbed the gaping wound, trying to hold his insides together. Hot blood gushed over his fingers and poured onto the marble floor. Dropping to his knees, he looked up at Jambres as the bloody knife descended for the finishing blow. "Why?" he gasped as his eyes clouded over.

"The gods demand it," answered Jambres as he thrust the blade into Luther's heart.

Stepping over the lifeless clay, the Egyptian headed for the exit. He sensed George waiting right outside the museum entrance. Fifty feet away lurked Jasper and Otis. It was time for them to serve the gods as well.

Stopping a few feet away from the door, Jambres

gripped the Staff of Fire with both hands. Slowly, he raised it over his head. He could feel its mighty power rippling through his body.

He spoke one word. "Darkness." And the darkness descended.

A thick, murky fog fell like a black curtain over the museum and the surrounding park. It blocked out the moon and stars, shrouding the entire area in Stygian night.

Relying on his inner eye and not physical sight, Jambres stepped outside. Carefully, he rested the staff against the wall of the museum. From now on, all he needed was the hunter's knife.

A few feet to his right, George Slater blundered around in the fog, waving his arms in circles and cursing the darkness. Jambres ignored him and instead went looking for the other two Blood and Iron members.

Neither Jasper nor Otis exhibited any signs of panic. They stood their ground, eyes scanning the murk for some sign of their enemy. Guns ready, they guarded each other's back.

Jambres walked silently through the blackness. He moved like a ghost, scarcely disturbing the air through which he passed. The dense fog clung to his cold body like a cloak.

He closed in on the two men quickly. In one hand he carried the hunter's knife, wet with Luther's blood.

"You hear something?" asked Otis, raising his automatic and peering into the gloom.

"Nothing," said Jasper, turning his head from side to side. "Not a thing. Nothing to worry about."

Jambres's knife whispered in the darkness. Otis gagged as cold steel sliced through his windpipe. His gun exploded as his fingers convulsed in a dead spasm, sending a lone bullet whining into the night. He fell to the ground, head nearly severed from his body.

"Son of a bitch," said Jasper, taken by surprise. Instinctively, he dropped to the ground and rolled.

Coming to a quick stop, he jumped to his feet, spraying his surroundings with bullets. Nothing stirred.

Hands shaking, he pulled out a book of matches. Using one hand, he lit one and raised it over his head. The dim fire cast a reassuring glow around him.

Otis's gun barked once, then again. Jasper, a look of shock and dismay written across his face, stumbled back. He never expected the dead man to use a gun. He sank to his knees, two bullet holes in his chest. Like a shadow, Jambres stepped behind him and, using the automatic, blew off the top of his skull.

That left only George. Cautiously, Jambres approached the angry giant. He wanted the big man's body in good condition. Which meant a killing blow from in close. Jambres had to match his strength against Slater's.

Knife held low and close to his side, Jambres approached his enemy. He walked slowly, trying to circle the giant from the rear. But George refused to be taken so easily.

"I know you're there," said the big man loudly. "You smell like rotten meat. No way you can hide from my nose."

Jambres shook his head in dismay. He'd never realized how acute the giant's senses were. Unable to surprise the big man, he stopped for a second to plan a new attack. Seizing the moment, George struck first.

Rushing forward, the giant seized Jambres by the shoulders. Effortlessly lifting the dead man into the air, George threw him into the nearby brick wall. Brittle old bones cracked on contact. Jambres staggered forward into a roundhouse right that knocked him back against the bricks.

Savagely, George gripped the sorcerer's forehead in one huge hand and slammed his skull again and again into the unyielding wall. Desperately trying to stop the big man, Jambres swung his knife wildly at the man's chest. The bloodstained blade cut a narrow line along his rib cage, drawing blood but doing little damage.

Laughing madly, George knocked the weapon out of Jambres's hand. Huge arms circled the dead man just below the shoulders, pinning his arms against his sides. Breathing hard, George started to squeeze. "I'm gonna break your back," he declared. "Let you squirm on the ground like a snake while I stomp your face to powder."

Jambres struggled with all of his strength to break the giant's grip. It was no use. The big man locked his hands together and continued to apply pressure. Jambres could feel the bones in his rib cage cracking; it would be only seconds before his backbone snapped. Frantically, his trapped hands tore at George's shirt, trying to find some way to pull free.

It can't end like this, thought Jambres, futilely beating his head into George's breastbone. *The gods must be served.* As if in answer to his plea, one of his hands came in contact with a crude bandage on the big man's side.

The giant howled as Jambres dug his sharp nails into the center of the dressing. The intense pain broke George's concentration. Jambres clawed at the stab wound inflicted the night before. He forced a finger directly into the hole, ripping away scar tissue to the muscle beneath.

George screamed, releasing his hold, his face sheet white. He wheeled away, trying to escape. Jambres scrambled in the darkness for his lost knife. He reached it just as George stumbled across the forgotten Skorpion machine pistol.

"Now I'll blow your head clean off!" he shouted, lifting the gun off the ground. Pointing it in the general direction of Jambres, the giant tugged on the trigger. Nothing happened.

Smiling, Jambres darted forward. Last night, when the men slept, he had made sure their machine guns were useless. Raising his knife high, he leapt at George.

"I ain't dead yet," cried the giant, swinging the Skorpion like a club. With a thunk of metal hitting flesh, the gun smashed into Jambres's side, sending him sprawling. By the time he regained his feet, George was fifty feet away and running fast.

Jambres shrugged. Better to let George escape than risk another confrontation. He regretted losing the big man's powerful body, but it mattered little to his plans. He considered himself lucky to escape the fight with no more than a few bruised and battered ribs. Even the gods feared madmen like George Slater.

43

▲ The small auditorium was nearly filled when David and Ellen arrived at ten to six. Draping their coats over two seats in the last row, they remained standing, searching the room for Moe Kaufman.

"There he is," said Ellen, catching a glimpse of the detective near the front row. She waved until he finally noticed them. Hurrying over, he reached their seats just as the lights began to dim.

"I'm sitting in the first row with my wife," he said after a brief handshake and hello. "Calvin is there, too. I left the school's phone number at the station if anything turns up. They've been checking the crime computer printouts for museum break-ins all day, but with no results so far."

"You're still convinced that something will happen this evening?" asked David.

"Positive," said Moe, his tone grim. "Tonight is the first night of Passover. History is filled with events of dread importance to the Hebrew people that took place on this date. The handwriting on the wall, Daniel in the lion's den, and the destruction of Sodom are three such events from the Hagadah. Can you blame me for being concerned?"

Then he shrugged and smiled. "If I'm wrong, though, Miriam told me to ask both of you over for Passover dinner at my house right after the performance. She's prepared enough food to feed an army."

"That sounds terrific," said Ellen, laughing. "I love it when somebody else does the cooking."

The loudspeakers at the side of the stage crackled and sputtered as the first strains of "Tradition" filled the auditorium. "It sounds like the show is starting," said Moe. "By the way, my daughter, Esther, is wearing a blue dress and has dark brown hair. We'll talk more during the intermission."

The curtain opened seconds after Moe regained his seat. A dozen students ranging from nine to twelve years old filed onto the stage. David settled back to watch the show. Casually, he circled one arm around Ellen's shoulders. She turned, smiled, and snuggled closer.

"Welcome to our Passover seder," announced a slender boy with dark hair and eyes, looking uncomfortable in a blue suit and red bow tie. "Please feel free to join in any of the traditional Pesach songs as we celebrate the story of the Exodus from Egypt."

The children sat around a long table covered with a white tablecloth. In front of each child was a gold or silver cup, traditionally filled with red wine. A near-empty bottle of fruit juice off to the side assured parents of a practical substitution.

Near the head of the table rested a large dish covered with a white cloth napkin. David, who had attended several Passover ceremonies while on assignment in Israel, knew that beneath the napkin were three matzos. Resting on top of the setting were the shank bone of a lamb; a roasted egg; bitter herbs; a mixture of apples, nuts, and wine known as Charoseth; a bundle of parsley, celery, and lettuce called carpas; and a container of horseradish. Along with the four cups of wine drunk during the seder, each item on the Passover plate symbolized an important aspect of the holiday.

"Please stand," asked another boy, a little older-looking than the rest. Raising his cup from the table, he faced the audience and recited the prayer over the first glass of wine, signifying the beginning of the seder.

"Blessed art thou, O lord our God! King of the Universe, Creator of the fruit of the vine."

In unison, the participants repeated the prayer and then sipped their juice. With that, all the people in the hall and onstage took their seats. The performance had begun.

The service moved along swiftly. Circling the table, each child read a short section of the Hagadah. Following tradition, the youngest attendee, a girl no more than six or seven, recited the Four Questions, the formalized queries that defined and gave meaning to the entire ceremony. In her clear, high-pitched voice, she asked, "Why is this night different from all other nights?"

David relaxed, listening carefully as the boys and girls responded to the questions with answers centuries old but still meaningful today. The seder was more than a retelling of the story of the Exodus. The Hagadah contained a great deal of commentary on the Passover holiday, including explanations of the symbolic meanings of all the items on the table. Though David had heard it all before, he always found the readings fascinating.

Sitting there, David closed his eyes and let the words roll past his senses. Listening to the story added a bizarre note to their unbelievable battle with Jambres. He wondered if something more than coincidence was involved.

Suddenly he froze, as one particular passage resonated through his thoughts. The muscles in Ellen's shoulder tensed beneath his fingers as she, too, reacted to the words being read aloud by one of the children.

"And I will pass through the land of Egypt, I *myself* and not an angel; and I will smite all the first-born, I *myself* and no seraph; and on all the gods of Egypt will I execute judgment, I *myself* and not a messenger; I am the Lord, *I am He* and no other."

In one crystal-clear epiphany, all of the events and killings of the past week tied together, and David comprehended exactly what evil Jambres planned for that night. Overwhelmed by his vision, he turned to tell Ellen when, out of the corner of his eye, he glimpsed Moe Kaufman and Calvin Lane hurrying for the exit.

"Time to leave," he whispered as the big black detective beckoned for them to follow.

Once out of the auditorium, Moe wasted no time breaking the news. "I just heard from headquarters. There was a museum robbery last night in a small town on the Mississippi named Gibson. Local police found signs of a struggle but no bodies. The thieves broke open one display case. Missing and presumed stolen was an ancient Indian ceremonial standard of unknown origins. From the description, it sounded a lot like a walking stick . . . or staff."

"Gibson," said Ellen, concentrating. Her expression darkened with worry. "In one of his books, Short described visiting that museum. At the turn of the century, residents supposedly discovered a number of early Egyptian artifacts in an Indian burial mound right outside of town. Most scholars deemed the relics obvious fakes, but Short wasn't so certain."

"Egyptians in Illinois," said David. "Unbelievable."

"Any more unbelievable than a three-thousand-year-old sorcerer returning to life?" asked Moe. "It has to be Jambres."

"If it is," said David, "I know what he plans next."

Ellen swallowed hard. "That passage from the Hagadah?"

"Right. The Lord God *himself* slew the first-born of the Egyptians. Jambres couldn't duplicate that feat because he wasn't a god. But, evidently, he finally realized his mistake."

"Using the staff," continued Ellen, comprehension

growing with each word, "he intends to raise one of the ancient gods of Egypt. And through its powers fulfill his vow of revenge made more than three thousand years ago."

44

▲ "Come closer." The figure on the throne beckoned. "I've been waiting for you."

Carl stepped forward and peered intently at the speaker. Though only a few feet separated them, he could barely make out the man's features. All around them, unseen creatures chattered in the darkness. "Who are you?" he asked.

"Don't you recognize me?" the man returned, sounding amused. He waved Carl nearer. "I am your brother."

"I don't have a brother," said Carl angrily. Grabbing the speaker by the collar, he yanked him out of his chair. Dark brown eyes, a short beard, and a sardonic smile brought no glimmer of recognition. With a snort of annoyance, Carl shoved the man to the ground and seated himself on the throne.

"No need for violence . . . brother," said the stranger, not the least bit perturbed. He chuckled. "I was going to offer you my chair anyway. It belongs to you now."

"Who are you?" asked Carl, starting to comprehend the strangeness of his surroundings. "And where am I?"

"Why, this is Hell," said the man. "My name is Judas, Judas Iscariot."

Shocked, Carl tried to rise from the throne. Instantly, a hundred cords darted out from the chair, binding him tightly in place. He struggled to escape, but without success.

"And you," continued Judas, his tone mocking, "are Carl Garrett. The *new* betrayer of Jesus Christ, Christian."

"No!" screamed Carl and awoke.

Covered with sweat, he tried to sit up. But the ropes circling his neck, chest, and arms held him firmly in place. It took a few seconds to regain his orientation. He was not tied to a throne in Hell. Instead, he rested face up on a crude wooden altar in the center of the yard at the rear of the hideout. A dozen hemp bands held both his arms and legs, stretched to their extremes.

Behind him, a huge fire roared, sending an occasional ember flickering onto his face. It was midevening, around nine o'clock, he estimated, and a fistful of stars twinkled in the night sky. Carl knew for certain he would never see another dawn.

He had fallen to Jambres without firing a shot. By the time the van returned late last evening, an unnatural fog had settled over the entire area. Carl never once associated the darkness with Jambres. When he spotted four men in the van, he immediately assumed all was well. Not until he reached the vehicle did he realize his terrible mistake. Seconds later, when the Skorpion failed to fire, he understood his mistake.

"Awake at last," said Jambres, breaking into his memories. The sorcerer carefully checked the ropes tying Carl to the altar. Evidently satisfied with his preparation, he walked over to the huge fire and threw a few more logs into the blaze.

"What are you going to do to me?" asked Carl, anxious to know what the sorcerer planned.

"I told you earlier that I needed you," said Jambres, returning to the base of the altar. He fingered the hunter's knife, caked with dried blood. "I didn't lie. You shall serve me well—as the sacrifice that raises Anubis from the Underworld."

"Why me?" asked Carl, anxious to keep the dead man

talking. The more he knew, the better his chances for escape. Carl refused to accept defeat.

"Your hatred attracted me like a magnet," said Jambres, sheathing the knife in his belt. "I needed a pawn filled with anger, willing to do anything to achieve his ends. One foolish enough to bargain with the dead. You were such a man. I touched the minds of many others in the world of dreams. But only in you did I find the necessary ruthlessness to match my schemes."

"You used me," said Carl.

"Of course," replied the dead man. "Just as you hoped to use me."

"Then it was all for nothing. My men died for no reason."

"On the contrary," said Jambres. "Your death will summon Anubis from his long sleep. In this modern world of lost faith and fragmented religions, no one lives to stop him. He is both immortal and indestructible. The slaying of the first-born shall take place a second time. However, this time it will be the followers of Mose, my son, who wail for their dead children."

"The followers of Mose," said Carl, licking his lips. His dreams filled his mind. "You mean the Jews. Like we discussed."

Jambres looked to the heavens. "Another hour before the moon reaches the correct position." His dead eyes stared at Carl. "You never truly understood my mission. My quarrel was not merely with the group you call the Jews. The gods of Kamt demanded revenge against all those who followed the One God. Each and every of them."

"All?" repeated Carl, his eyes bulging from his head. He couldn't believe what he was hearing. "Including white Aryan Christians?"

"Certainly," said Jambres. "Their first-born die tonight as well." The dead man smiled, a vision straight from the pit. "The gods require their full payment of tears."

Carl cursed. He ranted. He raved. He called down

vengeance on Jambres from the powers above, the powers below. He cried, he pleaded. All to no avail. The dead man only smiled.

"I once explained to you how minor events in the pool of time spread like waves throughout history. So it was with the revolt of Mose. Though thousands died, the rebellion was crushed by Pharaoh's army. My son and his followers, the Hebrew slaves, fled into the wilderness. By decree of the god-king, all record of those terrible days was stricken from the temple walls, the papyrus scrolls. But the damage was done.

"The God of Mose, the Lord God, *the One God,* had executed judgment on each of the gods of Egypt. And though they said nothing, the people saw and understood that this One God was more powerful than the combined might of Osiris and Set and Ra and all the rest. For the One God slew the first-born of Kamt, and the gods of Egypt remained silent.

"On this night, thousands of years ago, a new faith began. It was the belief in One God, a single creator, who tolerated no other gods before him. That ripple spread on the waters of time. Slowly, over the centuries, it grew until its shadow swept away all others in its path. The gods of Egypt, of Babylon, of Rome and Greece that followed, perished. Only the One God, the God of Mose, remained."

"You can't change history," said Carl. "What's done is done."

"The silent, forgotten gods of Egypt cry out for justice," said Jambres. "Their curse divides my soul from my spirit, forever denying me entrance to the Underworld. Only by exacting equal justice on the children of Mose can I earn their forgiveness. The first-born children of the believers in the One God must die. It is the only way."

"Christians, Muslims, Jews," whispered Carl. "They number in the millions, the hundreds of millions."

"When Anubis once again walks the Earth, the slaying

of the first-born shall begin. None will be spared. Blood begets blood."

For a second time, the dead man looked up at the moon. "The time of sacrifice draws near." He paused, as if listening to a voice in the distance. "I sense hostile presences nearby. They approach in two directions. No matter, my traps will stop them."

Jambres plucked at the rope drawn tightly across Carl's neck. "I leave you to make peace with your God," he said. "The God of Mose, the God of all those who followed his path. Explain to him how you sought to free this nation with the help of Satni Jambres."

The dead man laughed, a hollow sound that echoed endlessly in the night. "See if he understands or forgives."

45

▲ "I think we've located their hideout," said Moe Kaufman. "It's about twenty miles out of town."

"What if you're wrong?" asked David.

They stood outside the small brick building that housed police headquarters in Gibson. All four of them huddled around a detailed map of the surrounding area held by Moe. The two police officers had arrived fifteen minutes ago. David and Ellen pulled up just as the others finished speaking with the local police.

"Then we try somewhere else," replied Moe. "But I'm pretty certain about this farmhouse."

"We ran a computer check at the station," explained Calvin. "The program spit out every home rented in the area over the past week. FBI records we saw the other day indicated that Garrett always secured a hideout before moving to a new area."

"It provided him a safe haven," added Moe. "The authorities wasted lots of time hunting for him in the wilderness while he sat comfortably watching TV in a house not six blocks away from city hall."

"A Mr. Jones rented the house in question two days ago," said Calvin. "The entire transaction was conducted by phone and paid by credit card. We traced the charge to a clearinghouse for right-wing extremist groups that works out of Kansas City."

David nodded. "All right. I'm convinced. What's the plan?"

"The farm fronts a single-lane country road that runs diagonally between routes 6 and 11," said Moe, pointing out locations as he spoke. "It's around twenty minutes from here. Nobody lives for miles in either direction. I think we should split up and attack from both directions. You come in from the west while Calvin and I hit them from the east. It's a quarter after nine. You game for ten o'clock?"

"Right," said David. He turned to Ellen. "Are you sure you want to go through with this? I'd feel a lot better if you'd stay here in Gibson."

"No use trying to stop me," said Ellen. "I thought we settled this argument on the drive here. The three of you are confident guns will stop Jambres. I'm not so sure. Besides, you need someone to ride shotgun."

"Okay," said David. "But I still don't like it."

"Let's move," said Moe. "I kept the locals pretty much in the dark about things. However, I told them if we don't contact them by midnight, to call for the Marines. Or at least Anderson and the FBI."

David drove with Ellen navigating. The night air smelled crisp and clean while a thousand stars glittered above. Except for the Uzi machine gun between them, they could have been any young couple out for a moonlight drive.

"You scared?" asked David ten minutes later as he turned the car onto the single-lane country road leading to the farmhouse.

"A little," admitted Ellen.

"So am I," said David, patting her on the knee. "Fear's a healthy emotion. It keeps you from getting overconfident."

The narrow lane wove in and out of forest glades and small, overgrown fields. There were no lights anywhere. The moon and stars provided the only illumination. Ever cautious of being discovered, David drove with the headlights off.

"The farmhouse should be coming up on the right side," said Ellen.

"It's ten minutes till ten," said David, checking the clock on the dashboard. "No . . ."

"David!" screamed Ellen. "Watch out!"

The road ahead seethed with life. In the pale moonlight, thousands of shapes wiggled and squirmed across the narrow strip of pavement. A black tide of lizards, snakes, and bugs rolled toward them.

"Hell," said David, and slammed his foot on the brake. But he acted seconds too late. With a crackling, popping sound, the car hit the first line of vermin.

Unable to make purchase with the pavement, the tires spun wildly, sending the auto careening frantically from side to side. The steering wheel twirled uselessly beneath David's hands. A curtain of insects covered the windows, making it impossible to see outside. "Hold on!" he yelled as the car skidded out of control.

Whining in protest, steel-belted radials hit the edge of the pavement and dropped over the side into the adjacent drainage ditch. The metal underbelly of the car screamed as it slammed into blacktop. Angular momentum kept the vehicle upright for a second more. Then gravity took over and the car flipped over onto the shoulder. Glass windows shattered as the auto rolled across the meadow twice more before coming to a complete stop. The car rested sideways, driver's side to the ground, wedged against a clump of trees twenty yards from the road.

Groaning, David blotted the blood off his forehead with the palm of one hand. Next to him, Ellen swore like a sailor. "You okay?" he asked, unable to see her in the gloom.

"Other than a few bruises, bumps, and scrapes, I'm fine," she replied. "What about you?"

"Could be better," he admitted, trying to shift about on the seat. He grunted in sudden pain. "I think my right ankle's broken. And, to make matters worse, the steering wheel is pressing right up against my chest. I can't move."

"Maybe I can shift the seat back a few notches?" said Ellen.

"It won't work," said David. "The lever is on the side of the seat by the door. With the car in this position, it can't be reached."

"Let me try something else," said Ellen.

Unbuckling her seat belt, she slid down next to him. Carefully placing her legs beneath his, she stood on the door and tried moving the column holding him trapped. After a few minutes, she yielded in frustration.

"Don't waste your time," said David. "I'm stuck here for the foreseeable future."

Using the center armrest as a stepping stone, Ellen climbed up to the passenger door. After three tries, the door swung open, and Ellen peered out into the night.

"No snakes," she said after a few seconds. "We left them back on the road."

Turning in the other direction, she inched herself higher. "I see a bonfire burning a few hundred feet away. It sounds like a man chanting there." She hesitated for a few seconds. "That must be Jambres."

David shook his head. "Nothing we can do about him now. I even lost the Uzi. We're out of the game."

Ellen didn't answer. She remained standing. "I still have the .22 automatic you gave me earlier," she declared after a few seconds.

David felt a cold chill race through his body. "You aren't thinking of heading down there on your own?" he asked, already knowing the answer. "It's too dangerous. Let Moe and Calvin handle the Egyptian."

"What if they ran into the same horde as us?" she asked, sounding worried. "Nobody's shooting down there, and it's after ten now. They should have attacked by now."

She slipped back into the car and stared him in the eye. "Somebody has to stop Jambres. I seem to be the only one left."

"That's crazy," said David, tugging desperately at the steering wheel. "One woman against Jambres and Blood and Iron. You don't stand a chance."

"I love you, David," she said, leaning forward and kissing him gently on the lips, "but I have to try."

Hands clenched on the steering wheel, he tried one last time to free himself. After a minute of struggling, he surrendered. Tears of frustration filled his eyes.

"Shoot first and ask questions later," he said, admitting defeat. "No mercy. Catch them by surprise. You're no marksman, so aim for the body."

"I understand," said Ellen, pulling herself up through the doorway.

"No mercy," repeated David. "Those men are killers."

Ellen was out of the car, balanced carefully on the rear door as she prepared to descend. "I'll be back, David. I promise."

She left him with those words. He was alone, trapped in the darkness, with only his worst nightmares for company. Angrily, he gripped the wheel and pushed; there was nothing else for him to do.

46

▲ Ellen crept cautiously up to the side of the old farmhouse. The place appeared deserted. The only sounds came from the crackling of a huge bonfire in the backyard and a harsh voice droning in a language she did not recognize. A language, she suspected, dead and forgotten for thousands of years.

Crouched low to the ground, the .22 held tightly in her right hand, Ellen peered around the edge of the building. She was not sure what she would see, and it took a few seconds for the scene to register. She bit her lower lip to keep from screaming.

In the center of the clearing roared an immense fire, a circle of flame ten feet in diameter, sending red fingers shooting high into the sky.

Fronting the blaze was a crudely constructed wooden altar, five feet long and three feet high. Tied to the altar was a pleasant-looking middle-aged man, naked from the waist up. A dozen ropes circled his arms, legs, and neck, holding him tightly in place. His bare chest glistened with sweat in the bright moonlight.

Back a few feet from the altar sat three dead men. Arranged in upright position, each of them betrayed gaping wounds that spoke of violent deaths. Ellen avoided staring too long at the corpses. She knew they had to be the other members of Blood and Iron. Evidently, the alliance between Jambres and the terrorists had ended in violence.

A tall, lanky man stood facing the fire. Though she could only see his back, Ellen knew he had to be Satni

Jambres, sorcerer of ancient Egypt. In one hand, he held a long wood staff, five feet long and covered with arcane symbols. In his other, he grasped a hunting knife, the blade dark with dried blood.

There was something about the way Jambres gestured, the way he jerked his arms to and fro, that made it terribly clear he was dead. He moved with the ungainly grace of a marionette—an empty body animated by an undead puppet master.

The words of his chant blurred together in an unceasing mutter of undistinguishable syllables. Ellen felt certain that this was the ancient litany used to summon a god. The sacred fire burned. The sacrificial victim lay bound on the altar. There wasn't much time left. She had to act now.

David's instructions ran through her mind. She aimed the barrel of the automatic at Jambres's back. Bracing herself against the wall, she gently squeezed the trigger. The gun jumped in her hand, a loud crack shattering the dead man's prayer. Hastily, she fired a second shot, then a third.

Jambres staggered as all three bullets hit him in the back. The gunshots hammered him forward, causing him to drop the staff and the knife. Off balance, he dropped to one knee.

"Quick!" cried the man tied to the altar. "Shoot him in the head." He thrashed about violently, trying to rip free from the ropes. "You can't hurt him otherwise."

Ellen rushed forward, her heart pounding like a triphammer. The dead man was already rising to his feet. She could see the three bloodless holes in his back where the bullets had struck. The bound man's words made horrifying sense. She had to destroy Jambres's eyes and mouth to render him helpless.

The sorcerer turned just as she came within reach. Instinctively, she thrust the gun at his face and pulled the trigger. The weapon roared, jerking her hand up and away. The bullet screamed past Jambres's ear, causing no damage.

The sorcerer grabbed Ellen by the wrist. Powerful digits, cold as ice, tightened, causing her to scream in pain. The gun dropped from her useless fingers.

"Ellen Harper, I assume," said the dead man, in a voice as chilled and lifeless as his touch. His vacant eyes stared at her with unblinking intensity. "Somehow I expected you here tonight."

With a flick of the wrist, he hurtled her across the yard. Ellen collided with the rear wall of the farmhouse and fell to the earth, dazed. "Do not interrupt," he commanded. "My devotions to Anubis are complete. It is time for the sacrifice."

Jambres bent down and picked up the knife. Grasping it with both hands, he walked over to the altar. His intended victim struggled helplessly as the sorcerer approached.

Jambres raised his hands high, the darkened blade glowing red in the flames. Ellen gasped. The knife swept down.

Out of the darkness, a giant of a man charged. Arms outstretched, he slammed into Jambres with the force of an express train. Huge fists smashed into the surprised sorcerer's face, sending him flying.

Frantically, the dead man slashed at the giant with his knife. The stranger avoided the blow with ease. Laughing like a madman, he caught Jambres by the arm. Reaching down, he seized the sorcerer at the crotch. Without effort, the giant straightened, raising Jambres up over his head.

"Throw him into the fire, George!" cried the bound man. "Throw him into the fire!"

George did exactly that. Taking two steps forward, he tossed the dead man into the raging inferno. Jambres disappeared into the flames without uttering a sound. The sickening smell of burning flesh filled the clearing.

"I did it, Carl," the giant babbled as he set about tearing apart the ropes holding the other man to the altar. "I waited in the forest for exactly the right moment. He never guessed I was out there."

"Nor did I," said the man Ellen realized had to be Carl Garrett. Shakily, he swung his legs off the altar. "You shocked the hell out of—George, watch out!"

The blackened and burning form of Satni Jambres lurched out of the fire. In his hand, he clutched the hunter's knife. Propelled by a will stronger than death, the sorcerer headed straight for the unsuspecting giant.

George turned an instant too late. The red-hot knife sizzled as Jambres plunged it up to the hilt between the big man's shoulders. Gagging, the giant collapsed to his hands and knees.

Jambres wrenched the blade free, sending a fountain of red blood spurting into the air. "The ritual is complete," he declared as he drove the knife a second time into George's back.

The big man crumpled onto the ground, dead. Jambres, clothes and hair aflame, flesh smoldering, hovered over the body like a vulture.

"Anubis returns," he announced, straightening. He pointed a finger at the middle of the clearing. "And the slaying of the first-born begins!"

"You dirty son of a bitch," said Carl Garrett, his voice rising in anger. Wrenching the knife out of George Slater, he rammed the blade into Jambres's right eye.

The dead man screamed in shock. Without his eyes, he was completely helpless. Garrett had discovered the dead man's weakness.

Relentless, Carl yanked the knife loose. "One down, one to go," he said, teeth clenched in a mad grin.

Furiously, he jabbed at Jambres's other eye. This time, the sorcerer dodged to one side, but there was no avoiding the body sprawled at his feet.

Tumbling over George's legs, Jambres stumbled straight at the fire. With a shriek of despair, he plunged into the inferno. He did not emerge a second time.

Ellen scrambled to her feet. A circle of darkness was forming in the center of the yard. A hundred times blacker than the night, it hovered a few yards off the ground. Already a dozen feet in diameter, it expanded as she watched. Inside it, a vast shape shuffled slowly toward the perimeter. Squinting, Ellen could vaguely make out the titanic form of a manlike being with the head of a jackal.

"Anubis is rising," said Carl Garrett, coming up behind her. He asked no questions and showed no surprise at her presence. There was no longer any time for idle curiosity. "The door to the Underworld is open. And I am damned for eternity. Unless I find a way to stop him."

"What?" said Ellen, but Carl was no longer there. He returned in a second, holding the Staff of Fire.

"The gods of Egypt are immortal and undying," he said, more to himself than to her. "The Staff of Fire is everlasting and indestructible."

He raised his eyes to hers. "You know who I am," he said, his voice calm, his features serene. "My name is Carl Garrett. Whatever mistakes I made were done in the cause of freedom. Let the world remember me for that."

"No. You can't go through with this," said Ellen, realizing instantly what Garrett intended.

"Yes I can," he said, and pushed her away. Without another word, he reversed the staff so that it pointed like a spear directly at the center of the black doorway.

"Now," he cried, and charged into the darkness.

Something not human bellowed in anger. And pain—incredible, inhuman pain. The sphere flickered. For an instant, the stars and moon seemed to blink. And then, with a roar that shook the ground and trees like an earthquake, the circle disappeared.

Five minutes later, Moe Kaufman and Calvin Lane arrived.

47

▲ Wide-eyed, Moe nudged the dead body of George Slater. "Where's Garrett?" he asked Ellen. A few feet away, an equally incredulous Calvin studied the corpses of the three other terrorists.

"He's . . . gone," said Ellen. For the first time since he'd met the young woman, she seemed at a loss for words. "So is the Staff of Fire. He took it with him. I'm not sure if he's alive or dead. He's just . . . gone."

"That sounds promising," said Moe. "You want to tell me more?"

"In a minute," she answered. "I need some time to gather my thoughts. Where were you?" she asked, changing the subject.

"We experienced a close encounter of the worst kind," said Moe. "A horde of snakes and lizards overran the car. Damned things completely covered the windshields."

"I couldn't see a thing," said Calvin, coming up to them. "Which is why I drove us right into a tree."

"We abandoned the car three miles from here," continued Moe. "After fighting our way free of those infernal reptiles, we ran all the way here, arriving just in time to experience an invisible earthquake. Maybe you'll explain that phenomenon as well."

Ellen smiled and shrugged, leading Moe to suspect he might never learn the full truth of what happened before they arrived. He wasn't sure if he really wanted to know.

"Sure don't look like you needed any help from us," said Calvin, waving a big hand at the bodies scattered around the clearing. "Where's David?"

"Oh hell," said Ellen, her face turning red. "I nearly forgot poor David. He's trapped in our car, a hundred yards down the road. The steering wheel is jammed against his chest."

"Time to call the locals," said Moe. "I hope the phone works in this old shack."

"I'll hike over there and tell him help is on the way," said Calvin.

"Wait for me," said Ellen. "I'm coming along."

"Before you run off," said Moe, "how about telling me what happened to Jambres? Is he 'gone' too?"

"No," said Ellen, shuddering. She turned and pointed at the huge bonfire behind them. "He's in there. Or at least his ashes are."

Moe nodded, his features white.

48

▲ They celebrated their victory with a seder the next night at Moe Kaufman's house. Miriam cooked twice as much food as necessary, and Moe's daughter, Esther, proudly recited the Four Questions. Moe, Calvin, David, and Ellen alternated reading the Hagadah. All felt that in a special way the book spoke directly to them.

At the end of the meal, to neither detective's great surprise, Ellen announced that she and David planned to marry in the summer. Her fiance, hobbled by crutches, his ankle in a lightweight cast, cheerfully laughed off Carl's suggestion that he had learned from Jambres's mistake.

David could afford his merriment. After hearing his account of the past twenty-four hours, Eli Richter had personally delivered a very handsome check to him that afternoon. In doing so, the Mossad agent also managed to snare Ellen for a long, private chat out of David's hearing. Conceding defeat, David asked Ellen to be his wife minutes after Eli departed. Now he wondered if perhaps that had been exactly what the sly old man had planned.

Finally, with the dishes cleared off the table and the children playing video games in the parlor, it was time to discuss what had happened the evening before. Starting from when she had left David trapped in their car, Ellen described everything that took place until Moe and Calvin found her shortly after Garrett's incredible act of heroism.

"God works in mysterious ways," said Moe when she finished. "To think that two of the most evil, bigoted men alive today saved the Jewish race from disaster. For reasons I'm sure we will never understand.

"Garrett's officially accused of murdering his companions. Anderson doctored the FBI report so that it appeared he killed them in a rage over Sarah's death. Time-released poison was blamed for her demise as well as the people at the museum. The motive, of course, was robbery."

"He embellished my original theory," said Ellen, smiling. "When we found the gold statue of Anubis in the farmhouse, it provided the finishing touch to the story."

"What happened to Jambres?" asked Miriam.

"When the locals arrived," said Calvin, "they extinguished the bonfire. All they found in the center were a few bones, charred beyond any hopes of identification."

"He's dead for a second time," said Moe. "This time forever."

49

▲ On an island in the sea of dreams, separating the land of the living from the domain of the dead, a solitary figure stirred restlessly on a jet-black obsidian throne. With shaven head and hawklike nose, he resembled a human vulture waiting for his prey.

When the flames consumed his alternate body, Jambres's *ka* returned to the golden statue of Anubis. Ellen found the statue in the farmhouse and the idol was restored to the Petrie Institute, where it was once more on exhibit for all the world to see. His *ba* remained, as always, on the Isle of the Dead-Alive. As it had been, so it was again.

Eyes without pupils, blacker than night, stared unseeing into the darkness. He had failed in this attempt to escape his cursed existence. All his efforts had gone for naught. But a patient man never ceased trying. Three thousand years had made Jambres very patient.

His brief contact with the Staff of Fire had strengthened his inner will a hundredfold. Through dreams, he could easily contact others like Carl Garrett. There were always fools willing to sacrifice anything to realize their ambitions. He would try again. And again. And again. Forever.

Author's Note

This novel and all aspects of it are entirely the product of the author's imagination. However, the possibility of early Egyptian voyages to this continent are by no means fantasy. Interested readers are referred to *America B.C.* by Barry Fell for more details on this controversial but fascinating theory of prehistoric exploration.